The man

He's i
Endor
the same i   at
                                                                    in the
form of an average-looking man rushing straight at Mick and Robert.

Mick was half-turned toward her, oblivious to the danger, the killer ten feet from him. Without thought, Cassie threw a force field between the two men. Mick's attacker crashed headlong into it and fell back a step, momentarily stunned.

"Get him," she shouted. "He's the killer!"

To the POTL—Connie, Dana, Loralee, Nancy and Vicki.
And of course to Diva Dreyer.
Thanks and love to all. You truly are the best.

Other Books by Laurie C. Kuna

Writing as Laurie Carroll
A WAR OF HEARTS

Some Practical Magic

***

Laurie C. Kuna

ImaJinn Books

The sale of this book without its cover is unauthorized. If you purchased this book without a cover, you should be aware that it was reported to the publisher as "unsold and destroyed." Neither the author nor the publisher has received payment for the sale of this "stripped book."

Some Practical Magic
Published by ImaJinn Books, a division of ImaJinn

Copyright ©2004 by Laurie C. Kuna
Printed and bound in the United States of America. All rights reserved. No part of this book may be reproduced in any form or by any means (electronic, mechanical, photocopying, recording, or otherwise) without prior written permission of both the copyright holder and the above publisher of this book, except by a reviewer, who may quote brief passages in a review. For information, address: ImaJinn Books, a division of ImaJinn, P.O. Box 545, Canon City, CO 81215-0545; or call toll free 1-877-625-3592.

ISBN: 1-893896-37-4

10 9 8 7 6 5 4 3 2 1

PUBLISHER'S NOTE:
This book is a work of fiction. Names, characters, places and incidents are products of the author's imagination or are used fictitiously. Any resemblance to actual events or locales or persons, living or dead, is entirely coincidental.

Books are available at quantity discounts when used to promote products or services. For information please write to: Marketing Division, ImaJinn Books, P.O. Box 545, Canon City, CO 81215-0545, or call toll free 1-877-625-3592.

Cover design by Patricia Lazarus

ImaJinn Books, a division of ImaJinn
P.O. Box 545, Canon City, CO 81215-0545
Toll Free: 1-877-625-3592
http://www.imajinnbooks.com

Prologue

Southeastern Michigan, the present

Since he had a mild case of writer's block, Mirek "Mick" Sandor decided to go jogging that cold January day. He really didn't mind that the thermometer read zero degrees Fahrenheit. No wind blew, no snow fell, and no cloud marred the endless blue sky. There was nothing like a snowy Michigan landscape when the sun shone down out of a cloudless sky.

After a quick stretch, he set out from the back porch of his log cabin retreat, toward the barn and the groomed cross-country ski trails in the ten-acre woods behind his house. As long as he kept a moderate pace out of deference to several old athletic injuries, he knew he'd return to his computer with a clear head, ready to tackle the next chapter.

He arrived back at the house an hour and eight miles later. On the back porch, he knocked the snow off his running shoes and tights, then stepped into the mud room and went straight to the microwave. As he nuked a cup of tea, the doorbell rang.

"Shit." He looked like hell, all wet, sweaty and red-cheeked. But he lived alone, so if the door was going to be answered, he was the man for the job. Using a dish towel, he mopped the sweat from his face as he walked across the cabin's great room to the front door. A quick glance out the picture window showed a plain, dark blue sedan sitting in his driveway.

And two men in trench coats on his front porch.

He opened the door just enough to ask them their business.

"Are you M. S. Kazimer?" the taller of the two coats asked.

These guys didn't strike Mick as crazed fans, but there were the trench coats and unremarkable sedan to consider. They worried him a bit. On the other hand, if this was about his books, it probably wasn't anything catastrophic. "Actually, that's my pen name."

"Is your real name Mirek Sandor?" the shorter, younger coat asked.

The question made Mick's skin prickle. "Yes, and just who are you?"

Both men produced wallets with picture I.D. "We're FBI," the taller one said.

Man, these guys take that no-carrying-fruit-across-the-

California-border law seriously, Mick thought. *I'm probably going to get a huge fine. For two measly apples. Well, they were Michigan apples . . .* "What's this all about?"

"Mr. Kazimer," the younger agent said gravely, "the Bureau desperately needs your help."

This definitely doesn't sound like a contraband fruit issue, Mick concluded.

One

"Cassandra, why aren't you married?"

Stifling a groan, Cassie Hathorne grabbed a shock of her hair in a fist and barely restrained herself from giving it a frustrated yank. She briefly considered putting the phone on speaker, the better to pull at her short tresses two-fisted while her mother ranted. But doing that wouldn't make her feel good. Or less trapped.

"Good morning to you, too, Mom." Cradling the receiver between her shoulder and ear, she moved to the dishwasher. Might as well get some constructive work done during Mom's recurring rampage.

Just then, her huge, smoke-gray cat ambled into the kitchen.

"Endora, a little help here, please," Cassie whispered, indicating with a quirk of her eyebrow the now open dishwasher.

Endora leapt up onto the counter and sat down, a Cheshire grin on her intelligent gray face. She fastidiously licked first one forepaw then the other, then stared at Cassie with a smug feline smirk.

"Thanks for nothing, pal," Cassie grumbled before saying into the phone, "Any particular reason why you called, Mom? *Except to badger me about my lack of a significant other?*

"I thought that was obvious," came her mother's clipped retort. "You're getting on in years, and it's time you found a husband and settled down. Why, you're practically middle-aged."

Cassie bristled, bending to remove silverware from the dishwasher and glaring at Endora as she did. "I turn ninety this year, Mom. That hardly makes me eligible for a mid-life crisis!"

"Dear," her mother said with obviously strained patience, "witches don't live much past two hundred and twenty. Do the math. Ninety goes into two twenty—"

"Okay!" Cassie snapped. "I'm *almost* middle-aged. What's wrong with being single right now? I'm contemplating at least another century of life, so why rush?"

"I just want you to be happy," Medusa Morlock told her only child. "You don't have to be so defensive. I don't like to see you all alone." Her voice trailed off.

"Mom, you're alone."

"That's different. Your father . . ."

Cassie leaned back against the rustic kitchen table and stifled a sigh. "I know, Mom. I know. It's just that . . . well . . ."

"A good witch is hard to find?" Medusa supplied dryly.

"Something like that."

"What about that young fellow I introduced you to a decade or so back. Mort Morula. What about him?"

"Mort is his nickname. His first name is *Mortician*." Cassie heard the shudder in her own voice.

"Well, as Thae Bard said, 'What's in a name?'"

"Shakespeare obviously never knew Mort. He's so creepy, his name actually fits him." Goose bumps rose on her arms. She rubbed her hands briskly up and down from elbows to shoulders to dissipate them. "He's way too old for dressing Goth, but that doesn't stop him. Always wears black. No color at all. Paints his face white . . . Yuk."

"So he enjoys sticking out in a crowd. He's your age, dear."

"He's a hundred and fifty if he's a day," Cassie shot back. "Plastic surgery makes him look like he's in his nineties. And I can't stand people who lie about their age."

The pause on the end of the line lengthened to half a minute.

"Except for you, Mom."

"All right, maybe Mort isn't your cup of hemlock. But there has to be a nice young male witch out there just waiting to sweep you off your feet."

At Endora's loud meow, Cassie glanced at the coffee mug the cat was batting back and forth between her forepaws. The logo sported the Wicked Witch of the West skywriting "Surrender Dorothy" with her broom. Cassie rolled her eyes, then said to Medusa, "Listen, Mom, can this matchmaking craze you're on wait until I get back from my book tour? I'm leaving in half an hour."

"You're touring on the Ides of March? Beware."

"Today's the sixteenth," Cassie stated with waning patience. "And most likely the tour organizers just think of March fifteenth as two days before Saint Patrick's Day anyway."

"Most likely." Medusa gave an audible sniff. "Honestly, Cassandra, I can't see why you waste your time on such tawdry pursuits for the benefit of humans."

At that moment, hitting her head repeatedly against the cabinet sounded more enjoyable than further engaging in the conversation. But of course, Medusa would hear the banging, and Cassie would have to explain that her own mother was the trigger for her maniacal self-abuse.

"Mother, please. You know I need to keep busy. What's wrong with what I do?"

"What you *do* is write a newspaper column."

"And your point is?"

"It's to help humankind!"

Even though this was an old argument, Cassie felt her temper rising and consciously flattened her tone. "I'm a journalist, Mom. No coven I know of has a newspaper."

"But human beings!" Indignation crackled down the phone line. "They've persecuted us for eons. They're smelly, petty, and stupid. And they're so . . . so common."

Cassie gave up trying to accomplish anything and sat down at her kitchen table. Tracing the rich oak grain pattern with a fingertip, she said quietly, "Actually, I find them fascinating. Not common at all."

"Well, I suppose if you look at them in a strictly clinical manner, you could argue that they're a diverse, although vastly inferior, species."

"That's the spirit, Mom." Cassie smiled despite Medusa's grudging agreement. "No pun intended."

Suddenly, Medusa's voice tightened. "I can see there's just no reasoning with you today, Cassandra. So I'll say my good-byes. Call me when you return from your book tour."

"I will." Cassie hung up the phone and with an exasperated sigh turned to the dishwasher.

"Your mother just doesn't quit, does she?" Endora asked. She'd stopped batting the mug around and had trained her green eyes on her mistress.

Shaking her head, Cassie pulled out the top drawer of clean dishes. "You can say that again. She wants to see me in a permanent relationship."

"With Mortician Morula?" Endora snorted. "I'd rather date a troll."

"And you have, if I recall correctly."

"Huh." Endora stood and stretched. "Don't bother with those. I'll get them."

With a sweep of her long gray tail, she sent the plates, saucers and utensils flying through the air, heading for cupboards and drawers suddenly standing open and ready to receive them. All the cookware and table settings were quickly back in their proper places.

"Martha Stewart, eat your heart out," the cat purred.

At that, Cassie laughed aloud. Although she considered her something of a rival, she liked Martha and hoped all of the domestic diva's recent troubles would resolve themselves. Both Martha and Cassie had lots of positive things to offer, and it made Cassie sad to think other factors were clouding Martha's gifts. The difference between them, of course, was that while Martha actually had to work at making her projects look like effortless magic, Cassie just had to snap her fingers. Naturally, *La Belle Stewart* didn't know that, and Cassie wasn't about to enlighten her.

For the last ten years, Cassandra had written a weekly column on household hints entitled "The Kitchen Witch" for the *Salem Evening News* of Salem, Massachusetts. She'd deliberately chosen her most recent surname, Hathorne, because Judge Hathorne had presided as the head magistrate at the infamous Salem Witch Trials.

If nothing else, Cassie appreciated subtle irony.

She gave it her best effort to fill her columns with it, and with a light sense of humor that made her wildly popular with readers everywhere. She couldn't stand witches who lacked a sense of humor, having always felt more akin to the Good Witch of the North than to the rest of the witches in *The Wizard of Oz*. And even though the story was merely human fantasy, untold millions believed the stereotypes. Understanding this, Cassandra had kept a low profile throughout her near century of existence.

Now, even though she guarded her secret very well, her "human" persona was about to become not just a well-known columnist in the newspaper, but a body to go with the publicity photo on her book jacket.

She was due in Toledo that afternoon to begin a "down the Mississippi" promotional tour of her latest book, *When Dust Bunnies Attack*. A compilation of her best columns from five years of national syndication, it had already reached tenth on the nonfiction best-seller list. Her publisher hoped the tour would push those numbers even higher.

Cassandra was unashamedly proud of her writing skills. Oh sure, she didn't have to actually type or speak into special computer software like every other hack in the world. She just sat at her computer, let her thoughts organize on her topic, then teleported them onto the screen. Simple, efficient, and she never worried about Carpal Tunnel Syndrome.

But thinking up the topics and developing the best approach

and the best wording were still hard work. And there was always an editor to please. How did all those human writers do it?

Endora's leap from the counter to the table six feet away brought Cassie out of her reverie.

"Packed for the trip yet?" the cat asked.

Cassie glanced at the clock. "The cab won't be here for another half hour, so there's plenty of time. I've got lots of other things to do first."

"Like figure out how to keep Medusa from interfering in your love life. Or current lack thereof."

Cassie grimaced at her familiar's stark comment. "Mom just doesn't understand my fascination with human beings. Or how that affects my relationships with witches." All extraneous interaction with "inferiors" was regarded as completely beneath every male witch Cassie knew. "The males of my species are *so* arrogant."

"Sort of like every Ivy-Leaguer you've ever dated," Endora commented wryly.

"Well, there *is* that." Cassie opened the trip itinerary and her planner, but couldn't study either. Her mother's voice kept intruding in her mind. "I don't know what to do about Mom."

"Ignore her." Endora lapped from the creamer on the table.

"Like that would work."

After licking remnants of leftover cream off her face, the cat settled down on the table top. "Look Cass, I know you don't often see eye to eye—"

"Like never." Cassie closed her planner with a snap. "I don't think we share a single common opinion."

"I know this. I'm your familiar."

"Well, as my familiar, it's your job to listen to me complain." She scratched behind Endora's ears. "I'm on a roll here. Pretend to be sympathetic."

"I'm all ears."

A huge yawn spoiled Endora's attempt at empathy.

Cassie ignored her cat's antics. "Take the fact that she despises human technology."

"Why does she call you on the phone, then?"

"She thinks phones are quaint. And, she actually dated Alexander Graham Bell for a while."

"See, she's got human friends."

"Acquaintances," Cassie amended, "not friends. And she basically keeps them around to amuse herself. Her neighbor, Viv, is a church secretary, and one of her jobs is to contact parishioners if they've missed several consecutive weeks of services. You know, send Get Well cards and such. Mom suggested that Viv's message should be, 'Where the hell have you been?'"

Endora's eyes lit with humor. "That's Medusa for you."

Cassie sighed and rested her chin in her hand. "Once Mom's made up her mind, nothing stops her."

She sensed this marriage campaign her mother waged would not abate until Medusa had seen her only daughter "properly" attached to some macho witch. What had General Grant said during the Civil War? "I intend to fight it out on this line if it takes all summer"? In Medusa's case, Cassie could amend that to say, "if it takes the next century."

***

The book tour's major player sat in the main-floor restaurant of Toledo's convention center hotel eating lunch with his publicist. Sunny and airy, the establishment was not too crowded at midday, but the size of the crowd was of no import to at least one of the pair.

"Mick, I can't believe they've got you seated next to Cassandra Hathorne," Jennifer Bodin sputtered in a volume just a bit below ear-piercing. "Why, she's nothing more than a syndicated columnist!"

Mirek Sandor—known to his legion of fans as M. S. Kazimer—horror/suspense writer extraordinaire—frowned. He set down his fork, which had just been poised to dive into what looked to be an incredible piece of cheesecake, and gave his former fiancee-still publicist his undivided attention. "Do you think you could say that again a bit louder, Jen? I don't think the guys in the kitchen heard you."

"Stop being so sarcastic," Jennifer snapped, but she lowered her voice significantly. "This is important."

"They seat authors alphabetically for these group signings," he commented evenly. "It's not a big deal."

Jennifer sniffed, laying the book signing information with deliberate care onto the table by her plate. "She'll ride your coattails, mark my words. Her sales aren't a fraction of yours, and she'll milk sitting next to you to boost her sell-through."

Mick leaned back in the booth and crossed his arms over his chest. "She writes nonfiction. Sitting beside me will help her how?"

"The pity factor." Jennifer's posture had stiffened with her tone. "Your fans will pity her, sitting there without a customer while they wait in line for hours to get your autograph. They'll feel compelled to step over to her line—after they've gotten your book, of course—and buy hers."

Realizing logic wouldn't work, Mick chose to ignore Jennifer's rant. "Can we talk about this later? This dessert has my name on it."

If anyone could actually swell with indignation, it was Jennifer Bodin. "For God's sake, can't you focus on your career? That cheesecake can wait."

"No it can't."

Jennifer flushed. "What's a stupid dessert in comparison to—"

"Making tons of money?" Mick leaned forward, picked up his fork and said deliberately, "I've focused on writing for twenty years. Now, I want to eat this before it spoils."

Jennifer's crossing her arms over her ample chest snapped Mick's gaze up and drew his eyebrows down. It was more her expression than her mirroring his previous gesture that made his stomach churn with tension.

"Cassandra Hathorne is an award-winning columnist," he stated flatly. "Her books have sold millions, and she doesn't need me to help her sell more. Give it a rest."

The blonde's expression immediately turned to a pout. "I just have your best interests in mind, darling."

"I thought we dispensed with the 'darling' tag two months ago." At Jennifer's look of stubborn determination, Mick's anger at her posturing flared, and he added brusquely, "Ms. Hathorne isn't a competitor. She appeals to a completely different audience. A mostly female, *homemaking* audience."

"Of course she's a competitor." All remnants of a sulk disappeared, to be replaced by cold business savvy. "The buying public only has so much money to spend. Since you both sell the same product, she's competition. You're vying for the reader's hard-earned dollar."

Mick studied the woman that, up until two months before, he had been engaged to marry at Christmas. Just over five-feet tall, she was beautiful and curvaceous, with cornflower blue eyes and a mouth that, when not turned down in a pout, begged to be kissed. She'd been his publicist and manager for four years, his lover for two, and his fiancee for just over six months. He loved everything about how she managed his writing career, but he'd been foolish to think that his love of her professional abilities could carry over into a personal relationship.

Once they'd announced their engagement, it had become apparent that Jennifer was more interested in his net worth than she was in his individual value. As a business manager, her attention to detail made her second to none. But Mick realized he needed equal personal attention. Equal affection. And he needed to return them. Nearly four months ago he had discovered he didn't love Jennifer for herself, either, but for what she'd done for his career. So the fact that she loved his alter-ego, M. S. Kazimer, and all the wealth and prestige that went with that name, rather than Mirek Sandor shouldn't have bothered him so much. But it did. They were quite the pair. Maybe they deserved to marry each other.

He mentally sighed and stopped that line of thinking. Their engagement was over. Nothing would change that. Fortunately, God hadn't even joined them before they were split asunder.

He studied the pretty blonde a moment. "I'll likely sell a disgusting number of books on this tour, regardless of who sits next to me. No point in getting upset about seating arrangements."

"You should be off by yourself. Not only is that witch-person next to you, but Robert Whitman—whoever he is—is on the tour, too."

"He's new. Promoting his first book," Mick said stiffly. Mention of Whitman made his entire body clench. His stomach churned, making him glad he hadn't started eating his cheesecake. "Our publisher wants him on this tour with some of its big guns, to give his career a boost."

Jennifer's eyes lit up like a zealot's at a church revival. "You've just made my point. He'll really profit from your fame. I certainly hope you're being compensated in some way."

"As my publicist and business manager, you'd already know I'm not," came Mick's even retort. "And all this talk of money and compensation and riding my coattails stops now."

"I've offended you."

He shook his head and with a concentrated effort modified his sharp tone. "Look, Jen, I know you're supposed to promote me. But I'm not exactly failing at the author business. I've got more money than I know what to do with."

"Then why throw it all away by retiring from writing?"

At that question, the acid in his stomach did its best volcano impersonation. Knowing he was treading water in a shark tank,

Mick worded his answer carefully, putting as much calm conviction into his tone as he could. "When you've lost the joy in what you're doing, you have to stop. Find something else that makes you happy. Writing no longer makes me happy." *At least, writing horror novels doesn't,* he thought grimly. *But can I do anything else? What am I if I'm not M. S. Kazimer?*

His quiet declaration didn't have the effect he'd hoped. He knew it when he saw Jennifer's flush.

"I can't believe you made this decision without consulting me first," she said, volume increasing with each word.

Restaurant patrons seated at nearby tables stared at her and then quickly looked away. Mick had the sick feeling they were trying to pretend they weren't attempting to eavesdrop.

God, he wanted this nightmare to end. He kept his voice low when he leaned toward Jennifer. "I've said this before, but you've refused to listen. Listen now. I'm tired of all this. Tired of the deadlines, of the hype, of the pressure to live up to my readers' expectations. But most of all, I'm tired of creating demented serial killers who leave a grisly trail of victims behind them."

"But people adore your stories!"

"But *I* don't anymore. And doesn't my opinion count for something?" As Jennifer's silence lengthened and her mouth set stubbornly, Mick shook his head. Fortunately, his business manager couldn't feel the lump that had settled in his throat. Macho horror writers weren't supposed to get emotional. He was rather proud of the fact that his voice was steady and matter-of-fact when he said, "You never loved me as much as you loved M.S. Kazimer. And the money and fame that go along with that persona."

Looking the part of a long-suffering martyr, Jennifer rose regally from her seat. "Spare me the histrionics, Mick."

"I thought that was your ploy."

She continued with barely a pause. "You get moody before every tour. Come up to my room, and I'll see about arousing your interest in being here."

"Don't go that route. We haven't made love in months—and for the record, I don't count sex after our increasingly frequent arguments as lovemaking. Personally, I'm not interested anymore in sex for mending fences and not for passion."

Her chin rose. "Now you're being deliberately boorish."

"You were the one who broke off the engagement. And now you're coming on to me in the hotel restaurant."

"Sometimes, Mick, you really are a bastard." She turned on her heel and stalked from the restaurant.

He watched her leave, his mood sinking further with every step she took. The thought that she didn't love him had nagged at him for at least a year. She'd proven his suspicion when he told her this current book, *Mortal Sin,* would be his last by promptly threatening to call off the engagement if he retired. When he said his decision was final, she'd canceled the wedding.

Not publicly, of course. He knew Jennifer harbored the idea that she could lure him back to writing—and perhaps back into her bed. But knowing his bank account and international fame meant more to her than his emotional and physical well-being would shield him from her schemes.

And he had another, far more compelling reason for wanting out. A reason he couldn't discuss. Not with his family or his friends, not with his former fiancée.

He snapped his napkin closed and called for the check. Understanding that his affection for Jennifer was mostly due to her skill at running his career, he'd been prepared to call off the wedding. She'd beaten him to it, which hadn't surprised him much. And if she couldn't love him for himself instead of for the writing talent that had made him filthy rich and world famous, that was her problem. At the end of the book tour, when he officially announced his immediate retirement, she'd either decide she could live with Mirek Sandor, or take her severance pay and find work as someone else's publicist.

The realization that the latter scenario was the most likely to happen made his heart thud dully in his chest. But he set his jaw and squared his shoulders. Jennifer was going to spend this book tour mounting a furious campaign to keep him writing, but he wouldn't cave in. Couldn't. Mirek Sandor was not a coward; he could resist his former lover's persuasion.

But he'd sure as hell rather be facing a deadline for the editor from Hades than Ms. Jennifer Bodin on a mission that involved money.

***

"You're sitting next to M. S. Kazimer at all the signings." Endora studied the book tour itinerary as the limo Cassie's publisher had sent sped them from the airport to their hotel near the Seagate Convention Center in downtown Toledo. "Wow."

Cassie's head snapped around to look at her now very human familiar. "*The* M. S. Kazimer? As in, 'Every-word-I-write-turns-into-a-best-seller' M. S. Kazimer?"

"The very same."

"Did you arrange that, oh business manager of mine?"

Endora shrugged shoulders encased in a bright red suit jacket that perfectly complimented her steel-gray hair. Her ability to wear clothes that always harmonized with her coloring amazed Cassie. For Cassie herself, shopping solo was a recipe for fashion disaster. Fortunately, Endora was always more than happy to shape-shift into human form and accompany her.

Today, Cassie wore a royal blue suit coat with black slacks and a brightly colored silk scarf. As the tour moved south, she'd packed accordingly with lighter weight—and lighter colored—clothes. Of course, Endora had picked them out for her. Thank the goddess for color analysis, and a friend with a good eye for style.

"You know I'd take the credit if I could, Boss," Endora was saying of the signing arrangements, "but I can't. Luck of the alphabet, I guess."

Cassie sat back against the limo's plush leather seat. "That man's some kind of alchemist, I'm sure of it. He can certainly transform his imagination into gold."

"Good looking." Endora passed Mick's press kit photo to Cassie, who immediately sat straight up, studying it as if she thought it might speak to her.

"I'll say!" She continued to stare.

"I heard that."

"Heard what?"

"Don't give me that 'What are you talking about?' deliberately blank look. I heard your heartbeat."

One dark brow deliberately winged up. "Heartbeat?"

"Come on, Cassandra," Endora teased. "Your heart went into overdrive when you got a look at ol' M.S. here." She flicked the back of Mick's press photo with her index finger. "It's beating a regular tattoo right now."

Cassie shrugged. "He *is* very good looking...."

"No, he's devastatingly handsome. Admit it, you could go for a hunky human male like M. S. Kazimer in a split second."

"I'll plead the Fifth." Cassie looked at the picture again. "Or I'll *drink* a fifth, so I don't go into groupie overdrive at the signings and turn into a simpering puddle at his feet."

"I knew it," Endora crowed, then started chanting, "Cassie and M.S., sittin' in a tree, K-I-S-S-I-N-G—"

An elbow to the ribs brought an end to her banter.

"Great Mother Goddess, Endora, grow up! Okay, the guy's gorgeous. But he's probably married and the father of five."

Still snickering, Endora glanced at Mick's bio. "Says here he's forty years old and single."

"I thought I read somewhere that he's engaged."

"Engaged is not married. That means he's fair game. Grrrrr . . ."

Giving up any hope of heading off Endora's line of thinking, Cassie returned to studying the photo. "Black hair and blue eyes. Quite a combination."

"I prefer tiger-striped fur and yellow eyes, but then, that's just me." Her familiar grinned at the face Cassie made. "Ever read any of his books?"

"No! That psycho serial killer stuff scares me to death." She shuddered. "Disgusting."

Endora snorted. "You're hopeless. A witch who's afraid of the dark? Who'd a thunk it."

"I'm not afraid of the dark. I just can't stand to read novels about crazy people killing regular people."

"Of course not. Such actions would indicate that your precious human race aren't all saints."

Cassie's lips pursed indignantly. "*E tu Brute*? You're sounding just like my mother."

"Yet another service I, as your trusty familiar, supply," Endora stated blandly. "I must continually assure that your plane returns from Fantasy Island."

"How many lives have you got left?"

The Cheshire grin returned. "More than enough to do my job."

"I was afraid of that." Cassie moved to hand Mick's photo back, then paused, staring at it again. She gave a low whistle. "He's hiding something. Something very dark."

"Let me see that." Endora snatched the photo from Cassie's fingers. Flipping it over, she held it to the limo's interior cabin light to see Mick's image from the back. She glanced at Cassie. "You're right. His aura's got a definite darkness to it."

"I don't sense it as being something evil inside him, though."

Endora shrugged, then returned Mick's picture to the press kit. "Hard to tell from a photo. But you're the witch, not me."

Cassie's laugh was more like a snort. "You're practically as much witch as I am." She winced mentally when she saw how uncomfortable her remark had made Endora. The time was fast approaching when Cassie's familiar would have to deal with a critical issue, but that was months away, and Endora didn't seem overly concerned with the deadline. Instead of making matters worse by bringing attention to her gaffe, Cassie opted for a light tone when she added, "Everyone I know protects some secret. Why would M. S. Kazimer be any different? He uses a pseudonym. But then, so do I."

Her comment had the desired affect. Seeing Endora stiffen, she knew the cat was going into her familiar's role of witch protector. There was no need. But knowing Endora—despite her sarcastic manner and unorthodox ways—took her responsibilities to Cassie seriously was comfortably reassuring. Dora was a good friend, too.

"You know the reason for a pseudonym." Endora's voice held a touch of heat. "What might happen if you ever revealed your true nature to a human?"

Cassie's upheld hand staved off Endora's rising fervor. "You're preaching to the choir, here, Dora. You know I'm extremely careful. But everyone has secrets. M. S. Kazimer certainly does. And since I'll be sitting next to the most prolific and popular writer alive today, I should familiarize myself with his history. Just in case his ego's as big as his bank account, and I have to practice my ego-reduction skills."

Endora bristled. "You're as good a writer as he is."

"Thanks for the vote of confidence, pal, but he could very well not share your exalted opinion of my skills."

"If he's obnoxious to you, I can put a hex on him. Turn him into a zombie for you. I know you don't like doing that kind of stuff yourself."

Cassie knew Endora was only half-joking. "His fans might grow concerned when his body parts started dropping off at autographing sessions."

"You're right. I'll have to be more subtle . . . ."

Cassie reached over and gave Endora a quick, affectionate hug. "Thanks for being my friend."

"My pleasure."

"And *no* hexes."

"Spoilsport."

Two

"Endora, stop that," Cassie hissed, elbowing her familiar in the ribs. Her cat, still in human form, sat perfectly still, staring unblinkingly at the huge aquarium in the hotel lobby. Cassie elbowed her again. "Endora!"

"Huh?" Endora turned almond-shaped green eyes to her friend.

"You're doing it again!"

"Doing what?"

"Well, acting like a cat."

"I *am* a cat." Endora's gaze strayed back toward the huge assortment of tropical fish swimming placidly in the tank not five feet away. Her nose twitched.

Cassie shook her head. "Right now you're my manager. My very *human* manager. So, start managing. Go yell at some incompetent underling, or sign some book order manifest. I swear, you haven't moved a muscle in ten minutes."

"This tour is being run with military precision. There are no incompetents for me to terrorize." Licking her palm, Endora smoothed back her hair. It was the exact color—a dark, steel gray—as in her feline form. Not the ultra-white, pigment-challenged hair the aging referred to as gray. Hers was a startling, striking shade. Coupled with her green eyes and feline walk, Endora's human form always turned male heads wherever she went. "The hotel's first-rate, the bus would make a rock band's tour bus look like a V W beetle, and all your needs are being seen to. There's really nothing for me to do on this trip."

"Except keep me company."

Wordlessly, Endora patted Cassie's hand, and Cassie genuinely appreciated the gesture. It was difficult enough being a witch in a human-dominated world. Getting out among them as she did served to emphasize the vast differences between the two species.

Witches being so long-lived, Cassie had found it necessary to change her identity and location every twenty years or so to keep neighbors from becoming suspicious of her true nature. The Witness Protection Program could have learned some tricks from her. But since the average human can't accurately tell a person's age between approximately thirty and fifty—especially with hair products and surgical enhancement to alter the truth—

Cassie's identity changes generally consisted of moving to another part of the country, wearing a different hairstyle and color, and getting a new job. And, as a subtle precaution against detection, she changed her dominant hand with every one of her birth date upgrades. This time, she was left-handed.

A quick alteration of the date on her birth certificate, and then it was just a matter of filling out forms for the various required government documents. She had four Social Security numbers, twice as many different driver's licenses, and had filed tax returns in half the states in the Union. If she ever decided to do it, collecting retirement benefits would rival the trials of Hercules.

Unfortunately, she often had occasion to rethink her choice of dominant hand as part of her disguise. It was a right-handed world, after all. She had gotten so sick of smudging her left pinkie finger during autographings that she'd created an instant-drying ink which wouldn't come off on her skin when hand followed pen across page. The ink's rare main ingredient—henbane—was well worth the trouble to find, as it saved on many trips to the bathroom to clean up. To alleviate the "curled hand" writing style of so many southpaws, she'd also taken to turning the page and writing straight up. No more cramped fingers.

"C'mon, let's get you a cup of tea," Endora urged, rising gracefully from the chair. "As your manager, it is my duty to see that your every wish is granted, your every whim indulged."

"You sound like a genie, not a familiar," Cassie teased. Her friend's eyes again shifted in the direction of the aquarium, a wistful expression entering them. Linking her arm with Endora's, she said slyly, "I've heard salmon is the house specialty here."

"Wonderful," Endora purred.

***

Mick glanced at the check before reaching for his wallet. Man, eating out had gotten expensive. In Toledo, no less. Jennifer's vegetarian lasagna, approximately one cubic inch in size, almost cost more than his steak, which had a pretty hefty price tag. Add beverages and dessert to that, and the bill could offset part of Haiti's national debt.

He almost sighed for the "good old days." When one dollar could buy a burger and fries at a fast-food restaurant. And, of course, Mick's "good old days" included Thanksgiving dinners with his big Slovak family at their home in Detroit. A huge turkey with all the trappings, dumplings, Slovak pastries to send the cholesterol soaring, pies, cranberry sauce, and—his favorite—homemade sweet pickles. As a kid, he got a quart jar of his grandmother's sweet pickles as a Christmas present every year. It was the absolute best present she could ever have given him.

Times were not so simple now but, realistically, when had that fact ever been different for adults? Things were simple for kids. Adults complicated their lives and the lives of others. His life hadn't been simple for nineteen years, not since his debut novel made the *New York Times* bestseller list, and he'd become a twenty-one-year-old mega-star. Had he written as Mirek Sandor, his privacy would have vanished right then, so he counted his blessings for having the presence of mind to use his mother's maiden name as his pen name. How media and sports stars managed to handle the public idolization heaped on them, he'd never know. Of course many didn't, as evidenced by the number whose secondary addresses were rooms at the Betty Ford Clinic.

A sudden realization struck him. Jennifer would never have fit in with his raucous, fun-loving family. Her big-city style and metropolitan world view would have meshed with Mick's simple Old World roots like American Kennel Club members at a Humane Society dog adoption. It saddened him to think he and Jennifer were so completely unsuited for each other. Better for both of them they hadn't legally bound themselves to each other before they figured that out.

Movement beyond the approaching waiter drew his attention. Two women had risen from their table, and the taller one could be none other than Cassandra Hathorne. Since her book jacket photo was seared into his memory, he recognized the short cut of her brown-black hair even from across the room.

Stranded in Detroit's Metropolitan Airport a couple winters back and facing death by boredom, he'd picked up her first book. Then finished it in the three hours it took airport officials to de-ice the flight's wings. She was simply one of the best writers he'd ever read, even though her columns were definitely of more interest to women and male interior decorators than to a macho pop fiction writer like Mick. Thus, he'd never told a soul that he'd written her a fan letter. Using his real name, of course. He'd received a gracious, hand-written reply. Although he'd be surprised if she'd actually written it herself, the gesture was appreciated. He hadn't answered his own fan mail in over fifteen years. The volume was overwhelming, and some of it was way too bizarre to warrant personal comment.

Regardless of the authenticity of her letter, Cassandra Hathorne's "Kitchen Witch" column had become required reading for him, and he actually looked forward to autographing next to her on the tour. He wondered if non-fiction writers suffered the same self-confidence lapses he and his fellow fiction writers seemed prone to, and decided he'd ask. Besides that, she was extremely easy on the eyes. He'd not have been a red-blooded male if he didn't understand that on the most basic level.

The other woman, he assumed, was Cassandra's publicist-manager. Her startling gray hair and feline manner put him instantly in mind of a cat. Being allergic to the wretched creatures, he'd never owned one and had no desire to. His knowledge of them was pretty much confined to Animal Planet specials on cable TV, and only if that was the only program on. But as his gaze followed the women's departure, his throat started getting scratchy and his eyes watery. He felt as if an allergic reaction was imminent.

That had him shaking his head, amazed at his flight of whimsy.

Whatever good mood seeing The Kitchen Witch had put him in was doomed, however, as bleak reality rose up to snuff it out. He could have sworn he felt his whimsy draining out of him. Although he loved writing because he could control the outcome for his characters, he wasn't so egotistical to think that his fiction could translate into life. If he'd been that good, he'd have asked years ago if God needed some help. But the fact remained that Mick was a writer. He couldn't *not* be one. And though he had no intentions of ever penning another horror novel, the thought of never writing again terrified him.

Mick shook his head to clear it and glanced at his watch. Twelve-thirty. The first signing was set for four that afternoon. The first signing on the last promotional tour he would ever do . . . What crap to dwell on that fact. Mick didn't do maudlin. After all, life moved on, and it was time he did, too. The reason behind his retirement was what brought his mood low. That, and having Jennifer along in her business manager capacity.

The latter problem had definitely been caused by "man

think," he realized belatedly—the idea that they could get along in a professional capacity after their personal affair was ended. Too late to change that now. He'd just have to ignore her attempts to keep him writing. At this point, Jennifer's schemes were minor problems compared to the urgent reason for this tour.

Suck it up, Sandor, he chided himself. *You couldn't live with yourself if you didn't quit now.*

No multi-book contract, regardless of how lucrative, could be worth the possible damage if he continued his career.

No time like the present to get started on ending things.

***

The conference center would soon be open, and Cassie meticulously prepared her table for the book signing.

To her left, she prominently displayed a framed, autographed picture of Agnes Moorehead. A trophy from the years 1964 through 1973, when she was Cassandra Smith, staff writer for television's *Bewitched*. Of course, anyone who asked was told the photo had been her grandmother's, the *"Bewitched* writer" for whom Cassie was named.

Out of profound respect, she had always addressed Agnes Moorehead as Miss Moorehead. Had lobbied to name the character of the witch mother-in-law after her own cat-familiar, Endora.

They were all gone now. Agnes, Elizabeth Montgomery, both Darrins—Dick York and Dick Sargent—Paul Lynde; the original Mrs. Kravitz, Alice Pearce; her replacement, Sandra Gould; Aunt Clara, Marion Lorne . . . Dead of various forms of cancer, coronary artery disease, heart attacks, Alzheimer's, emphysema. The liabilities of humanity.

The logo for her syndicated column—which adorned her stationery, book covers, and every piece of merchandise the Kitchen Witch embellished—was the show's logo of Samantha Stevens, on a broomstick and wearing a pointed witch hat, smiling that million-dollar smile. Of course, Cassie had had to put a spell on her logo so that anyone who saw it would vaguely recognize it but never be able to say definitively where they'd seen it. One couldn't be too careful about copyright infringement or trademark violation these days, after all.

***

Mick's preparations for what promised to be a horde of autograph-seekers usually took all of thirty seconds. He'd sit down between a poster-sized picture of himself on his right and a mountain of copies of his latest book on his left, adjust his tie, and pick up his favorite Mont Blanc ink pen.

Since everything was ready to go, including the pen, he capitalized on his chance to clandestinely study Cassandra Hathorne up close. The Agnes Moorehead picture made him smile. Excellent touch. But the next touch was better. His nostrils flared when Cassandra set out a plate of hard candies made from a recipe in her cookbook. Cursed with a chronic Slovak sweet tooth and no time to devote to candy making, he had latched on to this particular recipe months before. It required a microwave and a maximum of twenty minutes in the kitchen.

Just looking at the plate of confections triggered his salivary glands. He knew how great that candy tasted. To spare himself the embarrassment of drooling in public, he reached into an open box sitting behind the authors' chairs, grabbed Cassie's book, then retrieved his pen from the table.

"Autograph this for me?"

She looked up, startled, and he noted that her eyes were a color he'd never seen before. A rich, dark caramel. Fascinating. A man could gaze into those eyes for a long time . . .

He gave himself a mental shake and refocused. He had a goal here, and right now it wasn't gazing into a woman's eyes. It was scoring some sweets. For a moment Mick thought Ms Hathorne wasn't going to answer him, then she snapped out of her daze and gave him a shy smile. A smile nearly as beautiful as her eyes.

"Sure, but you don't have to buy a book to get some candy."

It was his turn to be startled.

"You must be a mind reader as well as an incredible cook," he said, but when a sudden uneasiness crept into her gaze, added, "but I do want the book. I've got all your others, including the one with that candy recipe."

One dark eyebrow shot up. "You do?"

He didn't bother to tell her that he kept this fact from all of his friends and relatives, especially the male ones, and that her books were in his private office where no one would see them. "Actually, yes." Offering his pen and the book, he said, "Would you sign it 'To Mick'?"

"Sure thing."

As she bent to autograph the title page, he caught a whiff of spicy, exotic perfume. Suddenly, his mouth started watering for reasons other than candy. To cover his abrupt and shocking reaction to the smell, he grabbed three candies off the plate and popped them into his mouth.

Great seating arrangements, he concluded silently.

***

There. On the fourth page of the convention brochure. With a trembling fingertip, he traced the name of his idol. His god. Raising M. S. Kazimer's photograph to his lips, he placed a gentle kiss on the glossy forehead.

It was almost time to begin. Soon, not a living person would doubt his genius.

He locked the hotel room door, pulled the curtains, opened the latest book to the description of the first murder. There was no need to read the words, as he had committed them to memory. Eyes closed, he pictured the first victim's face. A drug-addicted businessman caught on his way to a connection in a seedy part of town. He'd died in a truly satisfying way, exactly as the plot depicted. Funny how life—or in this case, death—imitated art.

Aroused once again at the memory of his triumph, he stroked the book's pages as if caressing a lover.

Soon, two more murders in two more cities, culminating in a final orgy of death in New Orleans. The book tour would take him there, stopping in each of the novel's settings. And at every venue, he would carry out his destiny as depicted in the pages.

In New Orleans, all would know his true brilliance.

***

Five minutes before the doors opened on the Midwest Booksellers Association convention in Toledo, Cassie and Mick sat at their ten-foot-long table, ready for the crush of fans who had come to this event just to see one or both of them. Mick bent his fingers back, stretching them to prevent cramping, while Cassie closed her eyes and took four slow, deep breaths.

"Does this ever get to you?"

Surprised by the question, Cassie turned toward M.S. Kazimer. "Pardon me?"

Mick gestured to the huge exhibition hall. "This. All the booths, the crowds. The fans. Does this ever overwhelm you?"

Great Mother Goddess, this guy's gorgeous! Incredibly blue eyes were locked on hers like a laser guidance system, short-circuiting Cassie's rational thought patterns and replacing them with images of smoky jazz music and rumpled sheets.

She had to mentally swallow to steady her racing heart.

Earlier, when he'd asked her to sign her book for him, she'd barely made eye contact. She'd unthinkingly told him he could have the candy before he'd even asked, and his observation that she was a mind reader had put her on guard. That, coupled with dread that she'd have to confess to never having read any of his work—especially in light of the fact that he claimed to be a fan of hers—had kept her from looking at him for too long.

Now, she thought she could stare into those eyes forever.

But the underlying sadness in the blue gaze that studied her so intently grounded her flight of fancy. His aura reinforced what his eyes told her: M. S. Kazimer was a very troubled man.

"This is only the third time I've ever done this," she confessed. "The novelty hasn't worn off. I imagine—if I manage to stay as popular as you have for so long, Mr. Kazimer—the novelty will wear off."

She saw some of the tension ease from his beautiful eyes.

"I wish you continued success and boundless enthusiasm," he said in his wonderful baritone voice. "And, please, call me Mick. That's how you signed the book. Besides, 'Mr. Kazimer' sounds too much like some corporate raider's name for my taste."

Impulsively, she extended her hand to shake his. "Mick. It's Cassie for me."

"Cassie."

The sound of her name on his tongue practically made her swoon. *Pull yourself together, you idiot,* she ordered her reeling senses. *This guy's out of your league and probably spoken for as well.*

That latter thought tossed a bucket of ice water on her steamy thoughts. She could practically feel them fizzling out.

Just then, Endora glided up behind the table and set a large thermos and a coffee mug to Cassie's right so she could pour and drink with her right hand and sign books with her left.

"Here's your batwing tea," she crooned. "I added just a pinch of eye of newt and a sprinkle of unicorn horn. Enjoy." Smiling despite the glare her boss was sending her way, she raised in salute to Mick the small creamer she'd brought with her, drank its entire contents, then sauntered out, not bothering to wipe her new cream moustache from her upper lip.

Bemused, Mick watched her inimitably feline exit. He

blinked his suddenly itching eyes and sniffed once. "Can I ask you a question?"

Cassie looked over the rim of her tea cup as she sipped, then lowered it slowly. "Sure. As long as it isn't 'How do you come up with ideas to write about?'"

He gave a fake shudder. "Been asked that one too many times myself. That, and 'Your writing is so realistic, have you ever actually killed someone?'"

"To which you'd love to reply, 'Just the people who ask me that question,' right?"

"That'll be our little secret, okay?" He winked one piercing blue eye, and Cassie felt herself getting breathless. "Actually, I wanted to ask you about your publicist."

"Dora's not for hire," she stated. "I'm too selfish to let her work for anyone but me."

"Fair enough. Besides, I've got one of my own." His gaze focused on the far side of the room where Jennifer was in a heated discussion with the convention hall's manager.

Cassie's gaze followed his, and she honed in on the conversation. It involved which author deserved top billing. Jennifer, of course, insisted Mick get the largest lettering at the top of the marquee, but the manager maintained that, in the interest of fairness, authors were traditionally listed alphabetically.

Mick seemed to understand the content of the conversation, although Cassie was certain he couldn't hear it as she could. Expression tight, he stared at the imbroglio taking place just inside the entrance doors.

Sympathy swamped Cassie. Endora was often a trial—the little stunt she'd just pulled was evidence of that—but she did such things to keep Cassie from getting bored. Both of them knew no one would ever suspect Endora had really brewed batwing tea, so the joke was to call it what it was and let the humans laugh about the clever "Kitchen Witch" tie-in.

"About Endora," she prompted gently.

"Huh?" Mick turned toward her. "What did you say?"

"Endora? You were asking about her."

"Oh, yeah." He suddenly blushed. "Never mind."

Intrigued by this handsome, brilliant, popular man's sudden discomfort, Cassie found herself doing something she rarely did—pursuing a conversation with a human being. "No way, Mr. M.S. Kazimer. Mick. You're not ducking out now. Ask your question."

He visibly swallowed. "You're going to think this is a really stupid observation on my part."

"Try me."

He paused for so long, she thought they'd be overrun with autograph seekers before he continued. After clearing his throat twice, however, he seemed ready.

"Your publicist seems a bit..."

"Flaky? Ditzy? Eccentric?"

Mick shook his head, red creeping into his cheeks. "Actually, I was thinking more delusional."

Cassie managed to lock her jaw before her mouth dropped open, but she recovered instantly from such an unexpected comment. "Oh that. Well. The wonderful thing about Endora is she doesn't suffer from delusions." Cassie took a sip of tea and winked at M.S. Kazimer. "She enjoys them immensely."

Mick looked nonplused for a split second, then burst out laughing. "Touche."

The fact that she had managed to make him momentarily forget his publicist's embarrassing antics warmed Cassie straight through. *Not bad for a non-magic accomplishment,* she thought.

Although she had to admit that M. S. "Mick" Kazimer had managed to enchant her without using any magic, either.

It was going to be a *very* interesting tour.

Three

"My daughters are Betty, Alice and Florence," said a bright-eyed octogenarian as she stood in front of Cassie's table and patiently waited for her to sign the requested books. "Barb and Dorothy are my daughters-in-law." She paused as Cassie jotted down the names, then continued, "Granddaughters Diane, Kathy, and Ellen. Great-granddaughter Cindy . . . And when my five-year-old great-great-granddaughter turns twenty-five, I'm going to buy her a copy of this book."

Cassie glanced up into the woman's sparkling eyes and said straight-faced, "Let's hope it's still in print in twenty years."

"Oh, it will be, dear." The woman patted Cassie's hand. "It will. Good advice is always stylish, useful and necessary."

As she walked away, Cassie sighed. "I hope I've got that kind of energy when I'm her age."

"Relatively speaking," Endora said wryly.

"Relatively speaking." She winked at her familiar, who'd just restocked her pile of *Dust Bunnies*, then turned to the next person in line. "Whose name should I sign this to," she asked.

Totally absorbed with the many eager fans who had stood in line over an hour to get her autographed book, Cassie almost missed Endora's sudden tension. The hair on the familiar's arms abruptly stood on end, and she went completely still.

Something up?

Not sure, but I'd better check it out. Be back in a bit.

Endora rose and left, moving through the crowd with the lithe grace so typical of her species. When she returned forty-five minutes later, it was nearly time for the signing to be over. Silent, she took a seat.

The line had thinned to a handful, and Cassie caught the tautness still emanating from her friend. She shot Endora a startled glance, and immediately heard "Later" inside her head.

***

"What was that all about," Cassie whispered as they moved down the corridor toward the booksellers reception in the convention center's adjacent hotel.

Endora glanced quickly around. No one was within earshot. "Didn't you sense it?"

"Apparently not," Cassie returned tartly. "I was reading my fans' auras. What did I miss?" Endora shivered, and Cassie stopped, grasping her friend's elbow and turning to face her. A sheen of perspiration clung to her familiar's upper lip, and her eyes were a bit wild. "You're never like this, Dora. You're scaring me here."

Endora actually blinked before she turned to look at Cassie. "Pure evil. I sensed pure evil."

Cassie's grip tightened. "In the exhibition hall during the signing?"

Endora nodded.

"Human or nonhuman?"

"Human." Endora's green eyes were huge. "I've never perceived a darker soul in all my years on Earth."

"Great Mother Goddess!" Cassie swore. As flighty as Endora occasionally was, she never erred in her assessment of the karmic plane. A familiar's responsibility was to protect her witch from harm on any level, and Endora performed her duty flawlessly. "You couldn't determine who?"

"I didn't get a look at him." Endora ran both hands through her hair in a gesture of pure frustration. "By the time I worked my way through the crowd, he was gone."

"Male?"

"Aren't they all?" Endora snorted. "And here I was hoping it was Jennifer Bodin. No such luck."

The attempt at levity eased Cassie's anxiety somewhat, and she resumed walking toward the banquet room. "Most of my fans today were women. Was he waiting in my line?"

"No. All the men who bought your book got it for a significant other." Endora looked abruptly morose, but Cassie could sense she was putting on a front to lighten the mood. "That really cute blonde guy? Gay. The book was a gift for his partner, Bruce."

"I just assumed *his* name was Bruce."

Endora shook her head. "You are sooo naive."

"Back to this evil man," Cassie prompted, refocusing on their potential problem.

She slowed as they approached the head table. Their seats were next to Mick and his manager-girlfriend, and Cassie wanted all her questions answered before they sat down. Carrying on an in-depth telepathic discussion was difficult in a crowded room. And she didn't want anyone wondering why she and Endora had furrowed brows over the chicken a-la-king.

"I sensed him near Mick's line, but not to have a book

signed. Otherwise, I'd have found the ghoul." Endora shivered again. "If he's a fan of any of the authors here, he's definitely an obsessed one. Psychopathically obsessed, completely depraved. Someone who should be incarcerated."

"I don't sense him anywhere close by now." Cassie's gaze swept the room to reinforce her sixth sense.

"Neither do I."

Cassie gently squeezed her familiar's shoulder. "We don't know his intentions, and have no idea where he is, so we can't deal with him right now. Nor can we warn anyone just because spectral evidence points to evil. But we can't take this lightly. Let's stay alert to the possibility a wacko's hanging around the convention."

"I'm already on it," Endora muttered under her breath as they took their seats. "Trust me, Boss."

"I do. With my life."

***

The moment Cassie Hathorne and Endora Bast sat down at the head table, Mick felt his throat get scratchy.

That's the damnedest thing, he thought. *Happens every time those two show up.* Actually, he had to admit he'd sat at the signing all afternoon and not had any problems as long as Cassie was alone. *It's like I'm allergic to Endora Bast. Ridiculous!*

He cleared his throat, but his voice cracked when he started to greet the pair. He cleared his throat again. "Sorry," he said, still rasping. "It feels like I'm having some sort of anaphylactic reaction."

"Nonsense, darling," Jennifer cooed. She hooked her right arm through his left and quickly touched her head to his shoulder. "You're only allergic to cats."

Cassie, who had just taken a large sip of water, nearly spit the liquid onto the pristine table linen. It would be rude to laugh, so she concentrated on the fact that watching Jennifer paw Mick was discomfiting. She dared not meet Endora's eyes, but she could hear her friend's laughter in her head.

How ironic, the familiar telepathically commented. Aloud, Endora asked, "And do you have any allergies, Miss Bodin?"

"Strawberries," Jennifer replied on a much-too-bright smile.

Endora, I'm warning you. Don't go there!

Why not? She's a pompous ass.

She's Mick's fiancée, not to mention his manager.

Don't know about you, Cass, but I'm not reading any "lovey-dovey" auras coming from our handsome writer stud toward the obnoxious Miss J. B.

Cassie refused to admit she'd reached the same conclusion. In her quick reading of the room, she'd been surprised to see a trace of darkness in both Mick's and Jennifer's auras. His was darker, but each should have been much lighter to indicate a more relaxed state of mind. Obviously, he was annoyed with his publicist, yet Cassie didn't sense the type of loving tolerance in Mick one would expect he'd show his fiancée.

And something even more odd. She'd caught his gaze just as she'd sat down and could have sworn his eyes had actually lit with delight when he'd seen her. Then, of course, his allergy had kicked in, and the glint had disappeared. Probably pure fantasy on her part. She pushed the thought away.

I don't know what you're talking about, Dora.

Goddess, you're such a liar!

If her current physical familiarity with M. S. Kazimer is any indication, their relationship is just wonderful.

All the more reason to hex her, if you ask me. Eliminate the competition.

Unwilling to interpret that last remark, Cassie turned to Mick. "If you squeeze that lemon slice into your water, drinking it should take care of the tickle in your throat."

"Can't hurt to try." Mick promptly did as instructed and downed the entire contents. He smiled, a bit bemused. "You're right! The tickle's gone."

Only because you cast a protection spell on him.

Give the guy a break, Dora. This bus tour will be miserable for all of us if he breaks out in hives every time you're both in the same room.

Oh, I don't know . . . He could keep coming to you for remedies.

Jennifer's jumping into the conversation spared Endora from a scathing telepathic set down. She got a narrow-eyed stare from Cassie instead.

"You must save an incredible amount of money on doctor's expenses," Jennifer said to Cassie. Her tone wasn't the least bit complimentary. "Did you learn that in the Tennessee hills?"

Cassie sensed Endora's ire rising. *Down, girl. I can take care of this.* "Actually, it came out of the AMA's journal a few years back. An amazingly in-depth article about folk medicine."

Maybe you read it?"

Bull's eye, Endora crowed.

"I'm sure I was far too busy organizing Mick's career to take any note of it." Jennifer gave his arm another proprietary squeeze. "He's an industry unto himself, what with screen rights and signings and all."

"Jen—"

She turned innocent eyes to him, then smiled maliciously at Cassie. "After all, every book he's written has been a best-seller."

"If I recall correctly," Mick said, tone still full of warning, "Miss Hathorne's books have all been best-sellers, too."

"Oh? How many books would that be?"

Cassie met Jennifer's hostile eyes with a self-deprecating smile. "Only three. Compilations of my syndicated articles. Since six hundred newspapers worldwide carry me, it's hard to collect material most people haven't already seen." She shrugged as if apologizing for that "failing."

Boss, you don't need me to stick up for you, Endora groused. *But I'd like to hang around and watch Mick put Jennifer's pieces in a doggy bag.*

I don't think she even knows she lost this skirmish.

No, but Mick does. And from where I'm sitting, that's all that matters.

Sending Jennifer a quelling look, he raised his wine glass in salute to the authors at the table. "Here's to continued success for each of us."

As they toasted, Jennifer with obvious reluctance, Endora's plaintive cry filled Cassie's head. *Can I pleeeease put a hex on her, Boss? Please?*

Cassie bit back a chuckle. *No! Although I have to admit, I wouldn't be disappointed if every banquet on this tour served a dessert made with lots of strawberries.*

Endora's smile was purely feline. *I think I can do something about that.*

***

Back in the penthouse suite, Mick yanked his tie free, balled it up in one large fist, and hurled it into the dresser drawer.

"Jen, what the hell is your problem?"

She turned from where she stood perusing the contents of the fully stocked refrigerator. "What?"

"Don't play coy. That infuriates me." His glare halted the

protest he knew was forthcoming. "You were deliberately rude to Cassandra Hathorne. In front of half the authors on this tour. For God's sake, this isn't a pissing match."

"I was just paying her a compliment—"

"Backhanded at best." He poured himself a shot of straight scotch and downed it neat. "And what orifice did you pull that comment about Tennessee out of? You know she's from the East Coast."

"I thought I was being humorous."

"Well, your sense of humor and mine must be miles apart," he said evenly, "because I found your comment to be downright embarrassing."

Jennifer's blue eyes welled with tears. "Why are you being so mean to me?"

"Mean? You've had a burr up your rear end since you heard Cassandra Hathorne was going to be on this tour. Care to explain what that's all about?" He poured himself another drink and sat down in the chair closest to the window.

"Why should I have to justify doing my job?" Jennifer shot back. "She's competition."

His reaction more resembled a short bark than a laugh. "We've discussed this. She is not *my* competition." Then, with startling insight, he thought, *She's yours.* Jennifer saw Cassandra Hathorne as competition for Mick's affections. Shit.

He almost laughed aloud at the irony. His former fiancée viewed another woman as a rival for a position she'd voluntarily given up. Only the possibly cataclysmic importance of this tour kept him from laughing himself sick. He started to down the drink in his hand, but stopped. Alcohol had never been a salve for his problems before, and he wouldn't let it be now. He set the glass aside. "I think you're upset I'm quitting, and your misplaced aggression is being channeled her way. That's not fair to her, as she's got nothing to do with it."

Jennifer sat down in his lap and put her arms around his neck. He didn't respond. "Why didn't we discuss this career move?"

"I've tried to for a long time, but all you've been interested in was patching up our disagreements with sex." He saw her bottom lip begin to quiver, knew it was just an act.

"Something we haven't done in far too long." She rubbed her breasts against his chest.

"You called our relationship off. Remember?"

"Maybe I've changed my mind." She snuggled closer. "How about for old time's sake?"

"My heart isn't into it, Jen."

On a breathy growl, she said, "That particular organ doesn't necessarily have to be into it to do it, you know."

He gently pushed her away and stood up. "It does for me. I'm going to bed. Alone." He paused at the door of the suite's master bedroom. "Don't embarrass me like that again, Jennifer, or I'll fire you. I'm done with writing. Your constantly reminding me and the rest of the world that I'm a best-selling author isn't going to change that fact."

***

It had begun.

The television provided the hotel room's only light. On the screen, a grisly crime scene was the backdrop to the news anchor's account of brutal murder. The victim—a businessman in town for the booksellers' convention. Shocked witnesses, who in reality had seen nothing, appeared on camera, horrified looks on their stupid faces.

Idiots. Every last one of the drones of the world—the police, the news reporters, the riffraff at the scene. All were imbeciles. Only one person was worthy, and he likely didn't even know his worthiness yet. But he would. All in good time.

Today had gone well. He would glory in his triumph for a day then set the stage for the third stop on the bus tour. In less than two weeks this would all be over, and his legend made for all eternity.

Something even writing best-selling horror novels could not ensure.

***

The four-hour bus ride from Toledo to Chicago had proven to be completely uneventful, Cassie thought. Likely because she had managed to totally avoid conversation with Jennifer Bodin. That suited her just fine, as she found the pushy blonde to be distinctly unpleasant. Whatever Mick saw in her was not something Cassie could see. On any astral plane. And she had again sensed extreme tension between the two. Trouble definitely plagued that relationship.

Now she sensed even more trouble brewing. They'd arrived just half an hour earlier at McCormick Place, the Windy City's showcase convention center, and all the managers and publicists had been huddled in the corner with McCormick personnel since they'd stepped down from the bus. As usual, Jennifer was right in the thick of things. This did not bode well.

Endora confirmed that thought almost before Cassie had it. The familiar strolled up to where the authors sat at a table, drinking complimentary coffee, tea and juice, and headed straight for her witch.

"Well, Boss, there seems to be a bit of a problem." Endora glanced at the other authors, her eyes resting for a split-second longer on Mick's face than on any of the others'.

Cassie caught the relevance of the look, but oddly enough, she was more pleased with the fact her protection spell was keeping Mick from an allergic reaction to Endora than she was concerned about the latter's message. "What's up?"

"Apparently, the promotional materials have one author's name misspelled." There was a collective groan from the group. "The organizers caught the mistake about an hour before we arrived, and right now they're scrambling to put things right."

"Which means?" Cassie prompted, in no mood for Endora's dramatic flair for dragging out a story.

"The signing's been moved back two hours."

"To four o'clock?" Robert Whitman exclaimed, looking very disturbed by this turn of events. "It's only eleven now." He headed for the exit practically at a run.

"Must have a hot date," Mick quipped, obviously trying to put a positive face on things. "Well, we've got a long lunch break. Anyone up for grabbing a cab and going to Water Tower Place to check out the restaurants?" He glanced around the group, but everyone except Cassie claimed something to do and promptly left to do it.

"Cass, why don't you go," Endora suggested. "I'm needed here to help straighten things out, and it's pointless for you to sit around idle for four hours."

This is a set up. You can't tell me those other authors have pressing obligations.

C'mon, Cass, he's cute. Beyond cute—he's gorgeous. Take advantage of the Dragon Lady's hovering here, ensuring his name won't be misspelled again, and trade some household hints with the dashing Mr. Kazimer.

Remember what they say about paybacks, Dora. Turning to Mick, she said brightly, "Water Tower Place, it is. Just let me grab my purse."

As Cassie walked away, Mick scanned the exhibition hall,

then turned to Endora. "I don't see Jennifer anywhere."

"She went up to the office with the conference manager."

A bleak look entered his eyes. "I suspect it was *my* misspelled name that set things back." At Endora's wry smile, he shook his head slowly. "Thanks for not saying anything to the others. It's bad enough they have to put up with me on this tour."

"I don't hear any complaints. They're all probably big fans of yours to begin with and are happy to bask in your celebrity."

Mick laughed grimly. "Here's hoping they can stomach me for the next two weeks." He studied Cassie's manager. "Could I impose on you to deliver a message to Jennifer?"

"Certainly."

"Tell her I'll be back by three, would you?"

"Will do."

"Thanks."

Endora shrugged. "No problem. Have a nice lunch."

Mick's gaze fell on Cassie as she moved toward them. "I don't think that will be too difficult."

Boss, you're gonna owe me big time, Endora gloated.

***

Calgon, take me away, Cassie groaned silently when she caught sight of the pair heading toward her. Or, barring that, maybe the floor would just open up and swallow her without a trace.

Unfortunately, teleportation was out of the question with the McCormick Place Convention Center so crowded, and she'd never actually tried it, anyway. There was nowhere to hide. Trapped behind a table with a mile-long line of fans stretched in front of it, Cassie knew how postal workers on Tax Day felt.

"Medusa!" Endora's tone was just the correct amount of pleased surprise at the arrival of Cassie's mother. She subtly moved to intercept the older witch as the latter made her way, full steam ahead, past the lines of fans. A very tall, gaunt man dressed all in black followed in her wake. "Cassie has another half hour of autographing. Why don't we go to the concessions area until she's done?"

Medusa was not to be gainsaid. "I can't even greet my only daughter? What utter nonsense!" She adroitly squeezed through the twelve-inch space separating Mick and Cassie's table from Robert Whitman's and threw her arms around her only child. "Darling! I've missed you. You remember Mort

Morula?"

"Mom, I'm working," Cassie said tightly, barely sparing Mort a nod of acknowledgment. She turned back to the woman whose copy of *When Dust Bunnies Attack* had a thick line scrawled across the title page where an autograph should have been. "I'm so sorry. Let me sign another." She did so, added her signature to the ruined copy, and pushed both books across the table. "When you check out, tell them there's no charge for the ruined one. They can ask me if they need verification."

"However will you make a profit, dear, if you give your books away," Medusa asked, loudly enough for half the hall's occupants to hear.

"I ruined the autograph when you hugged me," Cassie said in a low, intense voice. "I couldn't charge that woman for a book I damaged."

Endora caught the spark in Cassie's eyes. "Medusa, I've got to insist we go to the concessions stand. There's really no room for all of us back here behind the table." She indicated the long line. "And plenty of fans want to buy Cassie's book. She'll be done in half an hour." She herded Medusa and her escort out of the autographing area and around the edge of the curtain separating the authors from the booksellers.

"Moms," Cassie said with a self-conscious laugh to the crowd in general. "You can't send them to their rooms without supper."

"It's so cute they dress like witches to support you!" gushed a middle-aged fan at the head of the line.

Lady, you don't know the half of it. Cassie glanced surreptitiously Mick's direction, wondering if he'd had enough of a lull in his crowd to hear Medusa's antics. Of course, he could have been stone deaf in the middle of a buffalo stampede and still heard her. At lunch, they'd traded writing industry horror stories, including problems with managers, and she'd sympathized with him over Jennifer's tirades . . . Would he now be returning her sympathy?

Why should I care? she thought perversely.

After all, Mick had hired his manager. Medusa was Cassie's mother strictly by circumstance. Anyone's sympathy—for anything whatsoever that involved her personally—appalled her. With a mental sigh, she admitted it wasn't the idea of Mick's sympathy or lack thereof that had gotten her worked up. It was the thought that his opinion of her mother might actually matter.

And it did. That realization shocked, to say the least. M. S. Kazimer was practically a stranger. She'd had a great time with him at lunch, but it was only lunch, after all.

He's spoken for, Cass. No sense setting your sights on something unattainable. But her sixth sense was telling her differently, and the vibrations she'd felt from Mick that afternoon were far warmer than anything she'd picked up between him and Jennifer. *This is too odd for you to sort out right now,* she reminded herself. *Besides, what if that weird bad guy comes back? I should be paying more attention in case he returns.*

That thought firmly in her head, she finished signing for her fans while mentally preparing for the upcoming battle with Medusa over the issue of matchmaking.

She'd have been mortified to know that, even as she dismissed Mick's opinion, he was concluding that Medusa and Jennifer had something in common, and it certainly wasn't tact.

Four

Cassie had to count to one hundred, twice, to keep her temper in line.

Always be polite to guests, especially in public, she chanted silently. *And always cast an obfuscation charm to scramble any thoughts other witches might read telepathically.*

Had anyone read her current thoughts, they'd have suffered scorched brain lobes for their efforts. She was seething.

While she'd finished the book signing, Endora had managed to get Medusa and Mort to the concessions area. A look at her frazzled cat, however, told Cassie it had come close to costing one of Endora's lives to keep the pair under relative control. The familiar's sleek hair was nearly standing on end, but she—having more sense than Medusa and Mort about public scenes—was subtly smoothing it into place. No licking her palm today, but she looked like the cornered animal that, in reality, she was.

Nothing angered Cassie more than seeing her friends abused, especially her familiar. And the abuse was about to end.

"Mother," she said as pleasantly as she could, "you certainly took me by surprise."

Medusa pushed back the sleeves of a robe that looked like the prototype for Disney's *Sorcerer's Apprentice* and smiled indulgently. "I thought you might need a change of pace."

"I didn't say it was a pleasant surprise, Mother."

Her maternal parent could win an Oscar for Most Obtuse Witch on the Planet. "My fear was that you'd be lonely on this silly book tour, so I brought you Mort for company."

If she ground her teeth any harder, Cassie knew some dentist was going to buy a yacht off the profits from her bridgework alone. "The tour started two days ago. Hardly time for me to be lonely at all. And you seem to forget that this isn't a vacation. I'm working."

Medusa waved a dismissive hand. "Work? You're merely indulging yourself, Cassandra. Isn't that what I told you, Mort? My Cassandra loves to amuse herself by slumming with humans."

The tall, cadaverous-looking witch nodded. "Indeed."

He could somehow manage to turn up his nose while gazing downward from his great height. The effect made him look like a giraffe reaching to eat from higher branches while watching the ground for predators. Cassie might have found the illusion amusing if she hadn't been ready to spit nails.

"Endora and I are going downtown for dinner," she said evenly. "Would you care to join us?"

Medusa shot the sleeves of the robe and flexed her fingers. "Where to, Cassandra? I'll have us there in a flash."

"No!" Cassie and Endora exclaimed as one.

Mort glared at Endora, and the familiar backed off, but his attempt at intimidation didn't stop Cassie.

"No," she said more calmly, moving to put a hand on her mother's elbow. She knew the tension she felt was reflected in her eyes for all to see, but at this point she didn't feel like concealing her feelings. "Don't cause a scene I'll have to undo with a charm. We're taking a cab, not teleporting to the restaurant."

"But, it's so much easier—"

"If you want to come to dinner with us, it'll be on my terms. No witchcraft in public. Please."

Medusa sniffed loudly, but her expression softened somewhat. "If you insist."

"I do." She turned to Endora. "Call the restaurant and change the reservations. I have to run back up to the room to get my purse."

"I could just—" Medusa stopped mid-sentence when Cassie turned a stern look on her. "Just a thought."

"No witchcraft, Mother," Cassie said with quiet emphasis. "None. Zero. Zip." Before anyone could say anything else, she added, "You and Mort make yourselves comfortable right here. Endora and I'll be back in a minute." She headed for the exit, knowing her familiar was right on her heels.

They split up in the lobby, Endora heading for the phones, Cassie for the closest bank of elevators just around the corner.

Hurrying around that corner, she nearly ran headlong into Mick as he left the men's restroom. His quick reflexes saved them from a collision, as he caught her by the shoulders and steadied her.

"Sorry," she said.

She started to add more, but his sudden move drove every thought she had right out of her brain. Still grasping her shoulders, he adroitly spun her into the men's room, pushing her gently but firmly around the partition that separated the urinals from the entry door.

"What the—"

"Shhh!" He held his index finger to her lips. "I thought I saw that weird guy who came to see you at the signing. To be honest, he creeps me out. So let's hide in here for a while."

Cassie would have bet her Witches Union card—if such a thing existed—that M. S. Kazimer was having a joke on her. He certainly didn't look "creeped out." In fact, he looked too sexy for words. And he was standing way too close for her peace of mind, even if her only alternative was backing into a urinal.

"Um, not to put too fine a point on it," she said *sotto voce*, "but if we're hiding from Mort, shouldn't we be in the women's room?"

Both of Mick's eyebrows shot up. His eyes glittered with amusement. "Isn't that illegal?"

Great Mother Goddess, but she wanted to kiss him. Wanted him to kiss her. But he was engaged, wasn't he? And if so, what was he doing hauling her into a men's bathroom on the pretext of avoiding one of her potential beaus?

Her heart gave a flustered little thump. He certainly wasn't acting like an engaged man. So, he was either a free agent or a two-timing bastard. Given that neither she nor Endora had picked up on any affectionate vibes between Jennifer Bodin and him, he could be unattached. If she thought for a moment that he really wasn't marrying the obnoxious publicist . . . Cassie pushed that thought aside. Right now, her problem was foiling her mother's latest matchmaking attempt.

"I'd better go," she said a tad breathlessly. *Is he wearing Stetson?* "Uhm, before Security arrests me."

"Sure you want to risk it?"

If he got any closer, they'd be wearing the same clothes. Cassie swallowed hard. "I'll take my chances."

"All right. I'll check to see if it's safe for you to leave." He waggled his eyebrows then peeked out the restroom door like a spy searching for counterintelligence agents. "All clear."

She smiled in relief and gratitude for not having to face any male besides Mick on her way out of their private domain. "Thanks. Really."

"My pleasure."

Something about the tone of his voice, coupled with that sexy smile and killer look, made her believe he really meant it. That thought turned her insides to massive tingles. Which made her want to conjure up some reality pills. What chance did she have with M. S. Kazimer, anyway?

***

That night, Mick invited Robert Whitman out for dinner in downtown Chicago, ostensibly to welcome him to the writers' fraternity. As anticipated, when he'd told Jennifer his plans, she'd sniffed indignantly and declared she had other things to do. Which saved him the hassle of telling her she wasn't invited anyway. Dinner with Whitman, Mick knew, wasn't going to be pleasant by any stretch. Nor was it open to anyone besides the two of them.

The urgency of this meeting added to his conviction of the complete surrealism of his life. Although the thought desolated him, he was quitting his career knowing it was the right thing to do. His ex-fiancée was coming on to him, and he'd practically accosted another author that afternoon. Completely surreal.

Pulling Cassandra Hathorne into the men's room . . . God, what had he been thinking? Then the truth hit him like a brick and he had to bite back a groan. He *hadn't* been thinking—with any organ above his belt. Why deny it?

At lunch that afternoon, they'd connected on a level Mick found nearly unbelievable. No one understood a writer like another writer, yet Mick had never compared experiences with a woman author. The horror genre was overwhelmingly male-dominated, and whenever the guys got together, they by and large acted like guys. Drank beer, watched ball games, ogled women. They didn't discuss writer's block or characters' motivations or readers' chat rooms. After a get-together, they'd go home, park themselves in front of their computers, and try to write their friendly rivals into the ground. They didn't share exercises for combating low back strain caused by sitting in a chair all day, or commiserate over rejection letters.

With all the turmoil in his life at that moment, with his doubts about ending his career–nearly tantamount to ending his life–a two-hour glitch in the schedule had proven to be a gift from above. He and the Kitchen Witch had gotten along like they were soul mates.

When he'd seen her hurrying out of the signing room, a worried expression dominating her lovely features, his impulse had been to surprise her worry away. And there was no point denying that his impulse had paid off for him, too. Having Cassie in his arms–getting to see her gorgeous, caramel-colored eyes at amazingly close range—made him want to grin like a dopey schoolboy. What had possessed him?

And who cared?

Now, seated in an isolated booth at the back of Trader Vic's, Mick's surrealistic life again intruded. His light mood turned immediately dark and grew increasingly disturbed as Robert spoke.

"... The guy was killed in exactly the same way as a victim in *Deadly Passions,*" Mick's companion informed him tersely.

"Shit. Shit, shit, shit, shit, shit!"

FBI Special Agent Robert Jamison—Robert Whitman for the duration of this particular assignment—grimaced. "The Director's exact words when Susan told him Detective Bird's hunch was right." He took a healthy drink of his coffee and sat forward over the table between them.

Mick knew that Susan was Susan Gannon, Jamison's FBI supervisor. Six months before, a Baltimore police detective named David Bird had contacted Gannon's office with some disturbing news. A devoted M. S. Kazimer fan, Bird had recognized patterns in a series of unsolved homicides he'd been investigating over the previous eighteen months. Each murder duplicated crimes in Kazimer's novels.

"Fortunately," Jamison continued, "Special Agent Gannon loves your books, too. She linked up to every law enforcement agency in the States and Canada for ongoing homicide investigations that might show the same pattern—" Mick raised his hand to stop Jamison's recitation, and the agent paused. "You know the rest."

Mick certainly did. Three other cities—Philadelphia, Dover, and Newark—had ongoing murder investigations that, taken in the context of five separate Kazimer novels, fit the profile of a serial killer.

A serial killer using Mick's books as blueprints for mayhem.

"My God, this is a nightmare." He resisted the urge to put his head in his hands. "How many homicides do they think the same guy committed?"

"This latest makes fifteen over a five-year period."

Mick shook his head, too stunned by Jamison's statement even to curse.

"Do *not* blame yourself," the FBI agent said firmly. "Serial killers are complete nut cases. They don't need an external reason to go off."

"But don't they sometimes kill to impress someone they

admire? If this guy fancies himself as my biggest fan, could he be killing the way my characters kill out of admiration for M. S. Kazimer?" When the agent didn't answer readily, Mick added in a low, intense voice, "Don't bullshit me, Jamison. Is this lunatic killing because he wants to impress me with his devotion?"

"I had hoped that wasn't the case, but after this last guy in Baltimore . . . "

"It looks like that's exactly what the killer is doing."

"'Fraid so."

Mick clenched his jaw until his teeth hurt. "You said the people associated with this tour would be in no danger. I'd never have agreed to this scheme if the Bureau hadn't assured me it was safe."

"It's as safe as we can make it."

"Meaning exactly what?" Not knowing what to do with his hands, Mick started pleating his linen napkin.

"It's a carefully screened group. Ninety percent of all serial killers are white males between the ages of twenty and thirty-five. The two female authors have a readership that's primarily female. Obviously, the author of the children's book draws parents and grandparents for the most part. And Jones, being a black man writing self-help books targeted toward minorities, is the least likely of all to attract a serial-killer type. None of their books are remotely like yours."

"Except the one you're selling."

Jamison shrugged, then smiled wryly. "Of course, that's because you wrote it. Thanks, by the way, for keeping that old unpublished manuscript around. It's brilliant cover for me."

"Back to this safety issue," Mick ordered.

The agent nodded. "We've got everyone on the tour, excepting you and Jennifer, on the same floor of each hotel. No other patrons are on those floors. Just my agents."

"I know the setup, but you never really said why Jen and I are isolated."

"Simple." Jamison assumed his most FBI-like tone. "Since we must consider you attractive to our perp, we've got you in a limited-access area. The penthouse floor is easily guarded, and my best agents and I are right across the hall from you at every stop."

The thought of being attractive to a serial killer made Mick's skin crawl. But maybe that would work to their advantage to catch this bastard. "If I'm a magnet, aren't we putting Jen in danger by having her with me?"

"It would look far more suspicious if she wasn't. As your publicist and fiancee, she's got to be staying close to, if not with, you." Jamison glanced at a small notebook he'd taken from his suit pocket then met Mick's gaze again. "For the record, I disagree with your not telling her about this."

"Trust me, Robert, there would be nothing covert about this operation if Jennifer knew." *Nor would I hear the end of her demands to cancel it.* Mick debated telling Jamison that the wedding was off, but decided he didn't need to know. Nor did he need to know that M. S. Kazimer was retiring from writing after the tour ended in New Orleans. "Anything else about security you haven't told me yet?"

"The local police in each city—as well as the nearest field operatives and the staff at every venue—have been alerted to watch for anything unusual in and around the convention centers and hotels—"

"A fact that didn't help the previous fifteen victims."

"That's because we only recently discovered a relationship. The latest vic went off to find a prostitute and got clocked by this maniac."

"Just like the final murder in *Deadly Passions.*" Morosely, he added, "The last book before *Mortal Sin.*"

"Yes."

Mick massaged his temples with his fingertips, contemplating all he'd been told. Then he leveled a stare at Jamison. "So, if the pattern is actually being followed, the guy should have struck in Toledo because the first victim in *Mortal Sin* died there."

"There have been no reports."

"Good." At Jamison's grim look, he added, "So far, you meant to say. And that also means he'll look for his next victim in St. Louis."

"That's our hope."

"Helluva thing to hope for." Mick crushed the napkin in both hands, then tossed it onto the table.

The agent barely flinched at this display of temper. "Actually, it's more than Detective Bird had to go on just a few months ago. If he wasn't such a big fan of yours and hadn't figured out the pattern, who knows how long it would have been before someone caught on to what this wacko is doing."

"Somehow, that's not much consolation," Mick said tightly.

"But it is something," Jamison persisted. "The guy's going to kill, regardless of whom he patterns his acts after. He's programmed to kill. Now that we know how he operates, we've got a great chance of ending his career."

"Let's get this bastard before he experiences any more career advancement."

"Amen to that."

The waiter brought their meals, forcing Mick to pick up his napkin again, but his appetite had long since left him.

Sweet Jesus, have I opened Pandora's box? he wondered desperately. He'd never forgive himself if anything happened to someone involved with this tour—a tour he'd agreed to headline partly because he couldn't comprehend anyone sick enough to kill to impress an author.

But reality had a way of biting a person in uncomfortable places, and Mick could feel the teeth marks. If he'd had any doubts about the wisdom of changing vocations, they'd been erased with Jamison's report of the Baltimore murder. As of that moment, M. S. Kazimer's novel *Mortal Sin* was his last. Mick would never write another horror story.

Jennifer had essentially chosen to leave him for following his conscience, even though she didn't know it. As much as that hurt, at least she'd leave untainted by the evil he could practically smell in the air around him. And she'd leave walking. Not in a body bag.

***

Mort made it clear he'd be sitting by Cassie when he crowded into the middle of the cab's back seat, trapping her behind the driver and forcing Endora to take the front seat or be squashed next to Medusa.

The ride to Gino's East was anything but comfortable, and not just because there was so much of Mort's long legs to fold into cramped quarters. The witch silently managed to be condescending and proprietary, and by the time they arrived at the restaurant, Cassie was ready to explode.

He sealed his fate as they were being seated.

Endora spoke to the concierge while Mort did his best to bore a hole into her back with his preternaturally bright gaze. However, being feline, she could easily ignore any other creature she chose to. As she blithely followed the hostess to their seats, Mort turned his glare on Cassie.

"You allow your familiar to dine with you?"

She cocked both brows, a sure sign to all who knew her that her tolerance level had gone above flood stage. But she held her tongue until they were seated—deliberately sitting between Endora and Medusa—and the hostess left. "You find something wrong with Endora's being here?"

"Indeed," came Mort's haughty reply. "Your familiar is, after all, your servant. Why ever would you condescend to allow her to remain in your presence in a social setting? Unless, of course, she was serving the meal. Or cleaning up."

Even Medusa had the grace to blush at that comment.

Cassie shot her mother a glance before she turned to face Mort. "Let me be frank here, Mortie. You're a guest. Dora's family. She's neither serving wench nor maid, and she won't be treated as such. Her duties are far more important. She's my guardian and my guide, and most importantly, she's my friend."

"She's an inferior being," Mort stated doggedly. "By dining here with us, she's acting above her station."

Cassie could feel her eyes almost shooting sparks and could guess her cheeks flamed from anger. But she kept her voice even when she said, "As she is *my* familiar, her station is where I determine it to be. And that is wherever I go. No one—and that includes you, Mort—will mistreat her, in my presence or out of it, without answering to me. Do I make myself perfectly clear?"

Belatedly, the witch sensed her suppressed fury. If possible, his skin blanched even whiter. "As crystal."

"Good. That will save me from having to curse you with impotence." She turned to the other two women at the table. "Are we ready to order?"

***

Mick should have ignored the note sitting on the bar in the penthouse suite, but some perverse sense of duty had him opening it to read. Jennifer had asked him to knock on her bedroom door when he returned from dinner. He didn't want to, but she was his business manager after all. And they were supposedly on a promotional tour. At no time until this little drama played itself out could he afford suspicion on the part of any other member of the group.

He walked the twenty feet to her door, wishing fervently that he'd not bothered to answer what amounted to a summons. Jennifer opened the door with barely a word of greeting, and Mick felt the chill immediately. Silently, she stepped aside to allow him entrance. The "bedroom" he stood in was the size of most regular suites.

"Did you get a load of that guy who came in with Cassandra Hathorne's mother this afternoon?" he asked as he moved past Jennifer into the room, hoping to warm the icy air with inane conversation. Unfortunately, his chosen topic had the opposite effect. *Nice going, Sandor,* he silently castigated himself. *Mention the one thing sure to get Jennifer's back up.*

"No."

He pressed on—perhaps he truly was a latent masochist—determined to act as though this was a comfortable conversation. "Probably some *Rocky Horror* cultist. Looks like he's been dead for a century." Jennifer's lack of response didn't stop him. "Maybe a reject from some semi-semi-pro basketball league. He's a good hand taller than I am–six-ten or eleven, I'd guess. But he looks like he'd blow over in a breeze." He faked a shudder. "Wanna bet he's an escapee from some asylum?"

"Give it a rest, Mick."

At her abrupt comment, he stopped in the middle of the room and planted his fists on his hips. "Why? I thought you liked chitchat."

"Not about women who vie with me for your affection." Jennifer moved to stare through the hotel windows at the glittering lights of nighttime Chicago. Back to Mick, hands crossed over her breasts, she embodied the word "inaccessible."

Uh oh. "What are you talking about?" The only thing he could do at this point was gut this out. He himself had brought on the tirade he felt brewing in Jen's compact body.

"Cassandra Hathorne, of course."

"Oh, come on—"

She spun to face him, anger contorting her beautiful features. "Don't deny it, Mick! You've defended her this entire trip: 'She's no competition, Jen.' 'I'll sell plenty of books even though she's here, Jen.' 'You're too hard on her, Jen.' Then you had lunch with her today while I stayed to make sure they spell your damned name right. I'm no idiot. I know where this is going."

If he was honest with himself, he couldn't deny that Cassandra Hathorne intrigued him. Attracted him on more than just a physical level. Even with his life falling apart around him, indelible images of being near her for the past two days had burned themselves into his brain. He'd gone so far as to haul her into the men's bathroom that afternoon! He gave himself a mental shake. What kind of degenerate was he? His ex-fiancee looked ready to fly apart at the seams, he'd decided to end his writing career, and a madman was making a reality of Mick's fictional mayhem. And he couldn't get Cassandra Hathorne off his mind? Maybe *he* was the lunatic here.

Torture couldn't have made him confess that Jennifer was right about Cassie. But he had to smooth this over somehow. Since he towered over his business manager, he decided to assume a less intimidating position by sitting down in the nearest overstuffed chair. As gently as he could, he stated, "You have no idea where this is going. And I can't tell you much more than that." He started to reach out a hand to her, then let it drop. "Please. You have to trust me on this. Cassandra Hathorne is not the issue here."

"Then why did you bring her up?"

"I didn't." *At least not directly.* "I brought up the weird guy who was with her mother."

Jennifer, pouting, kept her defensive stance. "Why did you even notice the guy? Or anything going on with her, for that matter? You were busy autographing books."

Mick took a deep breath and let it out slowly. Of course, he'd spent three pleasant hours in a restaurant with Cassie before the signing and another three hours sitting close enough to smell her perfume during it. And they shared a bond as authors. But he didn't want to go anywhere near the fact that she was extremely attractive. "Why wouldn't I notice some tall, scrawny geek in a black tuxedo and full-length opera cape, looking like sunlight hadn't touched him in a decade? Hard to miss that, even in the middle of a book signing."

"*I* didn't see him."

"You were too busy bullying the McCormick Place manager."

The minute he spoke, his heart gave that funny little burning-spasm beat it always did when he knew he'd stuck his foot in it. That hadn't sounded at all like the joke he'd intended. Jennifer flinched as if struck, and he was instantly on his feet gathering her into his arms. She resisted halfheartedly, but with a firm yet gentle hand he guided her head down to his chest.

"God, Jen, I'm sorry. That didn't come out the way it should have."

"You're a jerk, Mick."

"You're right," he agreed on a sigh. "I get tongue-tied under pressure."

Lifting her head, she stared up at him in disbelief. "Bullshit. You make a living with words, and you're telling me you don't know how to use them correctly?"

He shook his head. "Writing's not conversation. I'm terrible at talking face-to-face."

"You're terrific with your fans. And a terrific speaker."

"I make small talk with my fans and give scripted speeches. Neither of which is the same as a conversation, especially when that conversation is extremely important."

"I guess I don't see the difference."

And maybe that's part of why we broke up, Mick thought grimly. "Talking to people isn't like writing dialogue. I control every word my characters say, every action they perform. If they don't behave the way I want them to, I revise before anyone else sees it. Before feelings get hurt." He saw she hadn't understood his subtle apology and with sadness admitted this didn't even surprise him. "My witty heroes always have exactly the right thing to say in any situation—"

"And that's why your fans love you so."

"I'm not my heroes. I'm one of those poor schlepps who always comes up with a clever rebuttal, five hours after the fact." He released her, started to pace. "I'm only erudite at a keyboard. I can't be spontaneously clever to save my life."

Jennifer moved to the minibar to pour herself a shot of whiskey, then added the appropriate amount of tonic. "Why do you need to be clever?"

Having followed her, he stopped her hand from bringing the drink to her lips. He knew his eyes glittered. "I don't need to be clever, I just need to be myself. I'm not M. S. Kazimer. I'm Mick Sandor, a guy who has made a living turning a phrase, but who can't do it anymore." He turned her to face him. "I won't be convinced to keep writing. When this tour's over, I'm announcing my retirement. *Mortal Sin* is the last book M. S. Kazimer will ever author."

Anger flashed in Jennifer's eyes. "How can you throw away your career?"

"I just gave you some damn good reasons, although they're not the only ones."

"Tell me some others." She planted her feet apart, hands fisted on hips.

Mick grimaced. "I *can't* right now, but when you know the details, you'll agree I'm doing the right thing."

"Quit, and you'll be looking for a new manager."

Somehow, that threat had no impact. And he realized that her calling off the wedding hadn't devastated him, either. That lack of reaction couldn't be blamed on a demented murderer by any stretch of the imagination. With stunning clarity, he knew his love for her truly no longer existed. If it ever, in reality, had.

"You can still manage my career. I'll still be a famous writer, with all those backlisted books to sell. I just won't be adding anything new to increase my wealth. Or yours."

"You bastard!" Jennifer slapped his face, then stalked to the closet for her purse and coat. "When you get back to New York, I won't be there."

He stood frozen, watching her leave. "Jen, I'm so sorry. That was uncalled for."

"Tell someone who cares, Mick." With that, she was gone.

He stared at the door for a split second. Then panicked. "Jen!" Racing after her, he found the corridor empty. In a flash he was in his own bedroom calling Jamison on his cell phone.

"Dammit, Jamison, Jen just left. She's going back to New York, probably right now." He fought to control his rapid breathing as the agent gave calm orders on the other end of the line.

"We've got her covered, Mick. One of my men's following her right now."

A knot of tension eased a bit in Mick's gut. "Good. Keep her safe. If that crazy bastard gets her, I'll be your worst nightmare."

"Jennifer's not his target. And Chicago's not a murder location. The next killing is in St. Louis, and that's where he'll be next. Our agents down there are covering every venue your book mentions. And the agent assigned to your fiancee will keep her in his sights until this thing is resolved."

My ex-fiancee Mick wanted to say into the receiver but didn't. Besides, if this agent stuck as close to Jennifer as Jamison claimed he would, everyone at the Bureau would realize soon enough Mick was solo.

The thought of the FBI knowing he'd been dumped was nowhere near as terrifying as the thought of Jen's death. They'd never have a life together, but at least she would *have* a life. That was more than he could say for the fifteen victims of some crazed M. S. Kazimer fan.

For the first time in his entire life, Mick drank himself into a stupor that night. He passed out, fully-clothed, on the floor of his hotel suite.

***

"Mother, we have to talk."

Cassie, Medusa and Endora had gone to the ladies room together, and not because there was safety in numbers.

"About what, dear?"

"Mother——"

Medusa's hands fluttered in a gesture of agitation. "All right. I never should have brought Mort Morula here to see you."

"That's the understatement of the century, Mom. I'm almost to the point where I won't be responsible for my actions."

"I didn't even know you could perform an impotence spell."

Cassie's gaze met her mother's in the over-the-counter mirror, and she snapped, "Don't change the subject. You knew I wanted nothing to do with Mort, yet you brought him to the signing and made a scene."

"I just thought——"

"No, Mom, you didn't think. That's the trouble. I'm a grown-up now, capable of knowing my own mind. Just because what I want differs from what you want for me doesn't negate my feelings." Suddenly finding herself fighting tears, she took a seat on a powder room chair. A sigh escaped unbidden. "I love what I do, yet you refuse to accept my success. Why can't you be happy I'm good at something I enjoy? Why can't you be proud of me?"

Stunned, Medusa turned to Endora. The familiar stared back, expression stating she would stand by Cassie to the end.

Medusa knelt beside the chair and gathered her now-weeping daughter into her arms. "Darling, don't. Don't cry." She brushed back Cassie's hair with a shaking hand. "I *am* proud of you. Truly. I just don't want to see you alone all your life. Please, don't cry, dear."

After a few moments, Cassie was cried out. She raised her head from Medusa's shoulder and dashed away her tears with the back of a hand. Her mother's honest contrition had gone a long way toward easing the hurt. "You'd rather I spend my life with a loser like Mort Morula?" she asked wryly.

"Well, in retrospect, he's not a very good match for you," Medusa conceded softly.

"He's a pompous ass, Mom. And that's being kind."

"Unfortunately, I have to agree with you. His chauvinism astonishes me."

"Speaking of Mort the chauvinist," Endora interrupted, "we'd better get back out to see the show."

Both witches' attention snapped toward the familiar.

"Endora—" Her name on Cassie's lips was both warning and question.

She held her hands up in supplication. "Well, Cassie, he was being, as you said, a pompous ass—"

"Endora!"

"Okay, okay. I put live anchovies in his deep dish pizza," she confessed without the slightest bit of remorse. "They should be trying to swim back upstream right about now."

Cassie had a hard time keeping her jaw from dropping open.

"This I have to see," Medusa said on a laugh.

***

The women were destined for disappointment. They arrived at their table just in time to view Mort's back as he beat as hasty a retreat out of the restaurant as his stilt-like legs could muster.

"I should go after him," Medusa said halfheartedly. "Try to smooth things over."

Cassie shook her head. "Bad idea, Mom. If you follow him and see him tossing his anchovies in some alley, he'll be horrified. All that male witch pride and arrogance reduced to puking in the street, right in front of a respected elder. Why not just stay with us? We've got less than two hours before the reception starts back at McCormick Place, so let's eat."

"He left most of his pizza," Endora observed.

Cassie grinned. "Somehow, I don't think you're going to lose sleep over that."

"Are you kidding? Live anchovies are my favorites." Endora sat down in Mort's vacated seat and tucked into his pizza like a pit bull after a mail carrier. "Cream would go great with this."

Medusa and Cassie traded grimaces as they joined Endora at the table.

"I'll pass on that, thanks," Cassie said as Medusa nodded her agreement.

"Your loss."

"I don't think so," Cassie and Medusa chorused.

Mouth full of pizza, Endora muttered, "You two don't know good food when you see it."

With a wink at Cassie, Medusa said, "I think I'll trust my daughter's judgment on that one."

Cassie could practically feel herself glowing at her mother's subtle endorsement. She literally felt like flying. If she could pull off a stunt of that magnitude. Which she doubted. *One thing at a time,* she told herself. *Maybe Mom will stop her incessant matchmaking now.*

She was glad her obfuscation spell kept her thoughts from her companions, especially since images of Mick Sandor kept creeping in at the most inopportune moments. *One thing at a time. First, I need to find out if Mick's actually engaged or in a relationship with Jennifer Bodin. If he isn't . . .* She blushed when she realized Medusa and Endora were staring at her. She gave them a clearly fake smile. "Please, let's continue with this fascinating conversation."

"Actually, curing wood trolls of foot fungus doesn't thrill me at all," Endora deadpanned.

Cassie rolled her eyes. *One thing at a time,* she chanted. *One thing at a time.*

Five

"Good-bye, darling." Medusa hugged her daughter close, nearly smothering her in the voluminous folds of her purple robe. "Do have fun on the rest of your book tour."

Cassie held the embrace a few seconds longer, buoyed by the genuine solicitude in her mother's voice. The true intent behind spoken words could never be hidden from the witch who heard them. Medusa's sincerity was real.

"Thanks, Mom." She gave her a quick peck on the cheek. "And please don't say anything to Mort about tonight. Let's just let it lie, okay?"

Medusa laughed. "I doubt he'll show his face around the coven for quite a while. He really made a fool of himself, didn't he?" Turning, she embraced Endora before the startled familiar could get away. "Take care of my baby, Dora."

Cassie blushed as her friend, squirming slightly, replied, "You know I will, Medusa. It's my job, and I love it."

"You're good for her. See that she stays healthy and happy."

Endora's cocky smile only served to endear her more to Cassie. "I'm on it!"

Medusa shot the sleeves of the purple robe. Then glancing about and realizing they stood in front of the restaurant, she looked a bit sheepish. "Guess I'll just go around the corner before I pop out of here . . . ."

"Thanks, Mom."

"My pleasure." Blowing Cassie and Endora a kiss, she disappeared in an outrageous swirl of silk and satin down a nearby alley.

Impulsively, Cassie wrapped her arm around Endora's shoulders. She knew such contact went against the familiar's feline nature, but Endora permitted it. "Hey, pal, let's get back to the hotel and get freshened up for the big to-do."

"No problem, Boss." Endora hailed a taxi. "And on the way, you can tell me how your lunch with Mr. Gorgeous and Famous went."

Cassie winced, then gave her friend a calculating look. "Dora, what do you know about baseball?"

"Not a thing. I think it's a stupid sport."

"Good, then you'll have no idea what I mean when I say that, when it comes to M S Kazimer, I'm looking into his possible free agency."

Endora stared back at Cassie. "I can easily investigate into the meaning of that statement, you know."

"Sure. But while you're doing it, you'll be staying out of my private life." Cassie did her best impersonation of Endora's catty smile, an action which had the familiar snorting in disgust.

***

"Sweet Christ, Sandor, what the hell got into you?" Robert Jamison stood in the suite's master bedroom, hands planted on hips, disgust on his G-Man face. At his feet lay the prone body of the world's most famous horror writer. The agent studied the scene. "Ah, yes. A fifth of Crown Royal got into you. Buddy, you took today's bad news even harder than I thought you would."

Mick's loud snore convinced Jamison that checking for a pulse wasn't necessary, so he turned down the bed, lifted the unconscious writer in a fireman's carry and flipped two-hundred-fifteen pounds of dead weight onto the mattress. Taking pity on the poor sot, Jamison pulled off Mick's shoes, wrestled him out of vest and dress shirt, hauled off his slacks and socks, then tossed a blanket over the now loudly snoring lump.

"Glad I'm not going to be you in the morning," the agent murmured as he turned off the lights and left the room. "I'll give your regrets to the reception crowd."

***

The darkness of the hotel bar provided plenty of ambience and just enough light for patrons to read the carefully worded descriptions of exorbitantly priced drinks. In a final gesture of pique, Jennifer decided to run Mick's tab as high as she could. Her red-eye flight back to New York didn't leave until one-thirty in the morning. Since she hated airports and refused to sit for hours in some horrible terminal, she'd gone directly from her suite to the bar and hunkered down for some serious spending. In the three hours before she caught a cab to O'Hare, she figured she could order a dozen appetizers and get herself and every other bar patron plenty drunk on her former fiancé's money.

So, she set about doing just that.

She glanced up as he approached, expression telling him she saw a blonde-haired man of average height and average looks. And had immediately classified him as insignificant.

He knew he was anything but that.

He indicated the bar stool next to hers. "May I sit here?"

"Why not?" She took a sip of her drink, then cocked her

head at him. "You have very unusual eyes."

"Really?"

"So dark compared to your light coloring. Very intense." She turned away, and for a moment he thought she had dismissed him. Then she faced him again. "What's your name?"

He had no qualms about lying to her. Glancing at the bottles on the shelves behind the bar, he saw a familiar brand. "Jack."

"Just Jack?"

"Yes."

"Well, Just Jack, I'm Just Jennifer." The handshake she offered was flaccid and moist. "Can I buy you a drink?"

"Shouldn't I be the one asking you that?"

A predatory smile graced her wide mouth. "Not tonight."

He had never mastered a charming laugh, but it appeared Jennifer Bodin was beyond caring about the oddly rusty sound that left his throat. He saw her gaze become calculating. It seemed to say, "Let this loser think he has a chance with me." Bitch. Jennifer Bitch. He wasn't here to seduce her, but for another purpose entirely.

"Do you live around here, Just Jack?"

"No."

"In town on business?"

"In a manner of speaking."

She studied him over the rim of her highball glass. "Not very talkative, I see."

"No."

She laughed, then signaled the bartender for another round. "Just like my ex. You married?"

"No."

"Me either, and it looks like I won't be any time soon."

Stroking Jennifer Bitch's ego, though revolting, was necessary to his purpose. "Who wouldn't want to marry a pretty woman like you?"

She was so self-possessed she didn't even acknowledge the compliment.

"My ex-fiancé, that's who. The sonuvabitch is giving up his career! Didn't even ask what *I* thought. I tried my best to change his mind, but does he care what I think? Oh, no. M. S. Kazimer said he's quitting, and he's a man of his word." Jennifer tossed back the rest of her drink neat. "The bastard's going to regret he ever quit on me!"

The bitch's absorption in her own indignation caused her to

miss the expression of complete astonishment he knew flooded his face. She also missed seeing that emotion harden into cold fury. He could feel his cheeks burning with rage. Felt the walls closing in on him.

"I have to leave," he said curtly.

Her head jerked in startlement, and she turned to stare at him. "You just got here."

"Sorry."

He launched himself off the bar stool and had taken three steps when he heard her say, "Men are all bastards . . . Bartender, another round for the house."

He couldn't be bothered by her petty opinions, as she was nothing to him. But what she'd told him . . . He picked up his pace until he was practically running for an exit.

Quitting! M. S. Kazimer is ending his career. Impossible! Blind fury slowly gave way to more rational thinking. Could that bitch Jennifer Bodin have been mistaken? He had recognized her the moment she'd entered the bar. Recognized her from the meticulously collected publicity photos of his idol he had culled from magazines and newspapers over the past six years.

Her engagement to the great M. S. Kazimer was of no import to him. Nor was she. He had come hoping to gain more direct information on the man he worshiped. The man whose genius had provided a blueprint for his own life. But this was the last thing he'd expected to hear.

You can't quit! How will I continue my work? How will I prove my worthiness to you if I don't have your guidance to follow? M. S. Kazimer's wonderful books would no longer show him the way. Desolation struck hard. If Jennifer Bitch was correct . . . No, she lied! Vindictive harlot. Women lied. Always. Angry with M. S. Kazimer for some offense, she had chosen to punish him, spreading vicious lies about his quitting his career.

Necessity now dictated an adjustment in his plans. He'd have to get closer to his deity in St. Louis, where he'd already plotted his next spectacular act of reverence. That way, he could determine for himself the truth of the matter.

***

The main ballroom glittered with thousands of tiny white lights hung from the ceiling and walls to resemble a galaxy of stars. Men in tuxedos and women in ball gowns drank champagne, nibbling on exotic *hors d'oeuvres* while trading the latest publishing trends and insider gossip. They toasted the authors and gushed over their latest literary offerings with a fervor just short of sycophancy.

Cassie's innate insincerity detector stood her in good stead, and she and Endora spent very little time with those who sought to gain something from associating with the Kitchen Witch and her business manager. A quick kiss on both cheeks and a "Let's do lunch sometime" sufficed as contact with those particular types.

Starting at the buffet tables in the center of the room, they slowly moved in an ever-widening circle toward the outer rim of chairs and small cafe tables. Cassie didn't really care for large crowds, so her strategy was to start at the hub of the action—the food—see and be seen, and move slowly but steadily toward the exit doors. She found herself wishing she could talk to Mick about writing, rather than endure all the false praise coming her way from publishers and business moguls alike.

Where's your love interest? Endora said inside Cassie's mind.

Whomever do you mean?

C'mon, Boss, don't play dumb with me. You didn't get all dressed up in your favorite teal gown—the one you know makes men weak with lust—just to impress a bunch of uptight suits. Mick's not here, and that's bothering you.

Cassie grabbed a flute of champagne off a passing waiter's tray and took a sip to stall this unwanted conversation. So she'd taken extra time with her makeup and chosen to wear a gown that complimented in truly amazing ways her dark coloring. There were lots of big shots in the room tonight, and she wanted to leave a favorable image with them . . . Making them weak with lust was *not* her intent at all.

Get off it, Endora. I'm working the room here.

Sure, and my mother is a rottweiler. You've barely taken your eyes off the doors all night. That Brad Pitt look-alike made a pass at you, and you froze him out.

Sorry, but I can't stand it when men drool in my cleavage.

Or is that just when certain men do that? I'd bet you'd make an exception for one M. S. Kazimer. Who, I'm sure you've noticed, is conspicuously absent.

Really?

"You're absolutely impossible!" Endora groaned.

Cassie put the now-empty glass down on a side table. They had managed to work their way to the perimeter, and she sat down in an empty chair not five yards from the doors in question.

"Why do you say that?"

Endora took the chair beside her boss. "Obviously, you really like the guy. Why not go for it?"

"He's engaged!"

The general din in the room nearly didn't drown out the unladylike sound Endora made. "To the Dragon Lady of New York City. You'd be doing Mick a favor by breaking them up."

"That's not—"

"I found out what 'free agency' means."

"Mother Goddess you work fast," Cassie said, genuinely impressed. "I was banking on your extreme aversion to sports to keep you off that trail for at least a day or two."

Endora shrugged slightly. "I'm relentless when someone's love life is involved."

"Leave mine alone, Dora," Cassie warned in a low voice. "Just back off."

Robert Whitman took that exact moment to arrive at the party. Spotting them, he promptly moved over to their table.

"Good evening, ladies," he said politely. "Cassandra, you're looking lovely, as usual." He bowed briefly over Cassie's hand before turning to do the same to Endora. "As are you, Miss Bast."

"Thank you, Mr. Whitman," Cassie replied with a smile as Endora nodded.

"Please. Robert. I'm the rookie at this author business, and I feel like you're crediting me with too much experience by calling me Mr. Whitman."

"All right, Robert."

"Have you seen Ed Turner? I need to tell him Mick's not coming."

Alarm bells went off in Cassie's head, but she managed to ask calmly, "Is everything all right?"

"It will be. He's temporarily indisposed."

"Sudden illness?" Endora asked, shooting Cassie a glance.

"You could say that."

Allergic reaction to felines? Cassie speculated.

Whitman smiled enigmatically and walked away.

Quick, read his mind, Endora ordered Cassie. *He's lying.*

Cassie concentrated hard to pick up Whitman's thoughts before party noise swallowed up the connection. *Apparently, Mick got drunk and is passed out upstairs in bed.*

Not very romantic of your hero.

He's not my hero, Dora.

Right.

Cassie chose to ignore her familiar's mild sarcasm. *What could possibly cause him to get that drunk?*

Maybe he seriously began contemplating a life with Jennifer tied around his neck.

"You are evil!" Cassie laughed, but her humor didn't stay for long. She fought down a sigh. "Mick could be a closet alcoholic . . ."

Surprise lit Endora's face at that possibility. "I really don't think so," she countered. "He's been in the international spotlight for twenty years. No way could he hide a substance problem for that long."

"That's a point." A sudden thought struck Cassie, and she had to resist a totally different reaction. A picture of an indisposed Mick—and Jennifer ministering to him—sprang into her head full blown, and jealousy reared up.

The green-eyed monster, Endora warned, obviously thinking it safer to communicate telepathically on this subject than speaking aloud.

Oh, shut up!

With a laugh, Endora sauntered in the direction of the cash bar. *I'm outta here at midnight, Boss. Feel like taking in some of the nightlife down on Rush Street.*

Knock yourself out, Cassie glumly told her friend.

Mick won't be here, but you could always hang out with the charming Robert Whitman. He's pretty buff looking.

Cassie was tempted to take a swipe at her cat. *That's not even his real name, and you know it. And, come to think of it, why would he know Mick wasn't coming? Jennifer would have notified Ed Turner of Mick's being a no-show, not Whitman.*

Mick really must be blotto if he's not here. I'd think Jennifer would drag him out as long as he's this side of death.

Doesn't add up, Cassie countered. *Jennifer's too into image. Why tarnish Mick's reputation by bringing him to this event falling down drunk?*

She thinks Mick's more important to this tour than anyone else, even drunk on his very fine rear end. Ole Jen wouldn't allow anyone else to be fawned over more than her business asset.

Fiancé, Cassie reminded her, mentally gritting her teeth.

From the beginning, she's struck me as someone who's far more in love with herself and with money than she ever could be with another human being.

That was the distinct impression Cassie had gotten from Mick during their luncheon earlier in the day, but she chose not to confirm Endora's suspicions. Her familiar was getting far too cocky lately. Telling her of the feeling Mick had projected about Jennifer—and her own encounter in the men's bathroom with him—would only feed Endora's ego. Any such revelation would whet the familiar's appetite to brew something up between Cassie and Mick. As much as admitting so stung, she wouldn't mind that happening. But as far as she knew, Mick was engaged. *This tour is getting strange.*

Curiouser and curiouser.

Cassie gave herself a mental shake. "When did you say you were leaving to go downtown?"

"Midnight, but I can take a hint." The familiar gathered up her purse.

Cassie's hand shot out to grasp her friend's wrist. "You know that's not it at all, Dora."

"I know." Endora winked. "Thinking about coming along? Be glad to have you."

"No, thanks. I'm going to pull my Cinderella act and go back to the room right about the time you take off."

"Suit yourself, but you'll miss a great time."

When Endora rose from the table, Cassie followed. "Thanks for the offer, but I'll pass."

If you don't come downtown with me, you'll spend the night pining for Mick . . . Which, come to think of it, might not be all bad . . . Go skulk around his suite. Or conjure up an image of what he's doing.

That latter suggestion brought Cassie a flashback to her earlier picture of Mick and Jennifer together. She shuddered. *No, I'll spend the night pining for a familiar who doesn't try to run my life. Maybe a nice snowy owl, or a big old fruit bat . . .*

Strolling to the exit, Endora laughed out loud. *Owls are messy—all that molting—and bats get tangled in your hair. No, this cat is the perfect familiar for you, and you're well aware of that fact.*

Just keep reminding me, Cassie tossed after her friend.

Count on that, Boss.

***

Sleep had eluded Cassie most of the night, but she had never enjoyed the aftereffects of a sleeping potion, so hadn't bothered to brew one. Exhuasted, she felt out of sorts and sluggish the next morning boarding the bus for the trip to St. Louis. The rest of the authors and their various entourages also straggled to the meeting point. Obviously, a good time had been had by nearly all on the previous night.

Endora hadn't returned to the room, but all their bags were missing when Cassie got up—with the exception of the snug jeans and green gypsy blouse lying beside Cassie's bed—so she knew the familiar had already boarded the bus. And taken their luggage with her.

She found the familiar curled up in a bunk, and as she approached distinctly heard Endora singing "Memories" from *Cats*. Chuckling, she gently nudged her. "Hey, pal, up and at 'em."

"Geez, Tugger," Endora mumbled. "Have you been in prison for years or something?"

Cassie checked to see if they were alone, then snapped her fingers and produced a steaming mug of batwing tea. "Come on, Dora," she crooned as she waved the mug under her friend's nose. "At least look like you've got a couple lives left."

With an enormous yawn, the familiar stretched as only cats can, extending her limbs until both feet and hands hung over the edges of the bunk. Then one green eye popped open.

"Is there an emergency business meeting I need to attend at this unholy hour?" Her voice was raspy from howling. "If not, I'm going back to sleep."

"It's nearly ten-thirty, and we should check in with Ed Turner so he doesn't panic."

"Is Lover Boy on board?"

Cassie rolled her eyes at the comment. "Just came on with Whitman. Jennifer's not with them." She paused, sensed the air. "There's no reading on any of her stuff being on the bus, either."

"Curiouser and curiouser."

"You can say that again."

Endora roused herself enough to sip some tea. "Seriously, Cass, some very strange circumstances have occurred during this trip. The evil I sensed in Toledo, Whitman's lying, Mick's no-show at the biggest event before New Orleans. And now this thing with Jennifer."

"I know. And, much as I hate to admit it, I think it's time we started investigating things." Cassie could barely meet her friend's eyes, and this personal discomfort confounded her. "Starting with

Mick."

The cat's now-alert gaze lit up. "Boss! Does this mean what I think it means?"

Cassie knew she should start worrying when Endora had that particular look in her eyes. She warily eyed her familiar. "What?"

"That you and Mick are, you know, going to get intimate?"

"Only in the sense that I'll most likely have to get into his head—"

"When you really want to get into his bed."

"Don't interrupt me when I'm explaining, Endora."

"More like rationalizing."

Since her manager occupied an upper bunk, Cassie was eye-level with her. "Don't go there." The look she gave Endora was calculated to intimidate any creature on the planet. She knew it had worked when the cat blinked.

"Okay," came Endora's now humble acquiescence. "I'm not going there."

"Good." Cassie turned on her heel and moved stiffly away, angry that her feelings toward Mick had been so accurately assessed. Yes, she was incredibly attracted to him. He was amazingly sexy, but more than just that, she sensed a kindred spirit under that aura of self-confidence and fame. A shy and vulnerable heart, much like her own. Having Endora tease her about emotions she didn't yet completely understand grated.

Regardless of how she felt about Mick, though, Cassie was determined to investigate. As she moved up the aisle, she noticed him and Robert sitting in the frontmost seats, their heads together. It wasn't often that she allowed herself to pry into humans' minds, but as Endora had pointed out, enough strange and potentially dangerous happenings had gone on in four short days that she felt compelled to find out exactly why.

Taking a seat across the aisle and two rows behind the men, she opened her planner and pretended to study the itinerary. Then she closed her eyes behind her sunglasses and sent her mind forward to the front seat. Her supersensitive hearing engaged.

"Sorry about last night, Jamison," Mick said in a low voice. "When Jen left, I guess I just lost it."

So I was right. Our Mr. Whitman isn't at all who he says he is. And Jennifer isn't here. Neither of those revelations gave her a sense of triumph. Darkness lurked at the edges of these events. Cassie felt it.

"I told Ed you were indisposed. For all he knows, you and Jen spent the night doing the horizontal bop."

Both Cassie and Mick winced at Jamison's indelicate comment.

"Sorry. That was uncalled for," the agent muttered.

"Damn straight it was," Mick snapped. "Doesn't the Bureau train its agents in tact?"

Cassie could hear chagrin in Jamison's voice. "Yes, but sometimes its agents get stupid. It won't happen again."

Mick's grunt could have been acceptance. Or not. "Any word on Jennifer?"

The tension level eased slightly. "She got back to her apartment safely and is even now packing up to move. Our taps on your respective phone lines paid off. We traced her calls to several realtors."

Mick's sigh nearly ruptured Cassie's eardrums. The sensation made her jump, and she glanced quickly around to see if anyone had noticed her odd behavior. Every other passenger was either asleep or almost that way, thank the goddess.

"I told you before, Jamison, if anything happens to her, I'll be your worst nightmare."

"Understood." The agent rose from his seat. "I'm going for coffee. Want some?"

"No thanks."

"Suit yourself. I'm also going to call my field agent in St. Louis. I'll fill you in at lunch."

"I appreciate that."

Cassie tried to absorb all she'd heard. *Wow. Jamison is FBI, Mick's in on something with him, Jennifer's gone, and he still cares about her. But what does this information mean to me?*

It was time to go straight to the source.

Cassie rose from her seat and moved forward to stop beside Mick. She indicated the seat Jamison had recently vacated. "Mind if I sit down?"

"Not at all."

His tone was so neutral she wondered why he just didn't tell her to go away. He looked like hell, which was quite a trick given how handsome he was. His eyes were red-rimmed, and dark circles beneath them emphasized his recent lack of rest. A vision of him passed out on the hotel room floor, an empty bottle of whiskey nearby, flashed in Cassie's head, explaining his unkempt appearance.

"Where's Endora?"

Cassie couldn't resist. "Taking a cat nap."

"She looked under the weather when she boarded the bus." Mick grimaced, rubbing his stubbled cheek with one hand. "Guess I look like something the cat dragged in myself."

"That's far more applicable to Endora," Cassie said with a kind smile. "We missed you at the reception last night."

"I was indisposed."

"So Robert told us." It would have been simple for her to keep reading Mick's thoughts, but for some unknown reason she wanted him to be forthcoming with his information. "Is Jennifer meeting us in St. Louis?"

"No."

For a best-selling author, you're pretty stingy in the dialogue department, Kazimer. But you're not getting off that easy. "From your tone of voice, I'd say she's not going to be in Memphis, either."

Mick's look managed to be quelling and disbelieving all at once. "I only said one word."

"I'm not talking number of words, I'm talking tone and body language." His sudden scowl made her sigh. "Look, Mick, I realize it's none of my business, but if you need to talk, I'm a very good listener."

She was halfway out of the seat before he spoke.

"We broke up."

"You and Jennifer?" True concern tinged her voice, and she sank back down beside him. "You called off your engagement?"

"She did a while ago. Last night, she ended our business relationship, also."

Cassie hadn't seen any of that coming, and the question left her mouth before she considered the wisdom of asking. "Why?"

Mick shrugged his broad shoulders. "We'd been floundering for a while." He started to say more, then stopped.

Cassie had pried enough for the time being. "Sorry to hear that," she said truthfully, giving his hand a quick squeeze.

The moment she touched him, Cassie felt a lightning bolt of power arc between them. Only her cat-quick reflexes and supreme self-control kept her from yanking her hand back. A quick glance at Mick's eyes told her he'd felt it too.

Tread softly here, girl, she told herself, *or you could really get scorched.* Acting as though absolutely nothing had happened, she casually withdrew her hand. "If I can do anything, let me know." She paused, thinking. "Endora could help you with managerial details, if you'd like. She's amazingly competent, and I think a tad bored right now. She said earlier that this tour is so well-organized, it's like the Federal government is running it." She noticed Mick's slight grimace, acknowledged the irony of Endora's earlier comment. "Anyway, I'll ask her. That is, if you think you'll need help. I don't want to push."

"Not at all." Mick's smile had warmed considerably. "Thanks for the offer."

Cassie rose. "Let me know if I can help somehow."

"Sure."

***

"Dora, what did you do to Jennifer Bodin?" Cassie stage-whispered into her familiar's ear where she still lay in the upper berth.

Endora batted at Cassie's face to shoo her away. When that didn't work, she rolled over to face her employer. "What are you talking about?"

"She left last night and went back to New York. They've called off their engagement."

A large grin revealed pointed white canines. "Good. That leaves the field open for you."

Cassie wanted to pull out her hair. Endora's, that is. "Bat rumps, Dora! Did you hex her or something? Give her boils? Zits? Facial hair?"

"None of the above," Endora grumped, "although the thought of warts in a very inconvenient place did cross my mind." At Cassie's sound of disapproval, she added, "Look, I was too busy last night with Rum Tum Tugger to hex Jennifer. She left for reasons I wasn't involved in."

"I believe you."

"Good. Now let me sleep." The familiar rolled over, covering her head with the blanket.

Cassie yanked the cover away. "Not until I tell you what else I learned." When Endora didn't respond, Cassie prodded her in the shoulder.

"Ouch! Stop that." Endora slowly sat up. *"What?"*

"Now that I have your attention, listen to this. Whitman's name is actually Special Agent Robert Jamison, and he had another agent follow Jennifer back to New York City. I guess the Feds have tapped both Mick's and Jennifer's phone lines, and she made several calls to realtors."

This perked Endora up considerably. "Wow. She really is out of his life. Time to make a move, Boss."

"Endora, get that off your mind for a moment, would you? Mick's somehow involved with the FBI! Do you think it could have anything to do with the evil presence you sensed in Toledo?"

"Maybe . . . " Endora snapped to attention. "We need to be very, very careful, Cass. If that guy is somehow tied to Mick, and he comes back, everyone on this tour could be in danger."

Cassie stared solemnly at her friend. "I know. When we get to St. Louis we have to do some investigating on the astral plane."

"Maybe you should try to get information out of Mick, too." This time, there was no suggestion of seduction in Endora's voice.

"I've thought about that. That's why I volunteered you to stand in for Jennifer for the rest of the tour."

Mischief brightened the cat's expression. "I get to sleep with him?"

"No, you nitwit." Cassie bit back a laugh. "You get to help him with the business end of things."

Although she tried hard, Endora's look of dejection wasn't quite convincing. "You're no fun at all, Boss."

"I know. Time to work for a living."

"Slave driver." Endora's yawn was a jaw cracker.

This time, Cassie couldn't hold the laughter in. "You're impossible. Now, get up and around. We're almost to the lunch stop. We need to plan what to do for the rest of this trip."

"For once, you're making sense."

Cassie didn't bother to reveal that those plans included her getting closer to Mick Sandor, aka M. S. Kazimer, but she figured Endora would come to that conclusion on her own.

Six

Mick rested his head back against the bus seat and tried to sleep. But the pounding behind his closed eyes served as a reminder that a fifth of scotch on an empty stomach did not a pleasant road trip the next morning make. He managed not to groan out loud, but just barely.

Right at that moment, he loathed himself. What kind of pathetic loser avoided his problems by getting shitfaced in a hotel room? When he found himself in bed in his briefs that morning, he couldn't recall how he'd gotten there. Enter the Feds. Just before Cassie Hathorne appeared, Jamison had told Mick he'd put him to bed and then informed everyone at the party that Jennifer and he were indisposed.

Indisposed didn't even come close to the state of his relationship with Jennifer. They were completely over, in every way. He couldn't really say he blamed her for severing all their connections. His career had, in many ways, consumed her life, and his refusal to keep writing had been a greater personal loss than she could take.

Although he'd suspected she saw the tour as an opportunity to get him to propose again, he'd actually encouraged her to come along. Perhaps out of a sense of honor and integrity—he didn't know exactly—but he'd been brought up to believe that a man kept his promises. And although he hadn't considered marrying her after she'd broken their engagement, they still had a business arrangement. He'd planned to reward Jennifer handsomely for all of her hard work as his manager. At one time, marrying her had seemed like the ultimate reward. Of course, at one time he'd loved her.

In retrospect, he marveled at his own ego. Marriage to him was the ultimate reward? Pathetic. Now, he considered sending Jennifer something she'd actually appreciate—a large check as severance pay. Cold, but money appealed to her more than Mick himself had.

God, what now? He massaged his aching temples with both hands. *What have I gotten myself into?*

And how would he get himself out? He'd committed to seeing Jamison's scheme through, and he would, although the entire situation was too bizarre for belief. Chills raced to his core at the thought that some lunatic was following a pattern

Mick's writing had inadvertently given him. He wasn't equipped to handle someone like that, which made him feel vulnerable despite the FBI's presence. Next to hopelessness, vulnerability was the worst feeling in the world.

So, he'd stop being vulnerable. End of story. He sat up straight in the seat and looked around. None of the other passengers were doing much more than reading. With the exception of Cassandra Hathorne. He could see her standing near the berths, speaking with her manager.

Mick found himself suddenly swallowing hard. Had the temperature in the bus just risen? Had he been wearing a tie, he'd definitely have loosened it. Innate honesty forced him to admit his pulse had jumped about four hundred beats per minute at Cassie's touch moments before. He couldn't deny he found her incredibly sensual.

He winced inwardly. It was official—he'd completely lost his mind. All around him things were going to hell in a handcar, but he was all hot and bothered because a woman had touched him.

A touch that had been companionable, not sexual. Friendly. Empathetic.

Like hell it was friendly. My hand might damn well have ignited if she'd left hers there any longer.

Cassie hadn't seemed to notice the electrical jolt, but maybe she was adept at hiding her responses to that kind of stimulus. Suddenly, he hoped that was true and that the possibility of her finding him attractive was real.

She'd offered Endora's services for the rest of the tour, and Mick recognized that as the blessing it was. It gave him a natural reason to be closer to Cassie. He could point out that proximity would make Endora's double duty easier. If he kept close, she wouldn't have to split her time between them and could just see to them both together. Good, sound business sense, right?

His heart lighter than it had been for days, he prepared to approach the two women at the lunch stop and accept their offer of help.

***

Here comes tall, dark, rich and sexy.

Cassie almost snorted hot herbal tea through her nose at Endora's telepathic remark. *Great Mother Goddess, Dora, you did that on purpose! Saying that when I was about to swallow . . . That's low.*

Endora gave her a look of pure innocence and took a huge bite of her tuna fish sandwich. *I'm not the one who's warm for the man's form, Boss Lady. You are.*

Don't think with your mouth full, Cassie grouched.

"Mind if I join you ladies?"

Mick's smile had her wishing she'd opted for iced tea. "Not at all." As she mentally slowed her respiratory rate, she heard Endora laughing at her inside her head. Then she noticed Mick's eyes starting to redden and water and quickly reinforced her protection spell against his cat allergy. Instantly, his eyes cleared. "Have you considered my offer?" *My stars, I hope so!*

"As a matter of fact, I have." Mick looked from one woman to the other. "If it's all right with Ms. Bast, I'll take you up on your offer of her managerial skills for the rest of this tour." He focused his blue gaze on Endora. "And, I'm willing to pay you for the extra effort."

"That won't be necessary," she replied smoothly. "Cassie more than adequately compensates me."

"Nonetheless, I don't expect you to work for me for free."

Endora glanced over at Cassie, then back at Mick. Her eyes sparkled with mischief. "Working for the most popular novelist of our time is compensation enough."

"Did I mention sycophancy and sarcasm are two additional services Endora offers," Cassie wryly interjected. "Both for no extra cost."

Mick laughed, and her stomach did a little flip-flop at the sound. She found herself thinking of ways to make him laugh again.

Don't tell jokes. You're terrible at jokes.

Dora, mind your own thoughts.

I can't. I'm too busy minding yours.

Cassie firmly nudged her under the table while at the same time grinning at Mick like the village idiot. She knew she was doing it, but she couldn't stop. An adult trapped in a teenage fantasy was not a pretty sight, but all she could hope for was to emerge with some dignity still intact.

"Well, I guess if you can put up with Endora's highly suspect management style, it sounds like you've got yourself a temporary publicist." *That sounded more professional and rational than anything I've said all day.*

Endora rose at that moment and gathered up her tray and utensils. "I'll just leave you two to hammer out the details," she said brightly.

"No hammering necessary," Cassie responded immediately. "You're working for me twelve hours a day, and for Mick the other twelve. You'll get a three-hour vacation the day after the tour ends."

"Sounds fair." Endora turned her look on Mick. "That work for you, Mr. Kazimer?"

"Indeed it does, Miss Bast." Although he was addressing Endora, he looked at Cassie when he spoke.

She saw her familiar's patented Cheshire grin. "You'll have to start calling me Endora if I'm going to be terrorizing site hosts in your name," she cracked.

At those words, Mick's gaze snapped toward her.

"Just checking to see if you were listening."

"Endora, don't you have somewhere to go?"

"See you on the bus," Endora tossed over her shoulder as she walked away, whistling.

Cassie turned to Mick. "She's a bit eccentric, as I'm sure you've already realized. But she's extremely good at what she does."

He leaned back in his chair and crossed his hands over his chest. "Her style's different, but I'm not looking for a long-term work commitment, so she and I won't have time to get on each other's nerves."

"Be careful what you say," Cassie warned lightly. "A week could be all the time needed."

"Why Ms. Hathorne," Mick said in a tone of mock offense, "I do believe you've just insulted me."

Cassie played along, adopting a haughtily affected tone. "In what way, most gracious sir?"

"By insinuating I'm intolerant."

"Believe me, Endora could try the patience of a saint." *And most likely has in some past life.*

Mick made a gesture of dismissal. "We'll get along fine." Then his gaze became intensely focused on Cassie. "I really appreciate your doing this for me. Both of you. Thanks."

"It's nothing," she said through a suddenly arid throat. His look was definitely intense. "You'd have done the same for me, I'm sure."

"*I* might have, but I seriously doubt Jennifer would have shared my philanthropic urges."

At his pensive tone, Cassie's nurturing instinct kicked in

full-force. "Mick, I'm so sorry. About this whole situation. I didn't mean to upset you."

"I'm more disappointed than upset," he said slowly, and she could see his difficulty in saying the words. "I thought we had a strong relationship. Apparently, both of us were deluding ourselves. It's truly best things ended." He scrubbed his eyes with both hands. "Glad we figured out before the wedding that it wouldn't work."

Cassie couldn't help it. She reached across the table and squeezed his hand. Big mistake. Waves of awareness rolled up her arm, and she found herself pulling back as if she'd been burned. "I, I'm sorry I brought it up," she stammered. Heat burned her cheeks, and she knew she was probably doing a good impersonation of a boiled lobster right then.

"Don't beat yourself up over it. It wasn't your fault." With that, he rose to leave. "See you on the bus."

"Sure." She watched him walk away, and her heart sank lower with every step he took. *Way to go, Cass,* she chided herself. *Top marks in the Unadulterated-Lust-Scrambled-My-Brain category.* Why had she mentioned Jennifer? Sure, it had been indirect, but she should have kept her mouth shut. There was no way she was going to make him forget his old flame if she constantly kept reminding him of her.

Maybe you need a refresher course in making moves, like Seduction 101, her familiar suddenly said.

Shut up, Dora!

***

The Adams Mark Hotel was crowded that weekend, as a variety of events had served to pack the Gateway City, including the Midwest's largest science-fiction convention. The Detroit Red Wings—the St. Louis Blues' hockey rivals—were also in town, so the possibilities for excitement ranged from authors to Klingons to toothless men wreaking havoc with bent sticks and razor-sharp skates.

The concierge met the bus as it pulled up under the portico and ushered the party into the airy, open lobby. Within moments, they had their room assignments and were heading for the elevators. As in Chicago, the authors all had suites, but only Mick's was the penthouse. Since Cassie now knew the FBI was fronting the tour, this special treatment made even more sense. Before she'd overheard his conversation with Jamison, she'd just assumed Mick's overwhelming popularity had earned him first-class accommodations. Now, she understood that the Feds thought isolating him would make it easier to track their quarry while maintaining the illusion of a public relations event, not a manhunt. If the other writers stayed on a different floor, their chances of seeing something unusual would be diminished, as would any suspicions about the true purpose of this book tour.

She glanced at Mick and found herself gratified at his improved color. He stood with Agent Jamison near the closest bank of elevators, talking quietly, and suddenly she wished she was the one he was confiding in.

Where'd that thought come from? she wondered.

From your heart, Endora answered.

Dora, get out of my head!

It's not that I was eavesdropping, Boss. It's just that you're pathetic at masking your feelings for him.

Oh, so now I'm pathetic! Cassie swung around toward the elevators, the jerky motion causing her shoulder bag to slip down to her wrist. Since the hand attached to that wrist was grasping the handle of her Pullman, more than a little pain hit her when the shoulder strap hauled her arm down.

"Ouch!"

Endora caught the strap and pulled it back up onto Cassie's shoulder.

Come on, Cass. You're gaga over Mick. Your karma's been humming since he accepted your offer of my managerial skills. He sat down, and your pulse went off the charts. You can't keep from thinking of him, either.

I'm envisioning you in a pet carrier for the rest of this trip, Cassie huffed. *If you truly believe—*

The hair on Cassie's nape stood straight a split-second before Endora went completely rigid.

He's here!

Despite her familiar's previous warning, the dark wave of roiling evil caught Cassie completely unprepared, momentarily robbing her of breath. She gasped quietly and forced breath into her lungs and herself to action.

Find him, Dora! I'll protect the humans. Summon me when you locate him. Go!

Endora raced from the central elevator bank toward the escalators. Cassie cleared her mind of everything, brought up the protection spell from memory and cast it out over the lobby. Fortunately, their whole party stood close at hand. That made protecting them easier, but she was obligated to shield everyone nearby as well. It required even more concentration, but her spell would keep the hideous entity she and Endora had sensed from harming any nearby hotel patrons.

But there was one monumental drawback. The amount of psychic energy necessary to cover the lobby was staggering. Although an accomplished witch like Medusa could hold the spell for up to half an hour, Cassie was nowhere near her mother's league. With luck, she could get fifteen minutes, max. She fleetingly regretted not having practiced her spell casting techniques more diligently while growing up. Not listening to those coven instructors who'd all reminded every apprentice that "Some day, like algebra, this will come in handy." Although she'd never actually found a use for algebra, several spells would certainly have been a bonus right then.

Incompetence aside, no one—in the writers' group or not—deserved exposure to a monster the likes of which prowled the hotel. So, she'd do her best to shield them.

She slowed her body's functions to maintenance levels and concentrated as much energy as she could into holding the spell as long as possible. And as one part of her mind centered on protecting the humans, another part listened for Endora's summons.

It never came.

***

Just as she entered the service hallway where she felt the strongest negative vibrations—out of sight of any mortal—Endora changed into feline form to make herself less noticeable.

Evil pulsed all around her as she cautiously approached a pair of still-swinging service doors. Her quarry had entered these just moments before. She timed the gapping of the doors and slipped into the service kitchen next to the banquet halls. She guessed by the quiet that no luncheons were scheduled that day. And since night-shift banquet crews usually weren't required to report until late afternoon, this area would remain quiet for hours.

Sidling over to the closest wall, Endora began a slow reconnaissance of the kitchen. She peeked around a corner of a serving cart and scanned the area with extrasensory perception as well as visual. All the metal utensils and carts, the humming of the bright overhead lights, and the strong smells of food made it difficult to get a positive fix on her quarry, though. He was likely near the walk-in freezers at the back of the room—a great place to hide temporarily in an emergency. But she couldn't see him.

When she stepped out around the cart, he pounced. One large hand clamped down on her neck as the other pinned her hind legs together under her belly. She was helpless to escape.

"Nice kitty kitty," he hissed in a tone that was in no way gentle. He squeezed Endora's neck until her eyes began to bulge slightly. "I hate kitties!"

With unholy strength, he flung her against the closest wall and laughed as her limp body slid to the floor. Then he was gone.

Cassie, she managed to project with her last coherent thought before darkness claimed her.

***

Cassie heard the whisper of her name inside her head. She thought she'd also heard "kitchen."

Dora? she probed. The sound didn't come again, and she had to fight a sudden surge of panic. *Dora, you there?*

Silence.

Instantly, Cassie dropped the protection spell and froze everyone in place. Until she could find Endora, no one in the hotel would be able to move in any way, including the monster, provided he hadn't already escaped. Everyone would be safe from attack. Theoretically, anyway. She hadn't ever actually cast an immobilization spell, and her head pounded from her efforts with the protection spell. Those details had to wait, though. Her familiar needed her.

She conjured the spell as she sprinted toward the service area, knowing Endora had originally headed in that direction. And based on faith that the familiar had indeed put the word kitchen in Cassie's head. A thousand terrible scenarios flashed in her mind when she entered the corridor behind the banquet halls and honed in on Endora's aura. It was very weak.

Cassie burst through the kitchen doors, sliding to a halt where the cat's crumpled form lay at the junction of wall and floor. She was immediately kneeling beside her friend to gently lift her into her arms.

"Hang in there, pal," she murmured, brushing away the blood trickling from the cat's left ear. "Let's get you up to the room."

"He got the jump on me," Endora moaned.

"Shhh. Take it easy. You can tell me all about it after I've seen how badly he hurt you."

Cassie had started sending out waves of healing energy as soon as she'd seen Endora, and her friend's pain was already lessening.

"Do I get combat pay for this, Boss?" the cat wheezed.

"I'll have to think about it." Cassie gave her a quick, gentle scratching between the ears. "We've got to get you patched up first."

Endora suddenly stiffened. "Help the mortals, Cass," she urged. "That thing's still out there!"

Belatedly, Cassie remembered the spell she'd thrown over the hotel. "I've got everything frozen," she explained as she carried Endora on to the elevator and up to their suite. "I think. I'll put you to bed, then go back to the lobby and set things right."

"Be careful."

Cassie gently laid Endora on one of the beds and pulled the coverlet up over her. "I will. Now, you get some rest. I'll be back before you can twitch that tail you're so vain about."

Endora closed her eyes. "We've got to talk about this and what we need to do, you know."

"Believe me, I know."

Even though she felt the man had hurt her familiar simply because in her cat form she was vulnerable, Cassie put a protection spell on the suite as she flashed back to the lobby. Evil that powerful was never to be taken lightly. She didn't want to think about the fact that her confidence in her spell-casting abilities had never been very high before this.

What have you gotten us into, Mick? And could she get them out?

***

Mick shook his head to clear a slight buzzing in his ears. What the hell had just happened? He could have sworn Cassie and Endora were standing a few steps behind him as the group waited for elevators. Now, Cassie was definitely to his direct left, and his temporary manager was nowhere to be seen.

He glanced over at a glassy-eyed Jamison. The man was an FBI agent, how could he look that stupefied? Something very strange was going on.

"Hey, Robert, snap out of it." Jamison was slow to respond, so Mick nudged him with an elbow to the ribs. "Robert? Hello!

Anybody home?"

Jamison blinked, then his gaze again took on the intense focus Mick had become accustomed to seeing.

"That was weird. I just lost my edge and zoned out."

"It happens to the best of us," Mick casually quipped. But his mind reeled. *The exact same thing happening to both of us? That's too bizarre to be coincidence.* He was about to comment when he saw Jamison glance at his watch. The agent's eyes narrowed.

"Funny, I thought it was eleven-thirty. My watch reads almost eleven forty-five."

The hair on the back of Mick's neck rose, but he tried to pass it off as the lingering effects of last night's binge and the menacing reason for the book tour.

"What's taking this elevator so long?" Cassie broke in from behind him. "I swear, they've got three-legged squirrels on treadmills powering those things."

The sound of her husky contralto gave Mick shivers of a totally different sort. It conjured visions of rumpled satin sheets and morning-after breakfasts, and he found himself starting to become aroused. *Shit, Sandor, get a grip,* he ordered himself. *Remember Lake Superior.* That did it. Memories of August swims in water with a temperature hovering around sixty-five degrees effectively shrank his libido.

With a laugh he hoped sounded sincerely casual, he turned toward her to add, "More likely one-legged baboons on bicycles."

The impact of her caramel-colored gaze at a range of less than three feet nearly knocked him to his knees. The first time they met he'd seen her eyes were beautiful, but he had no idea how powerful. They nearly glowed. Funny, he hadn't noticed before. Of course, most of the time he'd seen her in subdued lighting. Not today, though. His original lack of perception that morning he blamed on a hangover and self-pity. At lunch, she'd been wearing sunglasses when he'd approached her.

Neither of those two barriers stood between them now, however. Had he fallen into a vat of caramel and been pulled under? Then he smelled that incredible perfume, so uniquely hers. It was a struggle to resist touching her cheek, he was so drawn by her physical presence. Drowning in sensations, he found himself loving his imminent demise.

It took him a moment to realize Jamison was speaking to

him.

"Mick, you getting on or not?" The FBI agent stood holding the elevator door open.

"Uh, sorry." Mick rolled his overnighter onto the car and, programmed in this situation to follow the rest of the herd, turned to face the car's doors. Then he spotted Cassie struggling with two sets of luggage. "Need some help?" He stepped back into the lobby to take a suitcase and garment bag from her.

"Thanks."

Her heartfelt smile warmed him completely through, and his chest tightened. *God, this woman is hot.* He cleared his throat. "Where's Endora?" He thought Cassie gave a start at his question, but wrote it off as imagination.

"She, uh, had to go talk to some of the service people," Cassie stammered. "Something about the menu, I think."

Mick hadn't survived growing up with three sisters without becoming a body language expert. And the language Cassandra Hathorne's body was speaking said she definitely wasn't telling the truth. He noticed a tightness around her mouth that hadn't been there any time before on this trip.

"Everything all right?"

That caramel gaze snapped in his direction, and a shade seemed to drop down over her eyes, shielding her innermost thoughts and effectively dampening the intense glow of just moments before.

"Fine," she stated. Not emphatically enough to be brusque, but there was no breeziness to her tone, either.

Mick chose to take her statement at face value, and when the elevator stopped at their floor, he casually said, "I could take this luggage to your room for you."

Cassie's response came after a slight pause. "I don't want to inconvenience you."

Mick laughed. "It's not like I'll be lugging this stuff for miles, then hiking Mt. Rainier to get to my room. I think I've got enough physical endurance to pull this off."

They were standing in the elevator lobby with all the other members of the tour streaming past them dragging carryons and various other bags and baggage, but Mick was really only aware of Cassie. God, he just wanted to take her in his arms and soothe away whatever was bothering her, but all the luggage in his hands quashed that impulse.

"So what do you say," he asked softly. "Can I come to your

room?"

Cassie jumped as if she'd been scalded. "Bat rumps, I'm sorry!"

Mick cocked a brow. "Bat rumps?"

"It's just an expression I use," she said hastily, completely nonplused. "The 'Kitchen Witch' thing and all that, you know."

It stunned him to realize he'd completely flustered her. She was really on edge all of a sudden. Lifting the garment bag he held in his left hand, he said, "Your room?"

"Oh! Sorry! I guess my mind just went south there for a minute."

That seems to be happening to a majority of us lately. He turned to the directional guides on the corridor wall. "What's your suite number?"

"Twelve-thirteen."

Before she could say another word, he was following the arrow pointing the way to her suite. He could hear her right behind him, and in a weird way that felt somehow comforting.

When he stopped at her door, she stepped past him to open it. He found himself fascinated with the back of her head as she bent to insert the key card. Her dark, silky hair, cut at chin level, parted almost perfectly down the middle to fall on either side of her face and expose the nape of her neck. What would she do if he kissed her there?

Whoa! Mick brought himself up short. *What the hell's my problem? I'm acting like a kid with his first Playboy.*

The purpose of this tour was to catch a serial killer, not start a relationship. Yet, almost from the moment he'd met her, and especially since their private lunch in Chicago, he'd felt an almost overwhelming attraction to her. And it wasn't just physical. When Cassie sat beside him at the first signing in Toledo he'd felt it. And it just kept getting stronger.

But the attraction could not take priority. This serial killer horror had him completely out of emotional control, and he had to regain it and return to his original objective. Taking a mental step back, he managed to throttle his hormones. A slow, deep breath helped, too.

At that exact moment, Cassie straightened and opened the door. She waved him inside. "Just set them in the closet if you would." She turned to indicate where. When he did so, she added, "Thanks, Mick. I'd ask you in for a drink, but Endora wasn't feeling well and planned to come back here and lie down after she talked to the serving staff. I'm hoping she's asleep by now."

Her polite dismissal gave him an opportunity to escape without embarrassing himself by carrying on like a lust-struck adolescent. "No problem. Hope to see you at dinner. Tell Endora to get better."

He was halfway down the hall before he realized his palms were sweaty and that a certain part of his anatomy had hardly been throttled back at all. In fact, it showed a definite interest in Ms. Cassandra Hathorne. He'd have to go to the gym and see if he could work off his sudden bout of hormones before he saw her again.

"I'm a pig," he muttered, turning by the elevator lobby into the corridor that led to his rooms. "All hell's breaking loose, and I can't get my mind off a woman."

Where was a priest when he needed one?

***

Cassie leaned her head against the door, mentally tracing Mick's retreat. She didn't need infrared sensors to detect his body temperature. Heat poured from him in waves. Longing hit her in the chest, and she found herself wanting to run after him and take him directly to bed. To see if the heat he radiated was anywhere near her own body temperature when she thought of him.

Goddess, she had a major problem. What had started out as simple lust was getting far too complicated. Come to think of it, it really hadn't started out as simple lust. That was dangerous, to say the least. And she had other real concerns to confront. Pining after a human being was one thing. Actually contemplating a serious relationship with one was a completely different cauldron of ingredients.

Not exactly a great time to start a courtship, Cass, she admonished herself. Arguably, there was *never* a great time to start a courtship with a non-witch, but she had it bad for Mick, and there was no sense denying it.

Now, what was she going to do about it?

Seven

Something had nearly gone wrong. For a few moments, he had been slowed to a near standstill, unable to escape from the hotel after having again seen the object of his adoration. Despite his most concentrated efforts, he could not move quickly, and panic had begun to set in. How could he avoid being seen by the Master? It wasn't time yet. He was not yet worthy.

Unexpectedly encountering a cat in the hotel kitchen had startled him, but he'd disposed of it. Then he'd just reached the hallway when he'd suddenly found himself moving in slow motion. No matter how hard he struggled, he could not increase his speed. It had taken close to fifteen minutes to travel only three hundred yards to the hotel's west exit. By the time his sluggishness abruptly ended, he was five feet from the door, soaked in sweat and terrified of discovery. His sudden release from this overwhelming lethargy caused him to stumble forward and nearly fall. He'd quickly regained his balance, fled the hotel miraculously unseen, and run into the street toward his temporary lair.

This time, he had drawn closer. Far closer than he had approached in Toledo. Of course, after the very proper sacrifice he'd made near the Seaway Center, his worthiness to come near the Master had increased. But he was yet too inferior to make eye contact, could only dare to see M. S. Kazimer from across the banks of elevators. Much work remained if he was to prove deserving of the one man in the world superior to himself.

Yet unforeseen circumstances had nearly impeded his schedule for accomplishing this triumph. Jennifer Bodin's revelation in the Chicago bar the previous night had infuriated him, but he had as yet discovered no support for her claim. The tour continued, as would he. But remembered frustration had him hissing through his teeth. Something about his idol's latest excursion didn't feel quite right. He'd definitely been held up by some invisible force in the hotel. Whether that had anything to do with the tour, he couldn't say. But it had disrupted his carefully laid plans, and that was unacceptable.

***

Cassie let out a shaky breath and pushed herself away from the door with a dispirited sigh. It took a concentrated effort to make her wobbly knees support her, and she laughed aloud at how ridiculous the situation was. That put some starch back into her spine. Laughing at herself always did.

"Better get unpacked," she said to the air around her and with a snap of her fingers put away all of Endora's and her clothes. "Too bad motion-freeze spells aren't so easy," she muttered, more than a little tired.

"I heard that," came Endora's disembodied voice from the suite's far bedroom.

Cassie shook her head as she headed for that room. "I should never forget your preternatural hearing, Dora."

"Don't worry, I won't let you."

Cassie sat down beside her familiar—bundled beneath the institutionally patterned, earth-tone bedspread—and ran a hand across the cat's furry brow. "You don't feel feverish. How's the rest of you?"

Endora rubbed her head against Cassie's palm and purred in contentment. "Almost as good as new, Boss, but you don't have to stop with the ear scratching just because I told you that. I like it when you show concern."

Cassie barked a laugh and gave the cat a soft pat on the head. "Like I never do! You're impossible, Dora."

"I know. It's just part of my feline charm." At Cassie's wince, Endora added, "What?"

Cassie managed through great effort to keep from grinding her teeth. But she couldn't prevent tears from welling in her eyes.

"I could've gotten you killed!"

Endora immediately returned to human form. Sitting up slowly, she took Cassie's hand between both of hers. "Nonsense."

"Dora—"

"Cass, listen to me! Your actions had nothing to do with what happened in the kitchen. That freakin' bastard got the jump on me."

"You shouldn't have been in there alone. I should have gone with you."

Endora rubbed Cassie's knuckles. "Stop hammering yourself over this. I'm not much the worse for wear."

"I should have been with you," Cassie insisted.

"Your responsibility was to Mick and the other humans. End of argument. I'm a cat, remember? And cats can take care of themselves."

"Most of the time." Cassie felt a tear spill out of her eye and run down her cheek, but she didn't brush it away. "If that man had killed you, I don't know what I would have done."

"Well, I've got a few lives left," Endora quipped, smiling wryly. "You could have brought me back to finish them out."

"Joke all you want, but you know I could never have pulled that off." Cassie put her head in her hands. "I'm just not good enough."

"You froze everyone in the hotel lobby—"

"A lot of good that would have done if that maniac had come back," Cassie cut in, misery in both tone and posture. "And I didn't stop time. Mick and Jamison noticed their watches had advanced. I tried to distract them from contemplating that phenomenon, but I'm not sure I managed . . ." She covered her face with her hands and sobbed.

Endora drew her friend into her arms and held her tight. Cassie sobbed harder.

"I hated witch training," she choked out. "All the other students were so mean because I didn't want to be there. Didn't want to be like them."

"You wanted to be human, didn't you?" Endora rubbed Cassie's back comfortingly.

Cassie nodded against Endora's shoulder. "I barely paid attention during spells and hexes training. I was much better at potions and cooking."

"And that makes you uniquely suitable for your chosen career path," Endora stated loyally. "While witches like Mort go around looking like Rocky Horror groupies who have no lives, you're beloved of human beings everywhere because of what you do. You actually help people, Cass."

"I'm a terrible witch."

"'C'mon! You can do lots of spells. Besides, you know as well as I do not every magick practitioner can cast the really complex incantations. Not with a high degree of proficiency. And especially not in a hotel lobby."

Cassie pulled from Endora's embrace and sat up. With a snap of her fingers, a box of tissue appeared on the bedspread beside her. At Endora's knowing look, Cassie hastened to say, "That's minor league. Any junior witch can do that one."

"I'd beg to differ, but it's obvious you're in the mood to feel sorry for yourself, so I'm not going to point out anything that disproves your theory."

"Nothing has ever stopped you before." Cassie eyed her familiar, hoping to compel her to continue that line of thought, but realized immediately a staring contest with a cat was doomed to failure. Sighing, she looked away. "I need your advice."

"Since you asked, Boss." Endora fluffed her pillows up against the headboard, then leaned back onto them. "Practice."

Cassie's gaze snapped back to her friend's, and she sat ramrod straight. "What?"

"I'm not the only one with preternatural hearing—you heard me."

"Practice."

Endora nodded. "Practice."

"How? *When*? We're in the middle of a book tour, and a crazy guy's out there stalking all of us. He almost killed you, and who knows when he'll be back—"

"Whoa, Cassie! Maintain." Endora leaned forward to grasp her friend's shoulders. "I'll teleport back to Massachusetts tonight to get your charm and hex books. We'll pretend you're taking your witchcraft certification boards."

"I barely passed a couple classifications—" Cassie started to say, but Endora's upheld hand stopped her.

"No negativity! None! We'll start out by reviewing the basic stuff you've already mastered. That will get your confidence back, then we can progress to the more difficult incantations. By the end of this tour, you'll be casting spells even Medusa will envy."

"Do you actually think we've got that much time?"

Endora shook her head. "Honestly, I don't know." She leaned forward, suddenly intense. "But we've got to try, Cass. You of all witches would do everything in your power to protect this group of humans. Especially Mick. This is no time to have a mid-life crisis! You're clever and smart, and all you need to do is brush up on your skills. I'll help you."

Cassie gave Endora a long, hard hug. When the two women broke away from each other, she grabbed Endora by the elbows. "Thanks for the pep talk."

"It's what I do." The trademark cockiness was completely missing. "You're *my* witch. No crazy, evil bastard with a death fetish is going to throw you off your game."

"I don't think I can protect anyone from this guy."

"You already did this afternoon."

"Even worse, I'm falling for Mick." Cassie's head bowed

slightly. "Hard."

Endora cocked a brow. "Honey, you were the last one to know. I've been aware of that vibe for days now."

"Lust would be simple. This is way beyond that." Cassie sighed unhappily and tilted her chin up so she could stare at the ceiling. "I achieved lust stage looking at his picture in the limo from the Toledo airport. But I thought Jennifer had him." This sigh came right from the depths. "But Mick's a free agent, and I'm halfway over the edge for him. What should I do about that?"

"I'd suggest the cat philosophy of 'love 'em and leave 'em,' but I know that advice will fall on deaf ears."

"You're right on that one." Cassie laughed ruefully and laid her head on Endora's shoulder. "I've never met anyone like him, Dora. He's so intelligent. Funny. Charming–"

"And handsome as sin."

Cassie elbowed her friend. "We relate on so many levels–"

"And he's built like a god."

"Because we're both writers, we know the troubles inherent in that profession."

"And he's got really big hands. They say the size of a man's thumbs correlates to the size of his–"

"Enough, Dora!" Cassie sat up, then stood. "You're not helping me think clearly, here, pal. And I need true clarity. Great Mother Goddess, I'm so confused!"

Endora licked her palm and smoothed a lock of her hair back away from her face. "You're going to listen to your closest friend," she said firmly. "Get Mick on the phone and tell him I'm indisposed this evening. Invite him to dinner in the hotel bar. That will give you two a chance to make out."

Cassie thought back to the heat they'd generated just standing outside the suite. Knowing Endora wouldn't leave it alone, she said solemnly, "We'd better be careful to stay away from the fire sprinklers."

"Spontaneous combustion, eh?"

"Oh, yeah."

"All right, order room service. Just make sure to use his room. In case the sprinklers actually do activate. I'll take off for home and be back by the Witching Hour with all of your school stuff."

Leaning back, Cassie stared at her friend for a moment, then shook her head. "What did I do to deserve you, Dora?"

"Skipped one too many spell casting classes, most likely." She shooed Cassie off the bed. "Now get out of here and go burn up the sheets with that hunky author."

"Don't call the fire department."

Laughing at her mistress' remark, Endora rose from bed and started for the sitting room. Halfway to it, she was back in feline form. "Later!"

Cassie chuckled, her mood once again optimistic. "Grab the book *Elixirs That Will Either Cure You or Kill You*. That information might prove extremely useful."

"Gotcha." Endora leapt onto the balcony railing and strolled along its length, then gathered herself to spring. *Keep your chin up, Boss.*

Will do, partner. Be careful, and hurry back.

Endora jumped from the twentieth-floor balcony out into the night. With a muffled "pop," she disappeared.

On a another sigh, Cassie pulled the balcony sliders closed and latched them. It was way past time for her to get serious about what she was.

And no better reason to do so.

***

He caught the phone on the third ring.

"Mick here." His heartbeat went into overdrive at the sound of the voice on the other end, and his fingers involuntarily tightened on the receiver.

"Cassie? Hi." He listened intently, mentally forcing himself not to groan at her invitation to dinner. "Oh, man, I can't. I'm ordering in and working on some of the New Orleans promotions," he lied smoothly. "And I'm still not one hundred percent after last night."

At least that last part was true. His stomach had been queasy since he'd dragged himself and his colossal hangover out of bed that morning, and even riding in the front of the bus on the trip down from Chicago hadn't completely helped. As to the fabrication about promotions ... Mick was meeting Jamison in the FBI's command suite to discuss profiles and crime reports they'd compiled on his personal wacko.

Since the Bureau had specifically planned the book tour to coincide with the settings in *Mortal Sin,* Jamison and his agents wanted to check all the details of the fictional crimes committed at each venue. In that way, they hoped to predict where the killer would strike next and capture him before he did.

The plan sounded good, but Mick secretly admitted he had little confidence in it. From his extensive research, he knew serial killers to be insanely clever fiends who were well onto their individual paths of destruction before authorities ever managed to stop them. Hence the term serial killer. That left too many corpses between identification of the pattern and the actual capture, and he was determined not to be the cause of more deaths.

So, dining with Cassandra Hathorne, although tempting beyond belief, had to wait.

"Can I take a rain check?" he asked, trying to inject enough casual interest into his voice to disguise just how much he wanted to be with her. *God, I'm reverting to my teenage years, trying to act cool and uninterested when I really want to jump in bed with her.* "Great! Tomorrow night then. Oh, and tell Endora to get well. Good night." He hung up.

Where had that last thought come from? He had never in his life been in to casual sex. He wiped his suddenly sweaty palms on the well-worn Michigan State hockey tee shirt he'd traded for his sport coat and polo shirt upon unpacking. Could he be having a mid-life crisis on top of all the other craziness in his world?

Though somehow he doubted a relationship with Cassie Hathorne could ever be casual for him. And he'd sure as hell like to find out if she felt the same way.

He hung his slacks in the closet and pulled on a pair of MSU sweat pants and his running shoes. Thus attired in clothes that brought pleasant memories, he went off to confront some very unpleasant realities.

***

Cassie huffed out a dejected breath as she hung up the phone. So much for Endora's suggestion. Mick had other plans for dinner. For the night, in fact. That left her out of luck in the romance department. Briefly, she considered walking over to the St. Louis arch—literally across the street from the hotel—but couldn't muster the enthusiasm. After all, if she wanted to see the city from that high up, she'd simply fly over it. And she wouldn't have to climb all those steps in that claustrophobic stairway to do it.

Thoughts of flying led to thoughts of other magical pursuits, and she momentarily allowed herself to wallow in self-pity. If she'd had any pride in her own kind when she was growing up, she'd have applied herself more diligently in school. Had that happened, she'd now be able to protect a special human being she found herself starting to care very much for. Instead of dusting off little-used skills, she could be enjoying Mick rather than just worrying about him.

Of course, she'd have to get into his room to enjoy him. And that didn't appear to be in her immediate future.

"Okay, pity party over with, Cass," she said aloud. "Time to get after it."

Even without the spell books and incantations, she had plenty to do until Endora returned.

After drawing a pentagram of light on the floor in the suite's sitting room, she sat cross-legged in the pentagram's exact center, facing north, hands resting palms-up on knees. She took five deep, cleansing breaths, closed her eyes and slowed her breathing to five breaths every minute. All her physical systems slowed, allowing her to concentrate her spiritual energy on mental activity.

She returned in her memory to her school days. Not regular school, of course. She'd simply attended classes to keep neighbors from calling school authorities. Since they moved fairly often, none of the humans ever suspected the dark-haired little girl who lived down the block aged about one year for every three of theirs. No, she mentally returned to her coven school days, when she and all witches of approximate age took their training in the magickal arts.

She pictured her first day—the excitement and anxiety, discovering others like her among whom she no longer felt so different. But also learning that there was a definite hierarchy among the students, and she was nowhere near the top of that pyramid. In the mortal school, she was an outstanding student. At the coven school, "disappointing" described her performance.

A pang of remembered hurt twisted through her. A boy named J. D. had relentlessly teased her because she was slow at spell casting. J. D. had grown up to become a coven leader. Though he was renowned throughout the paranormal world as a brilliant practitioner of the magickal arts, Cassie suspected he also illegally practiced Black Magic.

She, on the other hand, had become a writer for humans. A profession that brought no prestige among the coven's circles, although Cassie didn't begrudge her place in the universe . . . J. D. was a witch with no moral code beyond self-advancement.

She'd rather be like herself—a poorly-skilled witch with a big heart—than a soulless cretin like him.

Shifting her seated position, she entered into a trance and followed her past to the present . . . Each day of her magical education spun through her head as though she relived it in super fast-forward. The sights and sounds, smells and tastes, raced through her memories, reconnecting her to her spirit. She alternately laughed and cried as her adolescent triumphs and tragedies played themselves out on the movie screen of her mind.

***

Splatters of blood covered every wall, a veritable collage of red. The metallic smell of it filled the small room and added to his arousal. Bending to the floor, he dipped his fingers into the shallow pool then traced four lines of scarlet across his bare chest from his right shoulder to his left nipple. With his right hand he brought himself quickly to climax, ejaculating on the face of his decapitated victim.

Self-discipline dictated that he make no outcry of pleasure as he ended his latest rite. By remaining silent at the peak of his excitement, he again demonstrated his power over himself and all those around him.

Soon. Very soon, he would be worthy.

***

The phone had probably rung eight or nine times before the sound snapped Cassie out of her trance. She rose from the floor in one fluid motion, noting the time as she approached the phone and the desk clock beside it.

Ten-thirty. She'd been meditating for hours! But it had felt incredibly good to do so. And when was the last time she'd actually given herself over to concentration that intense and prolonged? More years than she was willing to count.

It was rather late for a caller, especially since she knew Medusa wasn't planning to dog her heels on this leg of the trip, and Endora wouldn't need to phone. Her nerve endings tingled slightly as she reached for the receiver, and suddenly she knew for certain her caller's identity.

"Dance with me," came the low baritone on the other end of the line.

It was a question she didn't have to ask, but it might seem odd to a human if she didn't. "Mick?"

"There's a dance floor in the restaurant at the top of the hotel," he stated without preamble. "We don't have to be up early tomorrow, so I thought I could make up for missing dinner tonight."

A wave of pure pleasure rolled over her. He wanted to make amends for turning her down earlier. She was liking him more and more as time went on.

"I'd love to. Give me half an hour to get ready."

"Uh-uh, Ms. Hathorne. This is strictly extreme casual. I'm wearing workout attire."

Although Cassie didn't consider herself to be a fashion snob, that made her cringe a bit. "You're a very brave man."

"I really don't care what anyone thinks of my clothes. They're clean. I'm not trying to sell them, and I'm planning to leave them on while I'm there. Besides, the place is dark, and most of the patrons should be well on their way to drunken bliss at this hour."

"Poor lighting and drunkenness notwithstanding, I think I'll opt for chinos and a nice shirt."

"Just as long as you've got them on when I arrive at your door in five minutes."

Cassie briefly wondered how he'd react if she greeted him wearing nothing but a smile. However, with her luck, there'd be a Publishers Clearinghouse representative right behind him—camera crew in tow—to inform her she'd just won a million dollars. That image pushed every thought of surprising Mick *au naturel* right out of her head.

She headed for the closet and her chinos and shirts, disgusted with herself for not being more daring. And hoping there'd be a chance later that night for her to make up for that fault.

Eight

When Mick arrived exactly five minutes after hanging up the phone, Cassie met him wearing khaki chinos, a lavender cotton shirt, comfortable flats and just a hint of White Diamonds perfume. As had occurred earlier in the day, her temperature spiked several degrees when he stepped in the door.

"Here." He brought a single red rose from behind his back and presented it to her. "As an apology for not being able to make dinner."

Inexplicably touched by the gesture, Cassie accepted the flower and brought it to her nose. "I love roses. Than you, Mick."

"My pleasure."

In order to avoid the intriguing look in his eyes, she turned her gaze elsewhere, taking in his dark green polo shirt and jeans. "I thought you were wearing 'ultra-casual.'"

"I decided not to embarrass you in public."

Cassie laughed. "I appreciate that."

The short-sleeved shirt and tight-fitting denim nicely complimented his athletic build. Topped off with his thick black hair and sky blue eyes, and Cassie saw trouble in capital letters. To keep from melting into a puddle right on the spot, she quirked a brow at the "Michigan State Hockey" logo on his shirt.

A smile of pure devilment lit his eyes as he put his right hand over his heart—covering the MSU logo—and gave her a courtly bow. "My lady, a humble Spartan, loyal unto death to his alma mater and pledged to his quest to give you an enjoyable evening, stands before you."

Smiling, she presented her hand for his kiss. And nearly went up in flames when his lips brushed her knuckles. She had to swallow twice before saying, "Noble sir, you show admirable judgement as regards your attire, as I've heard armor chafes right dreadfully."

He grimaced in mock horror. "And 'tis challenging to dance in chain mail, to say the least."

"Especially when the humidity is high."

At that, he laughed heartily and crooked his elbow. "Shall we, my lady?"

"By all means, kind sir."

***

The lounge was sparsely populated when they arrived close

to eleven. A weeknight, coupled with the late hour, kept the crowd small. Mick led Cassie to a table to the left of the dance floor, in dark enough shadows to be private but not isolating.

"Drink?" he asked her when the waiter approached.

"A glass of white zin."

"Make mine scotch on the rocks," Mick instructed. "And run a tab."

Sensing he wanted to say something, she sat quietly and took advantage of the dim light to study his expression. Although he did an admirable job of appearing nonchalant, turmoil radiated from him in waves. He studied the ice in his glass for so long, she was tempted to read his mind, but didn't want to violate his privacy.

Suddenly, he raised his head, pinning her with an intense stare. "Ever think about giving it all up?"

The question caught her completely by surprise. "What? Writing?"

He nodded.

For a moment, she turned her gaze to the nearly empty dance floor, then looked back at him. "Several times, actually. But never seriously." She shrugged. "Usually, professional disillusionment attacks about the time I get a new editor, or I've got what I think is a terrific idea for a column and everyone around me think's it's completely horrid."

"Yet you've never acted on that disillusionment." He took a sip of scotch, his gaze locked on her face.

Tension creased the corners of his mouth, but Cassie thought the intensity of his expression made him even more attractive.

"We work under completely different circumstances," she said kindly. "What I write is not at all the same as what you write."

"We're both authors."

Twirling her drink glass slowly between her hands, she answered, "Of course, but your volume of production compared to mine separates us almost as effectively as our different genres." At his nod of agreement, she added, "And my columns are rarely original material. I draw on real life, and many of my topics were suggestions. As a fiction writer, you draw your material almost completely from your head."

"I've been checking inside there lately, and I've come to the conclusion that it's awfully dark."

The sarcasm dripping from his voice wasn't lost on her.

She shifted slightly to lean closer. "Why not write something lighter? How about children's stories? You were a child once, weren't you?"

His laugh was more a snort. "About five hundred years ago."

So much for lightening his mood. "Okay, how about science-fiction. Or romance."

He did laugh at that last suggestion. "I don't know the first thing about romance, as evidenced by my fiancée's dumping me."

On impulse, Cassie reached across the table and covered his hand with hers. "Jennifer must have thought she had good reasons for breaking off the relationship. Isn't it better to find that out before the wedding rather than after?" Gently, she squeezed his fingers. "Or worse, what if the differences surfaced after you had children? They could very well have suffered because of the adults in their lives."

He turned his hand over and curled long fingers around hers. Heat shot straight up her arm and arrowed for her heart. From there, it spread to various other important body parts, and she was helpless to stop it. In fact, she didn't want to stop it.

"You're right." His voice proved to be the anchor she desperately needed at that moment to steady her spinning senses. She zeroed in on his every word like a parched desert traveler on sighting an oasis. "Marrying Jen would have been a disaster." His tone was more resigned than bitter. "She didn't want kids, and I realize now that I very much do. Better to drop it before long-term damage was inflicted by both parties."

If he didn't drop her hand soon, Cassie was going up in flames.

He rose at that moment and gave her a gentle tug.

"Dance with me. That's what we came here for, isn't it?"

"Sure." Although she wasn't at all certain her legs would support her, she followed him onto the dance floor, then went willingly into his arms. It was encouraging to find that, despite her knocking knees, she wasn't going to fall any time soon. Mick would catch her. For some reason, she was positive of that.

He proved to be an excellent dancer. Light on his feet and a steady lead. In just moments they were moving together as if they had channeled Fred Astaire and Ginger Rogers.

He pulled her close, and she rested her head against his shoulder, inhaling the spicy scent of after-shave. His body heat made her dizzy, but the steady heartbeat beneath her ear acted to right her reeling senses. At that moment, she didn't want to be anywhere else.

The small band ended the song and smoothly segued into the next. Within the first few bars, Mick was humming along, and Cassie recognized the tune as one of her favorite Beatles songs.

Apparently, Mick knew the song, because he began to sing the lyrics quietly into her ear. Lyrics about experiencing failed love and being reluctant to give his heart again. About understanding through experience that love wasn't just about hand holding.

When Mick got to the lines about needing to be sure before he committed his heart that his new love would love him more than his old one, Cassie's chest tightened. Tears welled in her eyes. Bless the Muse that had inspired the band to play that particular song at that exact moment.

She knew with certainty he was letting the song lyrics say what he didn't feel he could, and her heart filled with an emotion that felt a lot like love. Apparently, he was willing to try a new relationship. With Cassie. This realization unsettled her because she certainly wasn't looking for a short-term fling. And while she had never before experienced such an instant attraction to anyone, Mick wasn't, after all, one of her kind. When a witch found her true mate, it was for life. If that mate happened to be human, all sorts of problems presented themselves.

Don't jump the gun here, Cassie, she sternly told herself. *You may be totally misreading the signals.*

Mick finished with the band, and Cassie found herself staring into the endless blue depths of his eyes. *Thank you, Lennon and McCartney.*

That thought had no sooner flashed through her head than Mick lowered his mouth to hers.

***

It was nearly two when she entered her suite. Looking smug, Endora met her at the door.

"Hey, Boss, where've ya been?"

"Dancing with Mick."

Endora's Cheshire grin widened. "Doing the mattress mambo?"

The question snapped Cassie out of her reverie. "No, we just danced. Really."

"Get outta here! When I left, you were ready to burn the place to the ground with him. What cooled you off?"

Running her fingers across the top of the bar, she murmured, "He sang to me."

Endora collapsed onto the sofa, groaning. "Curse the Fates! His voice is so terrible it completely turned you off?"

"Actually, his voice isn't bad." Cassie smiled in remembrance, sinking down onto the sofa beside Endora. "It's just that . . . the song . . . it made me . . . " She trailed off, lost in her own private vision.

Endora snapped her fingers under Cassie's nose. "Hello, fair Juliet. Back-to-reality time. What happened?"

"We kissed."

"Kissing's good," Endora conceded. "Although not as good as some old-fashioned knocking boots."

Cassie leaned toward her familiar until they were practically nose to nose. "Check my eyes, Dora. See this scathing look? This 'back off now before I'm forced to consider hurting you' look?"

"Yes." But the familiar didn't look at all chastened.

"Then get off your obsession with sex. The evening was wonderful. We shared some really important things with each other. And even though I very much want to sleep with him, what we did tonight was unlike anything I've ever experienced with someone else." At her familiar's raised eyebrow, Cassie added a bit sheepishly, "And, I have to admit, he kisses better than anybody I've ever known."

"May I remind you that you haven't *known* Mick. At least not in the biblical sense of the word." Endora studied Cassie for a moment, then sighed. "You've got it really bad, don't you? As in head-over-heels bad."

A nod. "As in point-of-no-return bad."

"Bat rumps! What are we going to do?"

Suddenly energized, Cassie leaped to her feet. "We're going to study all those spell books you brought back." Reaching down, she grasped Endora by the wrist and hauled her to her feet. "Snap to it, familiar mine. There's a ton of work to do if I'm going to be up to snuff any time soon."

"Is it too late for me to regret talking you into this new course of action," Endora asked on a whine.

"Way too late."

"Oh, goody."

Cassie laughed aloud at her friend's dejected tone. "Hard work never killed anyone."

"That's easy for you to say. You're a witch. Now humans and cats, on the other hand, have been known to work themselves to death."

"Don't worry. If you manage it, I'll revive you. Just as soon as I find that particular incantation in one of these moldy old tomes."

Endora grimaced. "Somehow, I knew you were going to say that."

Chuckling, Cassie spread the spell books out on the coffee table. "Might as well get started right now."

"Would it do any good to point out that it's two-thirty in the morning?"

"Not at all."

"I knew you were going to say that, too." With a huge yawn, Endora settled on the floor beside the table. "Where do we begin, oh Task Master?"

Cassie quickly sorted through the various-sized books, selecting a small one bound in blood-red leather. "Here. *Simple Spells and Hexes*. It's the primer for all first-year witches. We'll start with this one."

By dawn, Cassie had worked her way through the primer and two other primary texts. She called it quits, promising herself there would be more of the same the next night.

Somewhere between Cassie's study of the first two textbooks, Endora had reverted back to feline form. She stretched from head to toe, then jumped lightly to the back of the sofa.

"I'm all in, Boss. I'll get a wake up call for nine. The autographing session is at ten."

Cassie scratched Endora under the chin. "Thanks, old friend. You're the best."

"I am, of course, putting in for overtime."

"Of course."

***

"God, what was I thinking," Mick muttered aloud as he plied his electric razor to his five o'clock shadow. "I *sang* to her. What in the hell possessed me to do that?"

Maybe it was the sincere concern in those beautiful eyes of hers . . . the smell of her perfume. Maybe the way she fit perfectly in his arms when they danced, or the electrical charge that seemed to spark between them wherever they touched. Whatever the reason, the fact remained that he'd sung one of the most intimate songs the Beatles had ever performed to a woman he'd known personally for less than a week.

Although knowledge was relative, he supposed. He thought about the copy of *When Dust Bunnies Attack* lying on his bedstand. She'd signed it "To Mick: I'm honored to be read by such an accomplished fellow author. Sincerely, Cassie 'Kitchen Witch' Hathorne." Her epigram gave him as much insight into her as the essays themselves. The title had made him laugh out loud, but he knew it would be full of her sparkling wit and practical good sense. On a written communication level, he knew her very well.

But he'd like to get to know her a whole lot better on an interpersonal level. Intimately interpersonal.

He checked closely in the bathroom mirror to see if he'd missed any minute whiskers, then stared himself in the eye. "You might have a chance with her, Sandor," he told his reflection. "Provided she's not a closet music critic."

On his way down to the continental breakfast the hotel provided the authors, he mentally rehearsed what he'd say if Cassie was there. He'd thought about asking her to meet him at the buffet, but the memory of his singing held him back.

Why did I do that? His subconscious at work, most likely. He'd always considered that his favorite Beatles song. And coincidentally, the lyrics fit his feelings and mood so well last night, he hadn't even thought about the potential connotations until halfway through the song. By then, it was too late to stop without calling attention to the significance of the words.

When he woke up this morning, embarrassed humiliation had set in, and he decided to let fate determine if he'd see Cassie at breakfast instead of doing the mature, adult thing and calling her. With Endora now technically working for him, he had automatic entree into their circle of two. How he handled that access was up to him, and he didn't want to make a mess of things.

He also didn't want to examine the meaning of a grown man reverting back to teenage behaviors over a female by letting fickle chance determine when he'd see her again.

It didn't bear contemplation.

Just as he was halfway out the suite door, the phone rang. Mick snagged it on the fourth ring, hoping there'd be a whiskey-voiced female author on the other end of the line.

"Sandor here." He was destined for disappointment. "Robert, what's up? I was just on my way down to breakfast . . . Uh huh . . . Right. See you in five minutes."

Running into Cassie at breakfast was out. He was eating with the Feds.

***

"Who's up for a night on the town?" Mick asked the group as they left the dining room where their latest dinner event had taken place. He had convinced Jamison it would look suspicious if there wasn't a casual event on at least one of the tour stops. The down time in Chicago had been a fluke created by a printing error, not something scheduled. By prearranged agreement, Mick suggested one of St. Louis's most popular pubs. "I've heard McGurk's has got great Irish music."

"And equally outstanding ale," Steven Jones, the self-help author, added. He looked around at the others. "Don't know about you all, but I'm up for it."

Cassie nodded to the huge black man who had played ten years in the NFL before embarking on a very successful career writing nonfiction. "I've heard if you're good enough to sing at McGurk's, you can sing in any pub in Ireland. Do you sing, Steven?"

Jones smiled broadly. "Only in the shower, although Louise claims I have a good voice." He patted the arm of the tall, ebony-skinned beauty at his side. Louise's smile was every bit as dazzling as her husband's.

"It could be the acoustics in the bathroom," she gently teased, and several members of the group chuckled.

"I couldn't get the audience drunk enough to fool them into thinking I can sing," Mick said somewhat sheepishly. "There isn't that much alcohol in the world." The quick glance he threw Cassie said he hoped his singing the night before hadn't completely appalled her. Her heart warmed. Then he quirked an eyebrow at her and Endora. "Either of you two sing?"

"I just caterwaul," Endora deadpanned. "But Cassie's got a great voice."

When Mick turned the full force of his laser-beam blue eyes on her, Cassie almost stuttered. From the heat she felt in her cheeks, she could guess her face was flaming. To make matters worse, now Mick looked like he was *really* regretting his impulsive dance floor serenade. She shrugged, hoping her voice sounded nonchalant. "I can hold my own. Although I don't have much experience in that singing style."

"Classically trained," Endora threw out blithely, then chuckled when Cassie rolled her eyes. "Arias and such."

It would be wise to stop Endora before she got on a roll. "Like I said, not much skill in pub-style singing." *No thanks for that completely unnecessary promo, Dora.*

My job is to promote you, Boss.

Not in the singing department. Mick looks ready to die of mortification over last night.

I can't help it if he can't sing and you can, Endora countered.

Keep it up, and I'm going to start calling you Jennifer.

That threat immediately wiped the smug look off Endora's face.

"I don't think singing's required," Mick quipped, apparently realizing Cassie wouldn't publicly criticize his vocal skills. "Unless you want credentials for pub gigs in County Cork." He glanced around. "I'll see the concierge about transportation. Let's meet down here in ten minutes."

Everyone hurried off to get whatever they needed for the excursion while Mick and Robert went to arrange for wheels. Mick could have left it to the agent, but he'd felt so out of control since January when he'd learned about the serial killer that he wanted to do something. And as simple as arranging transportation was, it was still something he could actually do.

Mentally, he sighed. He wouldn't be alone with Cassandra Hathorne at McGurk's, but he'd be damned if he'd pass up an opportunity to be with her under any circumstances.

Nine

Being winter, McGurk's patio was out of the question, which suited Robert Jamison just fine. An intimate interior venue made his agents' job of securing a perimeter far easier. That, combined with dark wooden paneling, equally dark wooden furniture, and low lighting allowed four of his agents to blend with the patrons.

The musicians were already on stage in the front room and starting a set when the group entered, so Steven Jones led them to several tall tables up front. As they settled onto the proportionally tall bar stools, diners entered from the back dining room and took up the remaining tables. Steven beckoned a server who sported Irish bar maid attire circa 1870.

"We've some serious drinkin' ta do, lass," he stated in an excellent Irish brogue. "Would ye be so kind as ta enlighten us on yer fare?"

Louise elbowed him in the ribs, but the server smiled and rattled off the list in an excellent brogue of her own. Orders were placed, and the group settled in to enjoy the music and the company.

Cassie took in the room. "This place looks like it was transported straight from the Emerald Isle. Great atmosphere."

Steven lifted his glass. "And great ale." He took a hearty drink.

"*Slainte*," children's author Janice Welton toasted, and followed Steven's lead. She sighed. "That tastes like a little bit of heaven."

When the music started, everyone's attention was instantly riveted on the small stage. Talk hushed to whispers as expert musicians wove the spell of a long-ago time and place. Pure enchantment. The crowd clapped in rhythm to the upbeat tunes, and sat in appreciative quiet during poignant ballads of love and loss.

And sitting in the darkened pub enjoying himself despite the situation that had brought him there, Mick watched Cassie immerse herself in the experience. Even in the dim light, her eyes sparkled with pleasure, and her alluring laugh carried easily to where he sat across the small table from her. Her incredible voice quietly singing harmony brought pure enchantment, and that clear contralto actually made the hair on his nape rise on several occasions. This completely new experience gave him pause. Then his heart lurched into a funny little beat he'd also never experienced, and he realized he was dangerously close to losing that particular organ to a certain syndicated columnist.

***

Two days passed in a pleasant blur for Mick, as the tour concluded in St. Louis and moved on to Memphis. He'd spent practically every waking minute with Cassie—next to her at signings, beside her on the bus, sharing every meal with her and Endora. He couldn't get enough of being near her, and his lack of a publicist made his association with The Kitchen Witch a natural collaboration that played into his growing attraction. He really did plan to pay Endora for her efforts on his behalf, as she'd proven just as efficient and far more amusing than Jennifer. Not that he'd mentioned that to either her or Cassie. Yet. When the tour ended, he hoped to speak to Endora about a business arrangement. And to Cassie about far more than that.

And although they hadn't had a chance to be alone, he knew it was only a matter of time before he and Cassie acted on the attraction building between them. Experienced enough to recognize that those feelings went beyond mere lust, Mick sensed a major life change approaching. A positive change after all the recent negative ones. He'd never felt so connected to another human being. Cassie seemed to be able to read his mind.

Of course, if she could do that she'd probably slap his face, as she figured very prominently—to say nothing of nakedly—in the overwhelming majority of alpha waves threading through his brain.

***

Stopping in Memphis hadn't been on his agenda. Instead, he'd planned to go directly from St. Louis to New Orleans to begin preparation for his ultimate tribute. But his conversation with the Bodin bitch had disturbed him enough to warrant an itinerary change. He felt compelled to follow the tour to its next to last stop.

Frustration had met him in Memphis. He'd been unable to gain admission to promotional events except the public signings, and he'd already attended one of those in Toledo. He had no desire to stand in line with a throng of parasites waiting to gush and coo over their "favorite author" while M. S. Kazimer signed his latest masterpiece for them. Pretenders! They would never rival his love and devotion. They would never kill for M. S.

Kazimer.

Everywhere the great writer went, crowds surrounded him, clinging like sycophantic limpets. He wanted to slaughter them all.

Maybe he would.

***

The reception in Memphis's famed Peabody Hotel dragged on. They'd spent six hours at autographings that day—three in the morning at the city's oldest bookstore, and another three after lunch at the newest chain store just blocks from the hotel. Throw in the Peabody's famous duck parade, and they'd been at it practically since dawn. For his part, Mick had had enough of his first day on the Memphis literary scene. Jamison might know how to run FBI field operations, but his concept of a book tour could have been taken from a Navy SEALS training manual.

Spotting Cassie next to the hors d'oeuvres table, Mick felt that odd thump in his chest. He paused where he stood, twenty feet away, to appreciate the view. Cassie's bright, multicolored skirt rode just above her knees, revealing as gorgeous a pair of legs as Mick had ever seen. She smiled at something the short, balding man next to her said, and Mick could see even from that far away that her reaction was genuine. Her caramel-colored eyes were trained directly on the little man and didn't waver.

Suddenly, Mick wanted more than anything to have Cassie's full attention trained on him. As he moved toward her, she shook the man's hand and headed toward the food table. Mick joined her.

"How's the grub?"

She turned a wry smile on him. "I can't exactly say, as I haven't seen any of the little things. Is that a Spartan delicacy?"

"Likely the ancient Spartans saw nothing wrong with them." Mick grinned. "Grub is the Big Ten equivalent of hors-d'oeuvres."

Cassie nodded. "I know. And it's pretty typical of these affairs. But there's plenty of it."

"I've got a suggestion." He lowered his voice to just above a whisper. "We've been doing the publicity thing all day. Let's go back to my room for a private party."

She started slightly, and for a moment he thought she'd skewer him with her sharp wit and send him packing. Then a smile spread like sunrise across her face. "How private?"

"You, me, and a chilled bottle of Korbel."

"That's private, all right." Her expressive eyes made endless promises before she turned and preceded him from the room.

***

Mick opened the suite door and ushered Cassie inside, surreptitiously studying her for signs of second thoughts. "I really do have a bottle of Korbel. Care for a drink?"

She gave a slight shake of her head. "No, thanks. I had a glass of champagne at the reception."

"Just one? Lightweight," Mick teased gently.

Cassie's eyes were full of mischief as she shrugged. "Who needs alcohol when you're high on life?"

Laughing, he set the bottle down on the bar and then turned back to her. Abruptly uncertain, he raised a brow in question. "No more drinking? How about a dance?" Her surprised look pleased him. He'd caught her off guard. "After hearing your voice firsthand last night, I'm not even going to try singing."

She recovered quickly from her startlement. "But I absolutely adore the Beatles."

"And, in deference to them, I won't repeat my performance. Care for jazz?"

"Love it."

"I was hoping you'd say that."

Mick went to the portable CD player on the table by the window and hit "play." The room filled with soft, sensual music, the jazz seeming to wrap itself around them in a visceral embrace.

"May I have this dance, Ms. Hathorne?"

"My pleasure, Mr. Sandor." She moved gracefully into his arms.

"Our pleasure," Mick whispered in her ear as he held her close. His body tightened in anticipation when she shivered. Her smell, her heat, the sound of her breathing filled him with an odd mix of sexual tension and contentment. He wouldn't waste time examining his feelings right then, though. That was for later.

"Is that a proposition?"

He pulled back enough to look directly into her eyes. "Only if you want it to be."

Reaching up with slightly trembling fingers, she brushed his hair back from his forehead, slid her hand down to cup his cheek. "Absolutely." Then she kissed him.

When she ended the kiss, he stated softly, "I haven't been

with anyone in over three months." When he saw the question in her eyes, he added, "Jennifer called off the engagement three months ago, and I haven't been with her since. And to be honest, the six months before that, we didn't exactly set any lovemaking records, either."

"Thanks for being candid." Cassie's chuckle was a bit wry. "It's been lots longer than that for me."

"I can't say that disappoints me." He lowered his mouth to hers, brushing lightly against her lips before deepening the pressure, coaxing a response from her.

Kissing as if they could delve into each other's soul through their mouths, they swayed to the music.

Mick ran his hand down Cassie's back; the zipper tab of her dress followed his fingers.

Responding to his silent challenge, she undid his tie and pulled it off his neck. In a split second, she had flung it over her right shoulder.

He countered by running his index fingers beneath the thin straps of her gown and pulling them down to her elbows. She returned the favor with his shirt, and as quickly as that, they were both naked to the waist.

He sighed at the feel of her skin against his. The cushioned press of her breasts—circles of warmth centered by the points of intense heat that were her nipples—brought him amazing pleasure.

"God, you feel good," he murmured into her hair.

Her chuckle reverberated through her breasts and into his chest as she ran her hands up his back and across his shoulders. "Right back at you."

As Mick hummed along with the music, they danced slowly across the carpet and into the bedroom. Pausing at the bedside only long enough to divest Cassie of her remaining clothes—and have her do the same for him—he swept her off her feet and laid her gently on the coverlet. Then he followed her down, searing her mouth, her face, with open-mouthed kisses. Hands sought and found sensitive areas to be explored more thoroughly after the initial fire was quenched. Mouths teased then soothed, stoking the fires. When he had her moaning and restless beneath his lips, he reached into the bed stand for a foil packet.

"That isn't necessary," Cassie whispered, her breathing rapid, her heart racing.

"It is." Mick kissed her gently. "Out of respect for you."

Her heart beat a quick, crazy cadence. "Then let me help."

He grinned. "Be my guest."

Finding her hands slightly unsteady, she gave a shaky laugh as she tore at the foil. "These little suckers are tougher than they look."

"God, I hope so," Mick quipped.

A laugh burst from her throat, and her nervousness dissipated, allowing her to make quick work of opening the packet.

"Very impressive, Mr. Sandor," she murmured, sheathing him. The compliment was completely genuine.

Mick's grin was equal parts wicked and masculinely smug. "I'm glad I measure up."

"You know what they say," she teased. "It's not the size of the wand, it's the magic in it."

It was his turn to laugh. "Ah. A challenge."

He took her lips with a slow, possessive kiss that curled Cassie's toes. He kissed her forehead and cheeks, ran his tongue around the edge of her ear, then kissed a path from her throat to her breasts. While kneading the left, he suckled the right, until she was arching to keep him close, gasping for oxygen. Then he took her left breast into his mouth and kneaded the right. The switch nearly drove her over the edge.

When his mouth moved down to cover her most sensitive flesh, she climaxed immediately.

Floating slowly down from the peak, Cassie opened her eyes to meet Mick's intense blue gaze. The air went right back out of her lungs as he slowly filled her, more completely than any lover before.

"Oh my stars. This feels so good." She cradled his face in her hands and kissed him, tasting herself on his lips.

"It's about to feel even better." His voice was a bit strained as he momentarily rested his weight on his elbows.

Then he started to move, and proved himself as good as his word.

Cassie quickly matched his rhythm. Locking her feet behind his knees, she moved with him. She kissed his face and throat and urged him on with her hands. Caressing his back and arms, guiding his hips. When she ran her fingernails lightly up his sides he broke rhythm on a gasping shiver.

"Jesus, Mary and Joseph," he groaned. Then he caught his rhythm again, and she was the one groaning.

Half an hour and several climaxes later, they finally came up for air.

"You're fantastic," Mick murmured into her ear on a panted whisper before gently kissing her temple.

"I certainly am," she returned saucily, her own breath still labored.

He laughed as he rolled to his back and pulled her half atop him. "No performance anxiety for you, Ms. Hathorne."

"I should hope not." She caressed his chest with her open hand. "Besides, that wasn't a performance."

Mick caught her roaming right hand with his left, trapping it against his chest before bringing it to his mouth to kiss the knuckles. "It wasn't for me, either." When her suddenly vulnerable eyes lifted to meet his gaze, his mouth kicked up into a half-smile. "I say we skip the conversation about previous lovers. It's just us. In the here and now." *And maybe in the future.*

She captured his thought in his eyes and dared to hope. "All right."

They traded kisses and caresses until passion surged again, necessitating more intense methods of dealing with the heat.

Wrapped in Mick's arms, Cassie awoke before dawn. Not wanting to disturb him, she cautiously slid out of his embrace, quietly gathered her clothes, then snuck into his dresser drawer to borrow a tee shirt and pair of shorts. She wasn't about to try to put her dress back on just to return to her own suite.

He stirred.

"Go back to sleep." She lightly kissed his stubbled chin. "I'll see you at breakfast."

His eyes slitted open, and he reached up to cup her cheek in one hand. "Don't leave."

"I have to. I've got nothing to wear."

At that, he awoke further. "Clothing is optional, even discouraged, for what I've got in mind."

"No doubt, lover boy. But I've got three words: Early business breakfast. Remember? And I don't want to look like I didn't get any sleep."

"Well, you didn't get much."

His smug tone made Cassie laugh. "All thanks to you. But despite the fact that you like me unclothed, our publisher suits would have themselves a fit and fall in it if I showed up at a meeting wearing just a satisfied smile."

Mick's blue eyes lit with humor. "Now that's an image I'll have in my head all day."

She leaned over to quickly buss his lips. "Let it sustain you until tonight, then."

He stroked her cheek, then deepened the kiss before releasing her. "Guess I'll have to survive on memories."

"We'll make more," she whispered.

"I'm counting on it, Cass."

***

He had searched every fan site on the Internet, called every fan club president, had even tried to contact M. S. Kazimer's editor, but nothing substantiated Jennifer Bodin's claim that his idol was retiring. Lying whore. His idol did not quit. M. S. Kazimer would pen brilliant works until the end of his days. And his greatest fan would by then be worthy to reveal himself to the world, not just to a paltry few law enforcement officials.

He had managed to discover that M. S. Kazimer's engagement had been called off. Most likely, Jennifer Bodin, the woman scorned, had sought to discredit her former fiancé by spreading lies that he was retiring. To soothe her shattered pride, no doubt. Deceitful bitch. He should have known enough not to believe her.

He had come to Memphis to prove the lying cunt wrong, and although he had yet to find any evidence to support his theories, he hadn't found any to corroborate hers, either.

But could it be true? What if the greatest writer who ever lived did plan to abandon his fans, abandon the fame and fortune his skills provided him?

Walk away from the blueprint he provided for his true acolytes.

Then M. S. Kazimer would have to die.

***

Yet another signing was about to begin, and Cassie found herself trying hard not to stare at Mick, especially certain parts of him. From the way he kept glancing at her, he was having the same problem.

So, aren't you going to tell me all about it?

Not on your nine lives, Endora.

Cassie heard a telepathic sigh. *You're absolutely no fun, Boss! You never kiss and tell. Why is that?*

Because, if I told you about my affairs, I'd then have to

sit through all the tawdry details of your innumerable peccadilloes. And frankly, Endora, you've got the morals of an alley cat.

Cassie had no idea how she managed it, but her familiar could sound vain even telepathically. *And isn't that just as it should be?*

For your adopted species, I guess. But mine has to have their hearts involved, too.

The mental pause stretched until Cassie heard ringing in her ears. *So, this isn't just a short-term fling? You're really serious about Mick?*

'Fraid so.

For once, Endora had no saucy comeback..

***

Busy with the tour schedule, Cassie had little time to contemplate the significance of making love with Mick. All she knew was that she'd be in his bed again that night, and that thought had her anticipating the event more than she'd anticipated anything in years.

She sent a mental "Good night" to Endora as they finished their dinner in the hotel restaurant and watched as her familiar gracefully excused herself and left.

Don't do anything I wouldn't do, Endora flung mentally over her shoulder.

Like that could ever happen, Cassie shot back. She grinned to herself when she heard her friend's mental chuckle.

And don't forget the reception from nine to eleven. Try to surface long enough to attend for at least a few minutes, all right?

Cassie stifled a groan, but as she turned and caught the gleam in Mick's eyes, that groan nearly became a moan. Feeling her chest tightening, she tried to take shallow breaths to avert passing out from lack of oxygen. *You've got it bad, Cass,* she chided herself. But at the moment, that really didn't matter.

"If we don't leave right now," he growled low in his throat, "I'm not going to be responsible for what I might do to you in public."

Their race to the elevator concluded itself on the carpet by the coffee table in Mick's suite, a trail of clothing from the suite door to the chair marking their progress to a shattering climax.

As their heartbeats calmed, Cassie ran her lips along Mick's collarbone and up the side of his neck. "I think I need Vitamin

E," she said between kisses to his jaw. "Intravenously."

"I'm fresh out." He pulled her to her feet and led her to the bedroom. "But we can go to the corner drugstore later."

She went into his arms, wrapping hers around his waist and resting her head on his chest. His musky scent, the tickle of springy hair beneath her cheek, filled her senses. "You have something in mind for right now?"

A purely wicked chuckle rumbled from Mick's chest. "Oh, yes."

***

"Make sure you take clothes for tomorrow, so you don't have to sneak back in here at dawn," Endora suggested as she watched Cassie brushing her hair and applying lip gloss. At Cassie's sharp look, the familiar shrugged. "Hey, I just want you to get as much sleep as possible tonight. Of course, you're probably not getting much . . . Sleep, that is."

"Endora!"

"Don't tell me you were napping after dinner." When Cassie groaned, the familiar added, "Very thoughtful of you to appear at the reception. It would have been bad form if you'd completely skipped it for dessert in Mick's room."

"I'm not going to miss a tour function, Dora." Cassie sighed. "Even if I'd much rather be otherwise occupied."

The familiar glanced at her watch. "Uh-oh. Red alert! You've been deprived of sex for three hours." She peered closely at Cassie's reflection in the vanity mirror. "I think I see signs of severe withdrawal. You need a nookie fix."

It was hard to give Endora a scathing look when all Cassie wanted to do was laugh, but she managed. "You're impossible."

Endora acknowledged this comment with a typical lack of repentance. Leaning on the counter, she caught Cassie's gaze in the mirror. "So, on a scale of one hundred, how good is he?"

Cassie sniffed and put her hair brush in her case. "You're the kiss-and-meow one, not me."

"Come on, Cass, don't get all prissy. I want to know if there's a legitimate reason I'm spending my second consecutive night in Memphis alone. I'm contemplating doing the Graceland tour all by myself."

"I'm sure the Jungle Room will be to your liking."

Endora fixed her best cat I-won't-blink-for-as-long-as-it-takes-to-break-you stare on Cassie. "Spill it!"

"You just won't let this drop, will you?" Crossing her arms

over her chest, Cassie turned her back to the mirror and leaned on the sink.

"Not a chance, Boss."

"One-fifty."

Endora's eyes popped. "What?"

"You heard me. Mick's a one hundred and fifty on a scale of one hundred." She turned back to the mirror to give her hair a brief finishing fluff, then left the bathroom to retrieve her purse from the coffee table.

"Wow," Endora breathed reverently, following in Cassie's wake. "Does he like threesomes?"

Cassie spun to face her. "Sweet Mother Goddess, Dora!"

"Just curious."

"You know what curiosity got the cat, don't you?" Cassie huffed.

Endora laughed until, gasping, she sank down onto the sofa. "I love getting you riled, Cass. It's so much fun." Her eyes shone with fondness. "And I love seeing you happy. He makes you happy, doesn't he?"

"Very much so."

"Well, what are you doing here talking to me? Go get happy." She shoved a small overnight bag into Cassie's hands.

"You're the best, girlfriend." Cassie grabbed her for a quick hug.

"I know. That's why I'm asking for a raise when we get home. Union scale at least."

One dark brow rose as Cassie paused at the door and looked back. "I wasn't aware that familiars had a union."

"The AFL-MEOW."

Cassie winced and reached for the door handle. "Call my attorney."

***

She was amazed at how the pace of her heartbeat accelerated as she knocked on Mick's door moments later. Her palms were actually sweating. Witches' palms didn't sweat! But here she stood, waiting for her lover to appear, fearing she'd leave a salt water puddle on the corridor carpet before he did. Was there a charm to stop palm sweat? Anticipation fogged her brain beyond practical thought.

When Mick opened the door a moment later, she exhaled the breath she'd been holding. Then he smiled, and she stopped breathing altogether.

"Lord, I just want to jump you." He took her in his arms and pulled her into the room. On a rather strained chuckle he added, "Look at me. Forty years old and acting like some horny teenager."

"I'll take that as a compliment." Cassie wrapped her arms around his neck and kissed him deeply, rubbing against him from knees to chest. "You taste good."

Mick groaned. "All right, that's it. We're going to the bedroom right now."

"Lead the way," she purred.

A sense of urgency permeated their disrobing, and within minutes the preliminaries ended. Mick held himself above Cassie just long enough to shift forward until his hips rode higher than hers. Then he lowered himself.

"This is new," she gasped, enjoying the sensation of total body contact. Mick's chuckle reverberated deep inside her.

"Good," he whispered in her left ear. "I wanted to surprise you."

"Mission accomplished," she breathed. "What do I do?"

"Follow my lead."

The minutes lengthened as they climbed steadily toward the peak. His hips above hers gave constant stimulation, and such sustained arousal made Cassie burn everywhere. Nerve endings thrummed like plucked strings as the heat spread all along her skin—everywhere they touched—from insteps to shoulders. She thought breathlessly that spontaneous combustion was truly possible. Just as she reached critical mass, she heard Mick's cry and felt his climax at nearly the exact time hers hit.

She had died and gone to heaven. What other explanation could there be for the aftermath of their lovemaking? Usually, she recovered her equilibrium and her breath at the same time. Tonight, she was dangerously close to never regaining either.

"I love you, Mick," she whispered, certain he hadn't heard her.

He was asleep.

Ten

The incessant pounding on his suite door woke Mick from a sound sleep. Careful to pull the covers up around Cassie, he slid out from under her pliant body and reached for the hotel robe lying on the bedside chair.

"Sandor!" Mick heard from the corridor. "It's Jamison! Open up."

"I'm coming," Mick muttered, unwilling to disturb Cassie's sleep by calling out. He closed the bedroom door behind him and made his way across the room to admit Jamison. "Jesus, Robert, it's four-thirty in the morning," he growled as he let the agent in. "Don't federal employees ever sleep?"

Jamison looked grim. "We've got to talk," he said brusquely, entering before being invited in. "Our boy has struck again."

"What?" Mick's heart leapt into his throat. "Jennifer?"

"No. She's fine. And yes, I've still got a man following her."

"Good." Mick glanced at the bedroom door and stated quietly, "Robert, I'm not alone."

Clearly startled, Jamison's gaze flashed to the bedroom door. Color crept into his cheeks. "Uh, sorry, Mick. God. I didn't know—"

"Before you jump to conclusions, Jen broke our engagement three months ago. She made this trip mostly to try to convince me not to retire." At Jamison's calculating look, Mick added, "That doesn't mean I'm letting you off the hook as far as tailing her goes."

The agent stiffened in indignation. "She's under FBI protection until this is over."

"Fine." The acid in Mick's stomach was building to toxic levels. He canted his head toward the smaller bedroom. "We won't be overheard in there."

Jamison entered first, taking the bedside chair as Mick closed the door and leaned against it. The Fed actually appeared nervous. Mick saw him swallow hard before adjusting his tie.

My god, he's dressed for work at four-thirty in the morning. This can't be good. "Spit it out," he stated harshly.

If Jamison took offense, it wasn't obvious. However, complying with Mick's demand seemed to give him trouble. He opened the night stand drawer and picked up the ubiquitous

Gideon's Bible. After turning it over twice, he placed it carefully back down and pushed the drawer closed. At that point, possibly sensing Mick was ready to leap across the bed and tear out his throat, Jamison said, "The Agency's Toledo office got called in on a homicide. Forensics set time of death as early morning, March seventeenth."

The sick feeling in Mick's stomach doubled in intensity. "And the vic was a white, thirty-ish businessman killed in the same way as the Toledo victim in *Mortal Sin*."

"Yes."

Mick slid to the floor, lungs refusing to draw air, fingers convulsively clutching the plush carpet beneath him. "Jesus, Mary and Joseph."

"That's not all."

Raising his head to look at Jamison was almost impossible, but Mick forced himself. However, he couldn't form the words to ask. The agent spared him from that.

"Around an hour ago, another body was found. In St. Louis. Same pattern—the killings follow your books."

With another epithet, Mick buried his face in his hands. "This isn't happening, Robert!"

"I'm afraid it is," came the not unkind reply.

"The bastard was supposed to hit your setup in New Orleans."

"I—"

"We were supposed to prevent this!" Mick surged up, advancing on the hapless Fed. In three strides he crossed the room, grabbed Jamison by the lapels and hauled him to his feet. "God dammit, we're supposed to be catching this guy, not letting him kill more!"

Jamison calmly pulled Mick's hands from his suit jacket and set his clothing to rights. "That's why I'm here. It's your call. How do you want to play this?"

It took Mick a moment to process that statement. When it finally registered, he turned away and paced the small room. Putting his fist through something held appeal, but he resisted the temptation by crossing his arms over his chest and tucking his hands into his armpits.

"How do *I* want to play this? I want to move to a deserted island and try to forget that my writing spawned a maniac who's killing people!"

Jamison resumed his seat on the bed. "You're not

responsible for this guy, Mick. You know that."

"Right now, I'm having an exceptionally difficult time swallowing that FBI profiler bullshit you've been feeding me."

The agent's tone remained matter-of-fact. "Serial killers are completely deranged. Your books have nothing to do with their mental health."

"That's easy for you to say. No wacko's using the FBI manual as a blueprint for slaughter." The image of making love to Cassie burst into Mick's head, and his stomach clenched harder. Had he put her in danger? "We're telling all the authors what's going on."

Jamison shot to his feet. "*What?* We can't do that!"

"You said it was my call. Either they're told the truth and allowed to decide for themselves whether to continue the tour, or I'm out."

"That's blackmail," Jamison protested. He took two steps toward Mick, anger clearly showing in his heightened color.

Mick refused to back down. Panic clawed inside his chest at the thought that Cassie, horrified by the truth, would bolt and never speak to him again. But he had to risk it. This was far bigger than his love life. "Take it or leave it. We don't think the other authors are in any danger, but we can't be completely sure. And I want them to know that. To know exactly what's happening and why. What they do with that information will be up to them."

Jamison rubbed his eyes with both hands. "What they do with it could be disastrous. If word gets out, our killer may go to ground."

"Then ask them to cooperate and keep this secret until we catch the killer."

"I'm beginning to dislike you, Mick."

"Too damn bad. These people won't walk blindly into potential danger. Either put our cards on the table for them, or bait your trap with another sucker, because I'm gone."

With that, he spun on his heel and left the bedroom. In ten angry strides, he was across the sitting room and into the master bedroom. He closed the door firmly but quietly behind him, leaving Jamison to find his own way out of the suite.

***

"What is it?" Cassie asked the moment Mick entered the room. She knew, of course. Jamison's aura had radiated urgency, and she'd had no qualms about using her preternatural hearing to eavesdrop on his meeting with Mick. The dark aura she'd seen in Mick's press kit photo now had an explanation. A horrifying one. Just how much would he tell her?

He sat down on the edge of the bed and leaned forward, elbows on knees and hands dangling. Cassie reached up to rub slowly between his shoulders. Comforting, encouraging.

"There's no easy way to say this." Mick swallowed hard, and Cassie knew he feared her reaction.

"Then just say it," she encouraged softly.

He caught a quick breath. "A serial killer's patterning his crimes after my books."

Cassie gasped despite having some inkling of this news. Endora's encounter with pure evil in St. Louis flashed into her mind, and she instantly understood who the killer was. "Oh, Mick."

"Jamison's FBI. He set up this tour to trap the guy, but apparently the bastard's not cooperating. He stepped up his killing spree." The anguish in Mick's eyes nearly broke Cassie's heart as he struggled to continue. "He's killed two more people just since the tour started."

And nearly killed Endora, Cassie thought grimly. *Great Mother Goddess, is Mick in danger, too?* "Could this maniac be after you?"

Mick laughed bitterly. "No. As a matter of fact, he's likely killing to impress me."

"Oh, no," Cassie whispered. "How can I help you?"

"I'm not sure." He drew a shaky breath. "Could you just hold me?"

"That's the easy part." Scooting backward until she was propped against the headboard, Cassie coaxed him back against her, then crossed her arms protectively over his chest. *Mick, I swear to you I'll do my best to keep you safe. I'm not completely up to speed with many of my skills, but I know some unique power brokers, too. In a league with the FBI for sure.*

Mick raised his hands to cover hers and leaned his head back against her cheek. "God, Cassie, this is a nightmare."

More than you even suspect, love. Maybe more than any of us suspect. She hugged him tighter.

***

"Now you know everything you need to know." Special Agent Robert Jamison closed his briefcase and sat down next to Mick in the small conference room the Peabody had provided. He looked around the table. "Are there any questions?"

"Just one," Steven Jones said. "How can we help nail this son of a bitch?"

Louise Jones squeezed her husband's hand and added, "Steven and I will do anything we can to help."

Mick, who had practically put dents in the tabletop with his fingers as Jamison debriefed the other tour participants, almost smiled. He released his death grip but didn't take his gaze off Cassie. It was one thing to have your lover disclose a terrible secret in the intimacy of a bedroom and quite another to have that secret made public. So far, except for a flush to her cheeks, she didn't seem ready to run screaming for the next plane back to Massachusetts.

"We'll let the experts can take care of that, Steven," he said.

Jones snorted. "Looks like the experts aren't making any headway."

Mick felt Jamison stiffen beside him. "The FBI made the connection between my books and the killer's routine. If they hadn't, this guy would still be completely anonymous. As Special Agent Jamison said, the killer is copycatting my plots. None of you write anything remotely like I do, so you won't attract this guy to you. "

It didn't take a witch's powers to perceive the tension in the room, especially between Jamison and Jones. Cassie turned to the Fed. "What can you tell us about the suspect? That isn't classified, that is."

"The standard profile," Jamison responded immediately, looking somewhat relieved that he could stop trying to stare down a former Pro-Bowl defensive end, a man who looked like he probably pulled the arms and legs off men Jamison's size just for warm ups. "Women and minorities very rarely become serial killers, so we're looking for a white male, twenty to thirty-five, who's obsessive about the details of his kills. He selects his victims with care. In this case, he's targeting people who resemble characters in Mick's books. He'll have all the props, the restraints, the venue." He paused a moment and looked around the table. "Personality-wise, he gets off on the suffering and death of another human. Sometimes sex drives him. Sometimes power. Sometimes both."

Mick took up the narrative. "None of you fits the profile of a single victim in any of my books, so there's little danger any of you are targets. As has already been said, the audiences your books attract don't in any way fit the killer's profile, either. But I insisted you be told what's happening so you can make your own decision on what you wish to do."

"Because this particular killer is following Mick's books," Jamison added, "we're trying to lure him into a trap in New Orleans."

"With Mick as the bait," Jones stated.

"More or less."

Cassie felt a rush of unexpected anger at the agent's words. Mick was risking his life? Trained experts should be setting this maniac up—not Mick. What a noble, heroic idiot. Realizing her face was probably starting to flush from raised blood pressure, Cassie took a mental step back and glanced around. Everyone with the exception of Jamison stared silently at Mick. And the agent wasn't looking at her, so most likely no one–except Endora—knew she was furious.

Right on cue, her familiar weighed in. *Should we say something, Cass? I'll bet the killer is that bastard who attacked me.*

Cassie suddenly took a keen interest in the water glass on the table in front of her. She stared at it intently, as if she could read the future in the ice cubes as they melted. *I'm certain he is. But if we intervene, we have to expose what we are.*

That's a point, Endora admitted, sitting back in her chair and glancing at the others. *And witches really don't get involved in human problems if they don't have to.* She was silent for a long moment. *But you're not just worried about ignoring coven policy, are you? You're afraid of Mick's reaction to what you are.*

Cassie nodded, unable to put her fears into any other form, telepathic or otherwise.

Under the table, Endora gave Cassie's knee a sympathetic squeeze.

The gesture broke through her mental daze. *If I did decide to intervene, how do I start the conversation? 'By the way, I'm a witch and Endora's my familiar, a shape-shifting cat. We think we've run into this killer a couple of times on this tour'?*

I suppose that's one way to approach it.

Cassie's frustration sizzled down their mental link. *Jamison would lock us up as psychos!*

C'mon, Cass, he'd never be able to hold us. We'd be out of there before he could say "Supercalifragilisticexpialidocious."

The glass actually shook, although Cassie didn't touch it. *This is no time for jokes, Dora.*

It's the perfect time for jokes, Endora shot back unrepentantly. *Some of the best jokes ever created came from bad situations. Someone in this group's got to look on the bright side. You do the worrying, and I'll take care of the comic relief.*

You'd be a lot less of a pain in the butt if you were a normal familiar.

Normal is boring. Ennui would paralyze you after ten minutes with another familiar.

I'll have to try that sometime. Soon.

Endora had to fake a coughing fit to keep her snort from being heard.

Mick spoke again, and Cassie gladly turned her focus back to him.

"You don't have to stay on this tour, Steven." Mick's intense blue gaze encompassed everyone in the room. "None of you do." He gave a half-laugh. "You can all go home, and I'll finish this alone."

"How much danger are you in?" Jones asked.

Cassie held her breath waiting to hear the extent of what her foolish hero risked.

"None," Jamison stated firmly. "The killer is following his idol's writings. If he harmed Mick, there would be no reason to kill, no blueprint to follow. And the killer has no guide to threaten any of you."

There was another long pause.

I swear that maniac bastard won't get his hands on Mick. No matter what it takes, Boss. Familiar's honor.

Those words warmed Cassie entirely. Endora had just unquestioningly pledged herself to protect Mick. *Dora, I'd hug you, but it's not the time or the place.*

I'll just settle for a good scratching behind the ears when we get back to the room.

You got it.

"Anyone who wants to go home," Jamison was saying, "is free to do so. The only restriction is that you'll have to abide by a gag order until this case is closed."

"I, for one, am staying right here," Steven Jones stated quietly. He flexed his massive shoulders, then reached for Louise's hand. "I'm not about to abandon my man M. S. Kazimer. And maybe by staying, I'll be a part of bringing an animal to justice."

"I'm with Steven," Louise said quietly.

Steven's physique and Louise's dignified courage and unshakable belief in her husband somehow made Cassie feel better. She looked at Endora. "We've got nothing on our calendar until May, right?"

"Actually, I don't think until the summer solstice," Endora confirmed.

"So, we're in, too." Cassie tried to keep her heart out of her eyes as she looked at Mick, daring to hope that the gratitude in his expression was mixed with true affection. It didn't matter, though. She loved him, and she could do little about it. Regardless of whether he loved her in return.

His eyes held her gaze alone as he stated, voice husky, "I appreciate all of your support."

Not a single author went home.

***

The afternoon's planned tour of Memphis had been canceled, and Mick and Cassie didn't really feel like venturing out on their own, even if Jamison sent agents with them. They stayed inside, ordering room service for lunch.

At 10:30 PM, the group would meet in the hotel lobby, board the bus and be taken to the train station. There, a sleeper car reserved exclusively for them waited on a side rail. In the wee hours of the morning, *The City of New Orleans*—on its run from Chicago to the Delta—would pick up the car. By midmorning, they would be in the Crescent City. New Orleans. The Big Easy.

Voodoo Capital of the World.

Cassie and Mick's lovemaking was poignant and intense that afternoon, as if the true circumstances of the tour had quelled any previous inhibitions regarding their emotions. They gave to and took from each other in equal measure.

Temporarily sated, Mick rolled to his side and smiled at Cassie. "Wow, lady, you're something. Where'd you learn that last move?"

"*Kama Sutra Monthly.* It was the featured position for December."

Mick laughed and pulled her to him, cradling her head against his chest. "How can I get a subscription?"

"I think you're doing just fine without one." She stroked his chest with her hand, then planted a soft kiss over his heart.

He squeezed her gently, and they lay together for several long moments, just holding each other close.

"What's your most prized possession?" Mick's question ended the companionable silence. "The one thing—besides friends and family—you can't picture not having."

"Hmmm . . . ." Cassie's fingers drew patterns in the black hair on Mick's chest while she contemplated her answer. "Tough question."

"C'mon, Cass. Fess up."

She cocked her head, still thinking. "From a strictly materialistic standpoint, it has to be my Mercedes."

"A car?" Mick's eyebrow shot up as he raised his head to look at her. "I took you for the type of person who'd say, 'My humanitarian award,' or 'My Nobel Peace Prize.'"

"Had I won a Nobel, that might have been the choice. However, if you're talking strictly an object, the Mercedes wins. No contest. I flat out love that car."

"I know I'm being sexist here, but isn't that more a male fantasy?"

She laughed. "Well, it's not just any car. It's a silver '55, 300 SL gull-wing coupe."

Mick sucked in an audible breath and sat up. "You're kidding!"

"One of the very few things I never kid about," Cassie stated solemnly as she slid up the headboard to sit beside him, "is my 300 SL."

Mick's incredulous look only got more comical. "My God, just fourteen hundred of that model were manufactured in four production years. Where'd you get it?"

From the factory in Sindelfingen, Germany the day it rolled off the production line, Cassie thought smugly. *My father's present to me on my fortieth birthday.* Since she assumed Mick could at least do simple math and draw some very uncomfortable conclusions, she didn't say that, though. Instead, she told a white lie. "I bought it from an ancient car buff who'd decided any ground conveyance that topped out at one hundred fifty-two miles per hour was too much for him."

"Straight six engine, Bosch direct fuel injection?"

Cassie nodded.

"Four speed manual transmission?"

Another nod, and when Mick groaned in appreciation, she added, "Zero to sixty in eight point two."

"You're killing me here, Cass."

"Well, let me nail down your coffin lid." She grinned smugly. "It's got an alloy body."

"One of *twenty-nine* alloy bodies? Twenty-nine out of the fourteen hundred cars?" He clutched his chest melodramatically and fell over in her lap. "Nothing short of preventing Armageddon would make me give that car up."

It was on the tip of her tongue to ask if stopping a serial killer counted as Armageddon, but that was far less a matter for joking than her car, and she wouldn't downplay the situation by making light of it. Instead, she ran her fingers through his hair. "I guess making someone really happy was his motivation. Believe me, I was ecstatic."

Mick's blue gaze turned serious, and he whispered, "I'd like to make you ecstatic."

Cassie's heart caught in her throat at his words. At the look in his eyes. "You do."

"Not just in bed. I'm talking about—"

The sudden hammering on their suite door had both of them jumping for clothing like a couple of teenagers caught necking in the back seat of a parked car.

"Cassie!" came Endora's call from the hallway. "Are you in there?"

You know I am! Cassie chided mentally. *And there'd better be a damn good reason you're here.*

The sound of a lock releasing echoed through the suite.

"Get decent, you two," Endora called from a now obviously open door. "I'm coming in."

"What ever possessed you to give her a key," Cassie hissed under her breath to Mick as they hastily put themselves back together.

He shrugged. "She is my manager for the time being." He reached out and caught Cassie's hand as she tried to squeeze by him through the bedroom door. "We have to talk, Cass. But the time's not right just now."

I'll say it isn't, Cassie thought. "Tonight, after we're on the train," she whispered before turning to confront Endora. "Dora, where's the fire?"

"You've got to come to the room with me right now," Endora stated, voice unusually tight. "We have important things to do before we leave for New Orleans."

Cassie shot her an annoyed look. "And this absolutely could not wait because . . . "

"Because it can't."

"Well, that explains it." Cassie turned back to Mick and bussed his cheek with a quick kiss. "See you later."

She could tell by the look in his eyes that he was more than a little frustrated with the interruption, but he kissed her back with a smile. "Okay, doll."

Endora quirked an eyebrow. "Doll?"

Mick grinned impishly. "I'm in retro-Forties mode," he stated. "Live with it."

Once out in the hall, Cassie turned the full power of her own frustration onto her familiar. *Dora, you couldn't have picked a worse time to show up. I think Mick was about to propose.*

I know he was. That's why I rained on your little parade.

***

They had reached the bank of elevators, and Cassie did a quick half-turn toward Endora.

"What?" Judging by Endora's wince, Cassie knew she'd shrieked the word, but she couldn't have cared less if she'd just shattered her familiar's eardrums. "What are you implying?"

"I'm not implying anything," Endora said with quiet intensity. "I'm saying I deliberately interrupted because I knew Mick was going to propose."

"Endora, that is way out of bounds!"

The familiar held her ground in the face of Cassie's fury. "I don't think so."

Without a word, Cassie spun on her heel and strode off toward their suite.

"You don't want to hear why I interrupted?"

"Not here in the corridor." *And not telepathically.*

More angry than she'd ever been in her life, Cassie deliberately cut the mental link between them.

Eleven

"I acted in your best interest," Endora stated for what seemed to Cassie like the hundredth time. "Just because you don't like it doesn't change the truth."

Cassie sat in the armchair in their suite's living area, feet propped on the coffee table and arms crossed tightly over her chest. She glared at Endora, standing at the wet bar. "I'm not speaking to you right now." When she saw her familiar flinch under the lash of that cold statement, realization of how deliberately bitchy she was being hit Cassie like a repulsion spell. In a softer tone, she said, "Give me some time with this, Dora."

The familiar planted her hands on her hips and stared. "Exactly how much time do you think you've got?" she asked evenly. "It's almost six. We're due in the lobby by ten-thirty to continue a book tour. Since *Mick* is the reason this tour was organized, he will also be in the lobby at ten-thirty. That gives you approximately—"

"I can do the math." Cassie didn't fight the sudden impulse to bite her right thumbnail to the quick.

The silence in the room lengthened to minutes, then finally Cassie straightened in the chair and turned to Endora. "All right. What is the truth, as you see it?"

"That you're a witch and Mick's a human and you'd better think long and hard about everything that could possibly happen if you married him." Endora managed the entire spate of words without pause, as if she feared taking a breath would allow an interruption.

"You don't think it could work between us?"

Endora paced from the couch to the wet bar and back, rhythmically rubbing the back of her neck as if she were swishing her tail. "I'm not saying that. But this is *not* a television sitcom. It's your real life." Sitting on the coffee table right where Cassie's feet had been propped, she leaned toward her friend. "Have you given any thought to the implications of a human-witch marriage?"

The heat Cassie felt in her cheeks could only mean she was blushing furiously. She swallowed hard. "Actually, I haven't considered much beyond the fact that I love Mick."

"Does he want kids?"

The urge to wring her hands was there, but Cassie successfully fought it. Her thumbnail again tempted. She leaned forward to let her hands hang between her knees and get that nail as far from her mouth as possible. "He told me he does."

"How does he feel about biracial babies?"

"Dammit, Endora!" Cassie shot to her feet, took two steps away from the chair, then feeling her familiar's gaze boring into her back, resumed her seat. Her chest tightened like a vice.

"Does he know what you are?"

"No."

"Plan to tell him, or just going to wait until he's eighty and asks why you don't look more than fifty?"

Incapable of speech, Cassie shrugged then stared out the window.

With a tenacity unusual for a familiar, Endora prodded, "What about Medusa? She's hell-bent on getting you married, but would she prefer a human to no marriage at all? Accept Mick as a son-in-law? Suppose you somehow convince her. How will you deal with the rest of your relatives? Not a single nominee for Open-minded Witch of the Year among them."

"I know," Cassie mumbled. "I know." Turning to face Endora, she tried to shrug nonchalantly but burst into tears.

Endora instantly moved to gather Cassie in her arms, hugging her close. "Oh, Cass."

"What should I do?"

"Tell him."

"What if he rejects what I am?" Cassie sobbed. "What if he can't love me enough to overlook our differences?"

Endora stared until her friend raised her head and met her gaze. "*Tell* him. Otherwise, your relationship is a complete lie."

Cassie pulled away. "You think I'm playing Mick because I haven't told him what I am?"

Even though she was very much in human form, Endora jumped like her tail was on fire. "No, by the goddess!" She paced again, hands and arms gesturing her points. "All new couples keep things from each other. That's a natural preservation instinct. It'll only become a lie if you marry him without telling him."

Cassie flopped down on the sofa, absently twisting the silver pentagram ring on her right hand. "Dora, quit pacing, for goddess sake. I'm not going to hit you or anything." She sighed, wiping away tears with the backs of her hands. "I need your honesty right now. More than ever."

Endora stopped moving but regarded Cassie warily from a good ten feet away. "What if my honesty hurts your feelings?"

Tipping her head back, Cassie studied the ceiling. "It already has, and I haven't attacked you, have I?" She straightened and turned her gaze to her familiar.

Looking guilty, Endora took three cautious steps closer.

"Come on, Dora, sit down." She patted a spot on the sofa beside her. "You have to help me."

"Sure?"

"Absolutely." An emphatic nod punctuated the word.

Endora complied, settled, cocked her head and launched her best cat stare at her friend. "What do you want me to do?"

The sigh escaped before Cassie could control it. "I'll probably regret this, but I want you to continue being brutally honest. Play devil's advocate, so to speak."

"I don't really like Lucifer all that much," Endora quipped. "How about if I just function in the manner Medusa would, were she here."

Cassie smiled wryly. "No need to be that extreme."

Impulsively, Endora reached for Cassie's hand, and knowing what a difficult thing that was for the familiar to do, Cassie didn't pull away. She waited patiently while Endora appeared to be weighing her words.

"Don't hold back for my sake. I want an honest opinion."

Relief swamping her features, Endora relaxed a bit. Yet, although she squeezed Cassie's hand and smiled slightly, she sucked in a deep breath before saying, "Until *you're* comfortable with what you are, you can't expect Mick to be."

Poleaxed, Cassie felt the blood drain from her face and suddenly feared passing out. "Wh-why do you say that?"

"Because it's true. You said yourself you were never good at being a witch."

Her constricted lungs were suffocating her, but Cassie fought off the dizziness. She thought of all the spell books she'd poured over before she and Mick became lovers. Before her spare time was occupied in making other kinds of magic. "I did say that."

"You think that way, and I suspect Medusa knows this. Maybe that's why she's pushing you so hard to marry a witch and settle down." Endora leaned closer. "Embrace what you are, then trust Mick to accept you for yourself."

"What if he can't handle the truth?"

Endora pulled back, a startled look in her green eyes. "Then I'd be very disappointed. He's got a lot of integrity for a human."

Cassie stopped twisting her ring and went to work with her teeth on her left thumbnail. She sucked in a huge breath, then let it out slowly. "I'll tell him tonight."

Endora bussed her on the forehead, cocky Cheshire grin showing for the first time in well over an hour. "That's the witch I know and love."

"Thanks, Dora." *But what if the man I know and love goes postal when I confess to what I am?* Her breath hitched. *What if I can't handle the truth about myself?*

The consequences to her heart should her fears prove out might just kill her.

***

Three days in Memphis, and he'd only twice seen his idol. And on each of those occasions M. S. Kazimer had squired two women. From the way Kazimer looked at Cassandra Hathorne, she had obviously replaced Jennifer Bodin in his affections. Likely, the bitch was spreading her legs for him at every opportunity. Whore.

It was 10:20 PM. He'd sat in the hotel lobby all day. Most of the group, without M. S. Kazimer and Cassandra Hathorne, had left around one that afternoon and returned at 2:30. That had been the only traffic through the lobby by any one of them. He had learned of a scheduled tour of Memphis, but that could hardly have been completed in just over an hour. None of the cortege had even come down to dinner.

The break in routine disturbed him. So much so that he had decided to abandon his vigil and seek another victim for his tribute. He would not find one here, however. Time to leave.

Then suddenly M. S. Kazimer appeared, another author—Robert Something or Other—with him.

Silently, he rose from the chair where he'd been ostensibly reading the paper and approached the men. They talked quietly, but his hearing was excellent and the lobby very still.

"I'm done after this, Robert."

"You're really hanging up your computer?"

A nod from M. S. Kazimer. "I am."

"Can't say as I blame you."

Rage exploded inside him. Blinding. Searing. Driving away logic and reason. The Bodin bitch had been *right*. His idol. His *god* was abandoning him.

He started toward the two men, thinking to grab his Master, to shake him, to demand he take back the hideous words he'd just uttered. Blind with rage, he quickened his pace. Little except the target of his loving hatred filled his mind. He must reach M. S. Kazimer! He must.

He drew even with the elevators just as one opened and half a dozen of the book tour participants spewed out, Kazimer's whore leading.

No! She must not reach his goal before he did. Mindlessly, he lunged.

***

He's in the lobby!

Endora's warning exploded in Cassie's head at the same instant a cloud of pure evil engulfed them all. In the form of an average-looking man rushing straight at Mick and Robert.

Mick was half-turned toward her, oblivious to the danger, the killer ten feet from him. Without thought, Cassie threw a force field between the two men. Mick's attacker crashed headlong into it and fell back a step, momentarily stunned.

"Get him," she shouted. "He's the killer!"

The split-second it took for everyone to recover from seeing a man slam full-tilt into thin air was all the time the monster needed to break and run for a boisterous wedding reception in the lobby's terraced bar.

Jamison's agents jumped to pursue, leaving a slack-jawed group of authors and tourists in their wake. Immediately, Cassie and Endora moved to flank Mick.

"I should have frozen him," Cassie spat out, disgusted. Her heart pounded so hard she was surprised the blouse she wore wasn't visibly palpitating.

"You probably saved lives here," Endora stated with quiet firmness. "Lighten up on yourself."

"They'd have caught the bastard if I'd—"

Endora glanced at the group's stunned faces. *Can you beat yourself up silently, Cass? We've got lots of curious people here, all with vivid imaginations, who just witnessed something they've likely never seen before.*

"Shit!"

It was a measure of Cassie's sudden awareness and agitation that the expletive escaped her mouth. She rarely used foul language of any kind in public.

The FBI agents returned within minutes.

"We lost him, Boss," one reported solemnly to Jamison. "There's a street entrance to the bar, and he got out. Bates and Johnson are still looking."

"Notify Memphis PD," Jamison snapped. "See if they've got any ideas where this guy could go to ground." He turned to the authors. "Board the bus. We'll get you to the train station and onto the car. It's a secure area . . ." His voice trailed off as he caught sight of Mick's expression. "Sandor, you all right?"

Mick never took his eyes off Cassie.

"Take the others to the station, Robert," Mick said quietly. "Ms. Hathorne and I have some things to talk about."

"Not without me there, you don't," Jamison retorted. He turned to the closest agent. "Get the others to the station, Reed. We'll be along later."

At least some of them would, Cassie thought.

***

For all its effect on the current occupants, the hotel manager's spectacular office view could have overlooked a brick wall.

"What the hell just happened?" Jamison asked the room at large. The normally calm, collected Federal agent couldn't seem to get his eyes to focus on anything for more than a split-second. Nor could he keep his hand from palming the back of his neck. He seemed to want to pace but didn't know if he should. Then he turned his gaze on Cassie and Endora, and his stare locked on them like a laser-guided cruise missile. "Would either of you care to explain exactly what that was?"

"A force field," Endora immediately replied, then directed her next remark to Cassie. "And a very fine one indeed, if I say so myself."

"A force field." Jamison's tone and raised eyebrow radiated skepticism. "As in *Star Trek?*"

"No, as in a spell caster's force field," Endora stated. "You know, witchcraft."

"How is that—-"

"Because I really am a witch," Cassie cut in, her statement sounding resigned even to her own ears. "The term isn't just a comment on my personality."

She glanced at Mick and Robert from behind the manager's desk where she sat. Then she lowered her gaze to the desktop. Robert had regained some of his usual composure, but she couldn't get a reading on Mick. He had a poker face on, completely hiding any reaction. And his reaction was far more important to her than the FBI agent's. Her fingers automatically reached to twist her pentagram ring. The gesture brought no comfort just then.

She wanted to reach out mentally, but refused to. If she couldn't trust Mick to truthfully express his feelings, then she couldn't trust his claims of love.

Endora moved to stand behind her, gently rubbing Cassie's shoulders. "I sense some doubts among the menfolk here, Cass. Perhaps a demonstration is in order."

"Endora—"

Giving Cassie's shoulders a quick squeeze, Endora stepped around the chair. "I'll take care of it."

Before anyone could blink, the familiar had shifted to feline form. Leaping gracefully onto the desk, the smoke gray cat sauntered directly to the middle and sat, long tail swishing slowly.

If she hadn't been so distraught, Cassie might have found the men's expressions amusing. Jamison's eyes were again nearly rolling in his head, and Mick had his jaw clenched so tight she could see the muscle bulging below his ear. To keep his mouth from dropping open, most likely. Under the circumstances, however, Cassie thought their reactions anything but funny.

"Endora, change back. Now!"

Cassie watched Endora swagger to the edge of the desk before leaping six feet to the room's small sofa and changing back to human form. She smoothed back her hair with her palm then smiled like the predator she was. Cassie could have knocked both the men over with a single breath.

"And I'm just the familiar," Endora purred. "Cassie has far greater talent than I do."

"Enough, Dora." Cassie couldn't take her eyes off Mick, who leaned one-shouldered against the wall beside the outer office door. His still clenched jaw proved he wasn't aloof at all.

"But Cass—"

Only her familiar's plea could shift Cassie's attention from the man she now knew without doubt she loved. She turned a heated glare on Endora that made the latter break off in mid-protest.

Finally, Mick moved. Expression still neutral, he

approached the desk.

"I'd like to have a word with Cassie," he said quietly. "Alone."

Her heart gave a hard thump before dropping into her stomach. This was it.

"Miss Bast, let's step outside for a minute." Jamison offered his arm when Endora rose from the sofa. She brushed by the agent, her stare only for Mick.

Mick immediately sneezed hard. Repeatedly.

Endora— Cassie warned.

Give me the word, Cass, and I'll make him feel like he's in the middle of the world's biggest hairball.

Stop. Now.

When Endora strode out of the office, Mick's allergic reaction instantly ended. Jamison followed on her heels, closing the door behind them.

Cassie and Mick were alone.

Funny, for such a big room, she couldn't find much air to breathe in it. It was impossible to look at Mick, so handsome in a midnight blue turtleneck that made his eyes practically glow. Why torture herself by wanting him. Loving him. In under ten minutes, he was going to walk out of her life, and she'd only see him on book covers and *Oprah.*

Her heart burned a hole in her chest. Rising from behind the large desk, she moved to the window, deliberately keeping her back to Mick. When the silence stretched out, she considered turning back around but, feeling tears welling in her eyes, stayed facing the city below.

"I know this likely denotes a certain shallowness on my part, but shouldn't you be thanking me for saving your life?" she asked brusquely. She winced at the harshness of her tone. *Great Mother Goddess, Cass, just deliberately bait him!*

"Thanks," he muttered.

His tone had her glancing back over her shoulder at him. He swallowed hard, then raised his head and offered a fake-looking smile. "This seems to be the part where I ask 'Are you a good witch or a bad witch?'"

That caused her to turn. She leveled a stare at him that would have made Endora cheer, all the while feeling her heart breaking. "There are good people and bad people, good witches and bad witches," she stated evenly. "I won't dignify your question by explaining what category I fall into." She struggled to keep her voice steady. Managed, but at the cost of relinquishing eye contact. She lowered her gaze to the floor. "I think you've already made up your mind on that count anyway."

He had no comment, and silence reigned in the plush office. After it seemed they would never speak another word to each other, he asked, "How much of what's between us is real?"

Her spine straightened to a ramrod. How could he even ask that? She imagined her eyes were blazing as she met his. It certainly felt like they were shooting fire. "Reality is relative, Mick. As a writer, you should understand that."

"I have the right to know if it was actually me performing, or you making me think I was."

He struck a belligerent pose, hands fisted on hips. Her insides felt like death. She smiled, knowing the expression did little to hide the hurt in her eyes, and shrugged in an intentionally dismissive manner. But no matter how much the question tore at her heart, she couldn't lie about their relationship. Even to save her pride.

"What's between us is magic even a witch can't conjure," she stated quietly. "It's chemistry. The kind that comes along once in a lifetime." Her sigh was soft but heartfelt, and she stared down at her feet. "And believe me, I've lived long enough to know the truth of that."

Mick moved closer, and she sensed that he wanted to touch her. He didn't.

"This goes way beyond my understanding of Wiccan."

"I'm not Wiccan." Cassie raised her head, nearly wincing when he took a step back. "I'm full-blooded witch. Both my parents are witches."

"Witches don't exist."

That comment instantly infuriated her, and she barely resisted setting his hair on fire. Instead, she broke her own rule. *I think what I just did out in the lobby blasts that theory of yours to pieces.*

Mick flinched, then shrugged away his surprise at her mental invasion. "So you're telepathic. I'm sure there are plenty of telepaths who don't claim to be witches."

"Very true. But I happen to be both." At the odd look that crossed his face, she asked, "What does telepathy have to do with us?"

Now Mick was the one who couldn't make eye contact. "Did you get inside my head when we made love?"

He couldn't have cut her more deeply with a razor. She'd only just then broken her vow not to use telepathy, and he wanted to know if she'd read his mind while they . . . His questioning the reality of the best lovemaking she'd ever experienced nearly crushed her. But anger quickly erased the sorrow. How *dare* he cheapen something so wonderful.

"Don't even go there," she growled. Then she started for the door.

Mick took two steps after her before stopping. "Cassie, wait. Where are you going?"

"To find a Black Sabbath," she shot back over her shoulder. "I'll drink some goat's blood, dance naked, fornicate with dozens of strange men. You know, typical witch behavior."

Mick ran his hand through his hair. "Look, Cassie, I—"

Turning at the door, she fixed him with her most potent stare. "As an advice columnist I feel it's my duty to advise you. Quit talking before you say something we'll both regret."

Then she spun on her heel and was out the door, leaving him staring at empty space.

***

He looked at the blood that coated his hands and arms, that had splattered across his face and chest, and he felt no satisfaction. None at all. The hot surge of life force and the power that had always come with the kill had abandoned him. Rage replaced them.

Rage that these two kills had been in blind fury—random victims slaughtered in the most expedient and violent way. No blueprint to follow. No planning, no selection process, no order or ritual. And the cause of that artless sacrifice . . . rage that his deity had forsaken him.

He had broken the pattern. Yet his idol had broken it first. His idol had decided to *stop writing*. The grief and pain of that realization doubled him over, brought him to his knees. He nearly cried out in anguish, but instincts honed to danger prevented him. He was vulnerable to capture. No matter that the authorities were moronic automatons, his carelessness in these two killings made him susceptible. He had to hide, to carefully assess his previous plans. To alter them according to the break in the pattern.

No choice existed. He would have to commit deicide.

***

Feelings of cowardice lowered her mood further, and Cassie

admitted she wouldn't qualify for any profiles in courage in this lifetime. Guilt stabbed her like a broken underwire. She'd stretched the bounds of friendship by having Endora cover the afternoon's signing, but she couldn't even face Mick, let alone sit next to him for two hours. The scene the previous night in Memphis felt like ground glass in her chest, scraping her heart raw. So instead of being brave and facing up to the source of her pain, she'd imposed on her familiar and then slunk away from the hotel, bound for New Orleans' French Quarter.

No destination in mind, she wandered, absorbing The Big Easy through every sense. Soon, she found herself on Royal Street in the heart of the Quarter. While most of her family frequented "N'Awlins," Cassie had only been there a handful of times. Never as an adult.

She'd never before in her adult life wanted to be here. Suddenly, a fundamental need to truly experience the city grabbed her. To connect with a part of herself she'd never completely accepted and answer questions she'd just discovered her heart had been asking for years.

Right down to her DNA, Cassie believed in fate. After all, she was a witch. She was here at this specific time for a precise reason, and duty to herself created the need to find out why. Hoping with all her heart it was to discover how to be with Mick, she nevertheless realized it might be to discover how to be without him. Her destiny was here, waiting to be seized.

Not one to waste an opportunity when it presented itself, she succumbed to the allure of the fabled Vieux Carre and went where instinct took her.

The architecture drew her eye first. Exotic and rich, completely unlike any other city in America. Royal Street embodied the entire Quarter. Every building sported lace iron balconies, most had fanlight windows. Flowering plants graced the wrought-iron railings, adding even more color and scent to the sensual mix of sights, sounds, textures and smells.

Perhaps her state of mind made her more sensitive, but she had never felt so much supernatural power surrounding her. Passing the Royal Cafe at the corner of St. Peter and Royal, she got an especially strong sensation. The air pulsed, and her skin tingled with kinetic energy. It engulfed her, making the fine hairs on her arms stand up, prickling the back of her neck. No doubt something terrible had happened here. The spirits of those involved in the tragedy still walked its floors.

New Orleans deserved its reputation of having the most concentrated paranormal activity on Earth. And for once, it didn't bother her to be responsive to that. It gave her a deeper layer of understanding than the vast majority of visitors to New Orleans could ever hope to experience.

A block over on Bourbon, she passed open-to-the-street jazz clubs, music wafting out to the afternoon shoppers. It was too early in the day to consider alcohol, so she let the music carry her along, past shops displaying Mardi Gras beads, intricate masks, and every imaginable souvenir. A plush purple alligator with a green felt swamp hat and a goofy, tooth-filled grin made her laugh out loud. She had half a mind to come back later and buy him.

Wandering farther afield, she played tourist at Cafe Du Monde in the French Market, where she ate beignets and drank rich coffee. Then she browsed the wonderful mix of trinkets and fresh foods the Market offered before heading back toward Jackson Square. The heart of the Quarter.

She was just off the square when a wave of negative energy hit her like a wall, chilling her skin. It emanated from a short, dead-end alley. Stopping, she peered past the wrought-iron bars and saw the back entrance to a restaurant that fronted the square.

Torrents of suffering and fear poured over her, nearly knocking her to her knees, and Cassie saw in her mind's eye the alley's original purpose. Slaves fresh from the slave ships and awaiting sale had been chained to its walls, left standing for hours without food or water, soiling themselves where they stood, some dying and hanging in their chains until their bodies were removed. She could smell the stench of death and human waste, hear the moans of humans suffering in stifling air and confinement. Startled by the strength of her reaction, Cassie gasped, recoiling several steps back into the street.

Right into her mother.

A youngish-looking man stood next to Medusa. Probably Cassie's age. Definitely a witch.

Oh, please, Cassie thought. *Not now.*

***

"Write the information here." Endora's most pleasant tone rolled from her lips as she gestured to a legal pad in front of a stack of Cassie's book. "Name, address, and how Cassandra should sign your book. As soon as she's better, she'll autograph these. We'll mail them postage free."

Mick silently revised his conviction that screaming in frustration was strictly for women and wimps. He'd sat for over an hour listening to Endora's patter—apologizing to a steady stream of Cassie Hathorne fans for Cassie's being unable to sign in person, that she'd mail the books . . . It was driving him crazy.

Despite having a constant line of his own autograph-seeking fans, his thoughts were only on Cassie. He hadn't seen her since the night before when she'd left him standing in the Peabody manager's office, but she filled his head. One of Jamison's agents had reported seeing her and Endora board the group's special sleeper car at the train station, but how the two women had gotten there was anyone's guess. And Mick didn't want to guess.

A witch and a familiar . . . He found that almost incomprehensible. And yet, supernatural powers certainly explained several things. Like his allergic reaction to Endora. And the man Cassie claimed was the killer who'd been charging toward Mick and Jamison when he bounced backward as if hitting an invisible wall. Then he'd run like he really had committed some horrible crime. And how could Cassie and Endora possibly have known who the man was if Jamison and his agents had no clue?

Afterward, in the manager's office, he'd managed to stay calm at Cassie's admission. But when Endora shape-shifted, he'd almost hyperventilated. Great respect for the supernatural ran in his blood, but respecting something in theory was a damn sight different from dealing with it in reality. Having the woman he loved possess supernatural skills would take adjusting to.

That is, if Cassie gave him the chance to make the adjustment.

Are you a good witch or a bad witch? Could he have asked a more idiotic question if he'd tried? Doubtful. Then he'd followed that brilliant line by questioning her honesty in their relationship. Mister Sensitivity. Not! In that moment, Mick admitted he loved Cassie more than anything else in his life. Yet he had acted like the king of Neanderthals when faced with the truth about her. He prayed he hadn't completely blown his chance in Memphis.

Damn his tongue-tied stupidity in the face of emotional crisis. Cassie should have turned him into a jackass for being one. What he'd told Jennifer in Chicago was true. He was miserable at off-the-cuff witticism. Why hadn't that knowledge stopped him from opening his mouth and sticking his foot so far inside that his toes were scratching his colon?

He had to keep his wits. Convince Cassie their differences wouldn't doom their relationship. Otherwise, the best thing that had ever happened to him would slip through his fingers, all because he was oratorically challenged.

But if he was honest with himself, he had to admit there might be little choice but to let her go. If she continued avoiding him, he couldn't explain himself or make amends for being a royal bastard to her.

His only hope lay in Endora. To get to Cassie he had to go through the familiar. A terrifying prospect. She was more than willing to defend Cassie to the death, and Mick knew full well that for starters she'd exploit his damned cat allergy. Maybe he should stock up on antihistamines before approaching Endora to attempt an alliance.

Amazingly, with ten minutes remaining in the signing, Mick realized neither he nor Endora had customers in line. Opportunity presented him the chance to talk to her—before she could bolt back to Cassie's suite and barricade the door. He mentally took a deep breath, checked that he had his handkerchief handy in case Endora hawked a hairball on him, and cleared his throat.

"Endora, we need to talk." His breath caught as she turned her exotic eyes toward him. Would she cooperate?

"We have nothing to say to each other."

He raised a brow. "I disagree. I have plenty to say to Cassie, and since it's obvious you're running interference, I want to talk." As the familiar contemplated his statement, Mick dared to hope. "Please, Endora. I love her. Help me."

A slight shake of her head preceded, "I'm afraid I can't do that."

"Can't or won't?" Panic rose in Mick's chest, and he fought hard to stem it. Endora was his only chance. He prayed his voice wouldn't crack when he said, "I deserve an explanation for your refusal."

Endora rose and began to pack up her briefcase. Mick thought he'd grind his teeth to dust as he waited for her to turn to face him, and it was obvious she deliberately took her time. Lockjaw was seconds away when she finally acknowledged his statement.

"Sorry, Mick," she stated flatly as she turned around, "but

a familiar's job is to protect her witch, and I don't think being with you is in Cassie's best interest."

His jaw had dropped, but he couldn't help it. He was about to demand an explanation for that asinine assumption when Endora volunteered the information.

"Longevity is an issue. The average witch lives twice as long as the most long-lived human. Even though Cass is almost ninety and you're less than half that age, you're going to die before she does." She picked up her case and headed for the convention hall's main doors.

Mick dogged her heels. "Not a good enough reason to keep us apart." When Endora kept walking, he grasped her elbow to stop her. "She and I need to discuss this, not the two of us."

Endora glanced down at his hand still on her elbow, and Mick's throat and eyes got scratchy. He pulled out his handkerchief, blew his nose. "I've had allergies all my life, and I've never let them stop me. You'll have to do better than that to keep me from Cassie."

Endora's green eyes fairly glowed. "Don't tempt me."

"Oh, I know you'd love to hammer me. But Cassie's feelings are holding you back." When he saw guilt flicker in Endora's eyes, hope again leapt in his heart. "She kept you off me last night, and I'm thinking she'd do the same today if she was here."

The familiar straightened to her full height—about even with Mick's shoulder—and bored him with a hot green glare. They stood toe-to-toe, neither giving an inch to the other, neither so much as blinking.

Finally, Endora's right eyebrow rose. "You want to talk, human? All right. Let's have words."

***

"Mom!" Unease crept up Cassie's back. "What are you doing here?"

Medusa was dressed in her usual garish outfit—this one in purples, blacks and reds—but in New Orleans she didn't look out of place.

"Visiting friends," she stated innocently. Her guileless expression didn't fool Cassie for a moment. "What are *you* doing here, dear?"

"Skipping out on a book signing," Cassie muttered under her breath.

Medusa's hearing was every bit as good as her daughter's. Both carefully plucked black eyebrows shot up. She started to speak, seemed to think better of it, then smiled warmly.

"Where are my manners?" She turned to the witch standing patiently beside her. "Cassie, this is Mandrake Tod. Mandrake, my daughter, Cassie Hathorne."

Cassie shook the witch's proffered hand, barely noticing that he held on a bit longer than necessary. "Nice meeting you."

"It's a pleasure to finally make your acquaintance," Mandrake said smoothly.

"Finally make your acquaintance?" Mandrake's words kicked Cassie's Parental Setup Detector into high gear.

Her expression must have warned Medusa that her ruse was discovered, because the elder witch's smile sweetened to insulin-shock-for-diabetics level. "Mandrake's a journalist just like you, Cassie," she said brightly. "What publication did you say you wrote for, darling?"

The witch's chest puffed a bit with pride. "I'm a feature writer for *Playbat Magazine*."

"*Playbat?*" What started in Cassie's chest as a bubble of hysterical laughter burst from her lips as uncontrolled sobs, and for the second time in less than two weeks, she found herself crying in her mother's arms.

Medusa looked at Mandrake over Cassie's bent head. "That went far worse than I'd expected it would."

At her words, Cassie cried even harder.

Twelve

They sat in a dim booth in the hotel's bar, the only patrons at that afternoon hour.

Mick could see Endora's eyes glowing like a tiger's in the low lighting, and he cursed his overactive writer's imagination for conjuring that image. No doubt she'd enjoy munching on his limbs. Or just breaking every bone in his body. He sucked in a breath. She wasn't going to intimidate him. Not much, anyway. Yet her predatory half-smile, full of gleaming teeth, almost made him revise that promise. As he cursed the acute powers of observation that had helped put him on the *New York Times* bestseller list, he wondered how he'd look in a full body cast.

"Speak your peace, human."

"Mick will do, Endora." Going for the appearance of casual confidence, he leaned back against the booth cushion. He hoped her feline hearing couldn't pick up the thundering of his heart. Should that be true, he'd never be able to fool her and would have to go to Plan B. And since he had no Plan B, running like hell sounded like a viable option. "And, for your information, I'm done talking. It's your turn. Tell me why you're keeping Cassie and me apart."

Would his bluff work? As they stared at each other, neither blinking, Mick tried to make his mind go blank. A futile attempt. Cassie filled his every thought, refusing to be put aside. If Endora, like Cassie, was telepathic and got into his head, that's all she'd see.

The familiar stared right through him, then stated coldly, "Historically, men have dealt with troublesome women by accusing them of witchcraft. Wife won't give you a son? Mother-in-law a shrew? Spread rumors they sneak into the woods at midnight. Get your neighbor's coveted land by suggesting to the local clergy that he shelters witches. The women are taken off to be raped, tortured and executed, and the accusers get what they want."

Mick stiffened, but held his comment until the waiter had set their drinks down and left. "I know the history. That has nothing to do with Cassie and me."

"It has everything to do with you two. Back in Salem, not a single woman executed for witchcraft was a real witch. Not one. Even Wiccans didn't die in 1692. Only Puritans."

"I'm not seeing the relevance."

Endora's sound of disgust was suspiciously like a cat's hiss. "A *real* witch wouldn't have been jailed in the first place. Witches can protect themselves. Humans can't control them unless witches allow it. That's where you and Cassie come in. Not being in charge—not dominating a relationship—drives some men crazy. Makes them abusive. Obsessive. You'll have to convince me you love Cassie, abilities and all, before you get to see her."

Mick's hand curled around his beer mug until his knuckles were white, but his voice was level when he said, "If you knew anything about me, you'd know I was raised to respect women for their capabilities. And I do. I also know good writing, and Cassie's the best writer I've ever read. I have tremendous admiration for her talents. I admire her for the career she's fashioned." He paused a moment to settle his emotions. "But even if she couldn't write a line, I would have fallen for her. She's incredible. I loved her before I knew about her supernatural powers. I won't stop loving her because of them."

"How do I know that?"

Something told Mick this was a test he had to pass. He locked down his temper. "Look, Endora, I'm a Catholic Slovak from Detroit. My ethnic roots run deep. Hell, my grandmother practically tore me a new one when I told a classmate my family spoke Czech. 'Slovak, Mirek. Not Czech! We speak Slovak.' I didn't get any of *YaYa's* pastries for dessert that night. Nearly killed me. But my family aren't bigots. If Cassie was Jewish or black or any other minority, I'd still love her. And they would love her, even *YaYa*. And not just for my sake, but because she's worthy of love in her own right."

Unblinking, Endora stared at him for so long he started thinking she'd gone catatonic. He badly wanted a sip of beer, but feared his hands would shake so much he'd spill it all over.

When Endora's eyes again focused, her voice had an edge to it. "Better make it right with Cassie, or I'll book you on the Extreme Swamp Boat Ride. Strictly for my own amusement."

"What's that," Mick asked uneasily.

"A ski boat excursion for the sociopathically macho. It literally costs an arm and a leg, and if you don't lose one of each during the course of the trip, there's no charge."

"You're kidding. Right?"

Endora's eyebrow rose. "It's across the street from a med center that sits beside Prostheses 'R Us." She paused a beat. "Kidding! You gotta lighten up, Mick. Where's your sense of humor?"

He didn't relax until he saw her Cheshire cat grin. "Considering I may never convince the woman I love to marry me, I'm rather short on that commodity right now."

"Well, ill humor is better than no humor at all." Endora cocked her head. "I actually like you. Of course, tell anyone I said that and I'll deny it. Then I'll bring down a plague of frogs on you." His expression must have looked as pained as those words made him feel, because she laughed. "You're doing it again."

"Doing what?"

"Getting that four-alarm-chili-heartburn look. I never tease people I don't like. I just torment them with, say, clouds of pet dander or somesuch."

Mick had to laugh, and the resulting release of tension made him feel better than he had in far too long. "What changed your mind about me?"

Although her shrug appeared nonchalant, the expression in Endora's eyes was serious. "You really love her."

"Will you help me get her back?"

"Probably." Endora sighed before knocking back half of her glass of Kahlua and cream. "It's no fun being a familiar to a depressed witch. They mope around the house, turning the rhododendrons to plastic . . . rain clouds hovering over their heads, pouring water everywhere they walk . . . Not a pretty sight." She shot Mick a look. "Think you can put up with that kind of mood?"

A smile threatened to ruin his sobriety. "I'll never give her a reason to be depressed."

"Ooooh, good answer, human."

"Thanks."

"Completely unrealistic, of course, but a good answer." Abruptly, Endora assumed her manager persona. "Enough pleasantries. Let's get to business. My first piece of advice for getting Cassie back is this. Write down your spiel beforehand. Frankly, you suck at spontaneous repartee, and I don't want you pissing her off so she turns you into a newt. That would spoil all my efforts on your behalf." She yawned, stretching. "And if you know me, you know I expend as little energy as possible. So, when I do decide to take on a project, I don't appreciate someone else messing it up. No offense, of course."

"None taken." Something that felt a lot like hope filled Mick's heart.

***

"Mandrake, darling, I'm afraid I must bow out of our shopping excursion," Medusa said as she handed Cassie all the tissue in her large, multicolored leather reticule. "I'll meet you at the voodoo temple at nine tonight."

Relief flooded Mandrake's face. Obviously uncomfortable in the presence of female tears, he awkwardly patted Cassie's arm. "Um, nice to meet you, Cassandra."

Cassie lifted her head from her mother's shoulder, sniffed once, and said, "My pleasure, I'm sure."

As they watched Mandrake hurry off, Medusa slipped her arm around Cassie's waist and gave her a quick squeeze. "We need to have a mother-daughter talk, don't we?"

"Big time."

"Then come along, darling. I have the perfect spot for a little *tête-e-tête*."

She led Cassie off, bound for Bourbon Street. Neither woman spoke as Medusa steered Cassie to the Old Absinthe House and into a back booth in the bar. She sat down across from her daughter and beckoned their server.

"Two house frappes." When Cassie barely mustered enough interest to ask what that was, Medusa said casually, "The drink of the gods. I remember when Cayetano Ferrer created the Old Absinthe House Frappe. Put this place on the map. He claimed I inspired his creation."

Cassie raised her head out of her hands and stared at her mother. "You must have been pretty close." When she saw Medusa smile and blush at the same time, Cassie gaped. "Oh."

"Oh, indeed."

Just like practically every child in the world, Cassie refused to imagine her mother with a social life. Especially one that involved sex. "I didn't realize you were, uh, dating. Thought you gave up on that after Dad."

"Heavens, child, Cayetano and I were an item long before I ever met your father." She adjusted her colorful turban and said, "Back in seventy-three, we were quite the thing."

Cassie did some quick math. "You're talking *eighteen* seventy-three?"

"Of course."

"You were, what, seventeen?" Medusa nodded, and Cassie took the time to really look at her mother. The elder witch had black-brown hair, just like Cassie's, though Medusa's featured a sprinkling of gray at the temples. Her skin was flawless, and her twinkling eyes jet black. *If I look that good when I'm a hundred and forty-seven,* Cassie thought, *I'll thank the Goddess every day.* She gave herself a mental shake. This wasn't the time for vanity. "So, tell me about the Big Easy in eighteen seventy-three."

Medusa's expression turned wistful for a moment, then brightened. "Such a wonderful time. New Orleans was as amazing then as it is now. More so. Calling cards and summers at the sea. Elegance. Gentility. No automobiles, fax machines or computers . . ." She closed her eyes on a sigh of remembrance. They were misty when she opened them a moment later. "Cayetano created the frappe the next year. It became an instant hit . . . and we drifted apart."

Something in Medusa's tone had Cassie asking, "Why'd that happen?"

"Fame, I suppose. Notoriety. Creating that drink made Cayetano the toast of the city."

"No pun intended."

"None at all." Medusa smiled at the memory. "He was a brilliant mixologist, and the frappe proved it to all and sundry. Being a celebrity suited him. He loved the soirees and the night life. Invitations to the races, entree to the men's clubs, associating with the very rich. As his fame escalated, we grew more distant."

What her mother wasn't saying seemed far more important than what she said. Cassie mulled it over. When it came, realization knocked her breath away like a punch to the gut. "He was human."

For once, Medusa didn't equivocate. "Yes."

A mixture of dread and curiosity filled Cassie. But she had to ask. "Did he know about you? About what you are?" At her mother's expression, regret assaulted her. But it was too late to take the question back. "You don't have answer if you don't want to, Mom. Really."

"Actually," Medusa sighed, "we should have discussed this a long time ago. But, honestly, I didn't wish to relive all the old hurts. Bury the past and leave it has always been my philosophy."

"So . . . did Cayetano—"

"No. I never told him." Medusa's eyes brightened with unshed tears. "I feared his rejection."

Reaching across the table, Cassie grasped her mother's hand. "Even in New Orleans? This city's more open to the other side than any I've ever seen."

Medusa concentrated on their entwined fingers as she explained. "Back then, the attitude toward our kind was far different from today. The Victorian Age and all that. The idea of witches, or anything supernatural, terrified most humans. Oh, there were cults who sought knowledge in alchemy, necromancy and such, but they were very much out of sight. Now, people are openly fascinated with such things, although I frankly don't see the attraction to all that dark occult nonsense. Modern Wiccans are working to change people's attitudes, too . . . ." Her voice trailed off as her eyes again filled with tears.

"You loved him, didn't you?"

Medusa merely nodded as the tears broke loose and streamed down her face. Cassie's heart hitched. Not only had she made her mother cry, but she'd used up all of Medusa's tissues during her own crying jag. Surreptitiously, she snapped her fingers under the table and produced a travel pack. Without a word, she handed them over, smiling when her mother gratefully accepted her offering.

"This certainly explains your attitude toward humans. And why you've pushed so many eligible male witches at me."

Medusa nodded then daubed at her eyes with a tissue.

Hoping to make her mother angry instead of sad, Cassie asked, "Did you take Dad on the rebound?"

"No." Medusa's tears stopped, and her black eyes glittered fiercely. "I was over Cayetano when I met your father, no longer fascinated by human males. Draco and I fell in love. He was one of my kind, and we got along famously for many years." She shook her head, melancholy evident in her expression. "But you never forget your first love." Squeezing Cassie's hand, she laughed self-consciously. "I'm sorry, darling. I didn't mean to rehash my life. I meant to help you with your troubles." She looked around the bar. "But I just love this place—it makes me feel close to Cayetano—and I thought perhaps you'd enjoy the ambiance enough to tell me what's wrong."

Cassie swallowed back her own tears before she smiled wryly at Medusa. "It seems the attraction to human males runs in the family."

She poured out her heart to Medusa, editing only the intimate details of her relationship with Mick from the telling of the book tour's serpentine events. When she finished, Medusa sat back in the booth and leveled a compassionate look at her.

"If he hurts you, I'm going to give him a temporary but vastly unpleasant and inconvenient rash."

Cassie caught herself before her jaw dropped. "You're not going to try to convince me things can never work out between us?"

"They might not." Medusa seized both of Cassie's hands. "But you must follow your heart. I'm your mother. Your happiness is paramount to me. You talk about Mick and your entire face lights up. That kind of feeling is worth fighting for." She released Cassie's hands and passed her a tissue. "If he loves you, he'll accept you for what you are."

"And if he doesn't, I'll be the second one in the family to have my heart broken by a human male."

Medusa's grin was equal parts wry and wicked. "Bastards. We might have to turn them all into eunuchs."

"I'm afraid I wouldn't be up for something like that."

"Neither would they when we got through with them."

"Mother!"

Medusa laughed as she signaled for the check. "Don't ever underestimate an old person, darling."

Medusa paid for the drinks, and they moved out onto Bourbon.

"I want you to go to the Bottom of the Cup Tearoom and have a reading."

That brought Cassie up short. "Why?"

"Because their reputation is spotless. Some of their psychics have worked there for over twenty-five years."

"Do you really think I need a reading?" Cassie's breath caught. "What if I find out my relationship with Mick is doomed?"

Medusa laughed. "Don't be silly, dear. I would have sensed if you and Mick wouldn't succeed together. But it won't be an easy road. You need to determine which forces are harmonious and which in opposition between you two. Knowing that, you can plan how to counteract the negative."

"Oh." Cassie felt her whole body momentarily sag. Then she straightened and glanced over at her mother as they walked side-by-side. "That likely won't help me. I just started studying the art again recently, and I'm incredibly rusty. Most likely a reading would be useless to me."

Medusa stopped walking, squared up to her daughter, and planted her fists on her ample hips. "You wouldn't consider asking me for help with this?"

"Well, given your history with humans, and all, I wasn't sure—"

"I would do anything for you, Cassandra. Just because we don't agree on every issue, doesn't mean I'm not there for you at all times. Now, go to the Bottom of the Cup. Get the reading, and I'll help you interpret it. Then we can make plans to correct the bad auras."

Impulsively, Cassie hugged Medusa. "I love you, Mom."
"The feeling's mutual."

***

"Bad news, human. Cassie's in the Quarter, and she's not alone."

Mick and Endora stood in the living area of Cassie's suite. Endora, holding one of Cassie's necklaces, had her eyes closed in concentration.

"Who's she with?"

"Shhh." Endora's eyes popped open, and she leveled her gaze at Mick. "Her mother."

"And this is bad news because . . ."

"Because Medusa's a very powerful witch, and she's not real keen on humans. Especially male humans who might have designs on her daughter." She placed the necklace on the wet bar and turned to him. "Let's hope she's not in 'protect her child' mode. If she is, you could be toast in nothing flat."

"That's encouraging."

Endora patted his arm. "If it's any consolation, Cassie will run interference for you."

"And what if Cassie's not in the mood to protect me?"

"Then, I'll hope for whole wheat. I just love whole wheat toast with raspberry jam."

Mick shook his head. "Hate to disappoint you, Slick, but it'll be Slovak rye."

"Probably burnt, too."

"Probably."

***

Cassie felt the need to take the initiative with her problem, so she promised Medusa a full report on the reading, then left her at the corner of Bourbon and St. Peter. Since Royal was the next street over, she only had to walk a block down St. Peter. Bottom of the Cup was just around the corner.

The moment she entered the shop a spirit made its presence known in Cassie's tingling skin and the raised hair at her nape.

A pleasant-looking young man standing behind the counter smiled. "F'sure you got the Sight, *chere*." Cassie was certain her expression made him think her IQ had dropped precipitously the moment she'd entered the shop, because he added patiently, "Julie's our res'dent haint, and usually don't never mess wit da customers da minute dey walk in da door."

Once she'd mentally translated this into language she

understood, true curiosity prompted her to ask, "How did you know I felt a presence?"

"Dat look on yo face, *chere*. Like someone pesterin' you, but ya too polite ta get yosef shut a him. Or in dis case, her."

Based on her knowledge of the words *pestering* and *polite*, Cassie deduced that the clerk thought she wouldn't be rude to someone who was bothering her. She immediately warmed to this fine judge of character. By now, the two customers at the counter were staring, and she felt herself flush. "Julie?"

"Dat's our haint's name." The clerk gestured to the back of the tea room. "George Rodriguez gave us dat portrait of her. 'Course, dat's his interpetation a what he thinks she looked like. She died a couple hunnerd years ago."

Cassie moved to study the painting up close. A young, beautiful woman of color wearing a fashionable gown of that bygone era stared back at her. Cassie's awareness of her surroundings faded, and while the clerk launched into the tragic story of the mistress who died in a futile attempt to prove herself worthy to marry her lover, Cassie saw the story in her mind's eye, heard Julie telling the tale herself. She sensed the aching cold of that long-ago December night, the feeling of chilled flesh as Julie perched naked on the roof, freezing to death before dawn came.

The vision faded, but Cassie still felt the spirit's presence. And something else.

"She has a cat, doesn't she?"

The clerk beamed. "Lordy, ya really are sensitive! Not many people pick up on da fact she got her cat wit her."

"Just an affinity for that particular animal, I guess." Cassie studied the schedule for readings. As luck would have it, the only spot available for the rest of the afternoon was in ten minutes. She signed up.

***

"A very dark force hangs over your field right now." The tarot reader, a woman who looked to be somewhere in her fifties, turned over more cards and studied them. "A man." When she looked up at Cassie, her expression showed true concern. "You'll need help in dealing with this man. His aura is dark. Purely evil."

Cassie wavered between relief that the dark force wasn't Mick and dread that the serial killer was. "Purely evil" described that monster completely. She signaled with a wordless nod for the reading to continue.

"You possess unique skills, special powers. But until recently you haven't been interested in developing them. In fact, you've purposely ignored most of them."

"Go on."

Julie's presence returned as Cassie listened to the reading. Her hair was riffled, and her right cheek tingled with energy. She felt a brushing against her right leg, as if Endora were greeting her in the time-honored feline way. Her hand was halfway down to scratch her greeter behind the ears when she remembered this particular feline didn't require a human touch. She smiled wryly to herself and returned her attention to the tarot cards.

"Julie bothering ya, *chere*?"

"Not in the least."

With a nod, the psychic looked down to her cards, arranged between Cassie and her. "There's also emotional conflict on another level." This time she smiled. "You're in love, but worried your lover won't accept you for what and who you are."

Cassie almost didn't catch her jaw before it dropped wide open. Then she managed a half-smile. "You've got that right."

Once all the cards were arranged, the reader leaned back in her chair and leveled her faded blue eyes at Cassie. "Great danger is very close. Please don't disregard this warning."

"I won't. Believe me, I wouldn't be here if I thought you were frauds. Any suggestions?"

"Accept yourself for yourself. Let your love see you for who you are. If you can do that, then you'll overcome the danger, and the troubles you now face in your relationship."

Relief flooded Cassie. Problems still lay in wait, but Medusa had been right about how knowing what the problems were made them easier to face. She rose from her chair.

"Thanks for the advice."

"My pleasure."

Halfway out of the curtained-off reading area, Cassie turned back. "How did you know I've got certain . . . skills?"

The reader chuckled. "*Chere*, your aura looks like solar flares, you've got so much power."

"Really?"

"Yeah, you right."

Cassie blinked, then smiled in understanding. Her question had been answered in the affirmative. "Thanks again." On her way to the front of the shop she stopped at Julie's portrait. "And thanks to you, too, Julie." Instantly, she was wrapped in an embrace of pure energy which felt like a quick hug. Apparently, Bottom of the Cup's resident haint was lending her support to

Cassie's quest.

She chose to walk back to the hotel, not from dread of facing Mick, but because she needed time to process her newfound knowledge. Being in the Quarter helped her do just that. Understanding dawned as to her family's love of this city. It was completely unique, filled with paranormal power and totally at ease with that power. Like her relatives. Like Endora.

And so unlike herself.

Her mother had many friends in the Crescent City—fellow witches, voodoo practitioners, probably some zombies . . . Cassie laughed to herself at that silly notion. Although in this amazing place zombies might well exist. Many very real paranormal and supernatural beings dwelled here, enough to make life amazingly exciting. Medusa had actually known Marie Laveau, the Voodoo Queen of New Orleans. Cassie was willing to bet several decades off her life that Marie knew how to party. Mardi Gras when she was alive would have been even crazier than it was at present.

She had to admit she'd intentionally avoided this city exactly because it was so steeped in the supernatural. Had she embraced her heritage, she would have reveled in the paranormal excesses here. She sighed mentally. Why had she allowed aversion to her true nature to keep her away? Exposure to so much cosmic energy still frightened her, but now as she came to grips with her true self, she understood the basis for her fears. She lacked confidence in her magickal abilities. She'd never trusted herself in channeling her powers. Understanding this lifted a huge burden. Knowing what caused her fears would allow her to master them.

And what of her mother's confession? She'd loved a human! The thought was almost as staggering as Medusa's accepting Cassie's love for Mick. Relief lightened Cassie's heart.

She sincerely hoped she'd someday share her family's level of comfort with what they—and she—were. She'd made headway in that area, but much was yet to be done.

***

Plans were progressing far more quickly than he'd hoped. Once he'd gotten over his rage, once he'd again set a goal and focused on attaining it, things began falling into place. As they had countless times before.

Soon, the stage would be set for his final spectacular demonstration. The crowning achievement in his astonishing success.

Too bad he wouldn't perform this spectacular climax for his one-time idol. Oh no. He'd perform it on him.

Thirteen

Mick figured Cassie would head directly back to her suite at some point, so he'd camped out on her sofa. If it took next to forever, he wasn't planning on going anywhere else until they'd worked out their problems. Endora's advice still rang in his mind, and he tried to formulate his case, backed by clear-headed and solid reasoning, to present to Cassie when she arrived. But fear blocked his logic, casting everything out but complete terror at the thought that she'd just turn him into some slimy creature and leave him to his fate. His stomach lining was threatening to disintegrate, and he fought the urge to pace frantically around the suite. If Cassie didn't get there soon, he'd have no nerve left.

Just when he was about to pound something in frustration, Endora abruptly snapped to attention. Startled, Mick dropped the copy of *When Dust Bunnies Attack* he'd been trying to escape into for the last hour. He cocked a brow at her as he bent to retrieve the book from under the coffee table. "Neural twitch?"

"Cassie's coming." Endora, now on her feet, shot Mick a glance over her shoulder. "Luckily for you, alone."

Mick hadn't realized Medusa'd had him worried until he felt his shoulders relax at those words. Trying to deal with Cassie would be enough of a handful. He didn't need the Wicked Witch of the West in the room with them. He studied Endora as she moved to the refrigerator for a bottle of water. "Should I be here?"

Endora took a long drink of the hideously overpriced beverage. "I don't sense any agitation, so this is likely the best chance you're going to get. Better now than later."

He suddenly couldn't think of how to act. Should he be sitting? Feet propped up? Reading her book? No, that would look like he was angling to get on her good side. Which he was. He rejected reading as too obvious. Or too desperate. Maybe standing. If so, where?

"Take a few deep breaths," Endora advised kindly. "You look ready to pass out."

"It humiliates me to admit I just might."

The familiar's stunning green eyes rolled. "You volunteer to be serial-killer bait but can't face your girlfriend after you have a fight? You are one pathetic human."

Mick was too nervous to be insulted. "I, I guess I've never been in love before. Cassie's the most important thing in my life . . . What if I blow it with her? I—"

"Did you write down what you wanted to say?"

"Shit no!" Mick started to pace. "I haven't been able to concentrate. I'm just so—"

"Breathe!" Endora must have taken pity on him because she smiled with genuine warmth. "You don't need a prepared speech. Listen to your heart and be honest about your feelings. Things will be fine."

"Thanks, Endora."

"And if you completely screw up, I'll be around to clean up the mess." She quirked a brow at him. "That's the mess I'll make when I kill you."

To Mick's stressed nerves, her laugh sounded more evil than lighthearted. Some day, Endora's teasing might tempt him to toss her into the air to see if she landed on her feet. But with his luck, she'd land on his head in cat form, and he'd die instantly from a massive allergic reaction.

Fortunately, thoughts of paybacks steadied him somewhat. He'd just gotten his breathing under control when the lock rattled and the door opened. His heart rate kicked up to wind-sprint levels as he waited for Cassie to enter.

A plush purple alligator head appeared in the gap between door and doorframe.

Mick shot Endora a quick glance, but the familiar was already moving toward the creature. "What's this, Barney does Bourbon Street?" she asked with a laugh.

"Hey purty lady," the 'gator said in a voice strikingly similar to Cassie's with a Cajun accent, "wanna suck da haids uh some crawfish wit me?"

"Oooooh, *chere,*" Endora purred. "Ya know I jus' love seafood." She seized the toy and pulled Cassie into the room with it. "But I think dis gonna be jus a date wit me an Barney here." She glanced over her shoulder. "Yuze got mo impotent thangs ta do dis aftahnoon."

With that, she grabbed the alligator, spun behind Cassie and pushed her toward the center of the room, leaving her staring at Mick as he rose from the chair.

Cassie could hear her pulse thundering in her ears as she drank in Mick's handsome features. She shot a look over her shoulder. "Cross to the other camp, Dora?"

"Absolutely not, Boss," Endora stated with false adamancy. "Just guarding him until you could interrogate him. Remember, you're on your own to clean up any blood you spill." She indicated the stuffed alligator. "Cajun Barney and I have a hot date. See ya'll at the reception tonight."

Just like that, she was gone.

Moving seemed to have become a motor skill Cassie couldn't master, although her mind was screaming at her feet to close the gap between Mick and her. His stillness mirrored her affliction. He'd stood, looking totally at a loss as to what to say, when she entered but hadn't taken a single step further. Like him, she couldn't seem to form coherent sentences.

"Mick—"

"Cassie—" he said at the same time.

They both broke off, standing tongue-tied and awkward.

Say you love him, she commanded herself. *Ask him if he can live with what you are.*

Easier thought than done. So much depended on his answer, she couldn't force herself to ask the question.

Speak from your heart, human.

Endora's voice in his head startled Mick into action. "God, I feel like I'm in junior high again," he blurted out. "Nothing I want to say to you comes out of my mouth."

Words broke both the silence and their frozen tableau.

As he moved to the wet bar, inspiration hit, and Mick shot her a glance. "Can I buy you a drink, *chere*?" Her slight smile encouraging, he rummaged through the refrigerator. "Let's see . . . lots of cream, but you'd likely have Endora in a snit if you drank it. Imported beers and a very fine merlot. Orange juice if you're not up for alcohol . . . ." He looked up at Cassie. "All right, I'm officially babbling. Say something to shut me up."

She took two shaky steps toward him. "Like what? 'There are more things in heaven and earth, Horatio, than are dreamt of in your philosophy'?"

Mick set a bottle of beer atop the bar and reached out to cup her cheek. "I prefer 'oh brave new world that has such people in it.'" He sighed as she leaned into his touch. "I love you so much, Cassandra Hathorne."

"Enough to ignore the fact that I'm a bonafide witch?" Despite her best efforts at nonchalance, her words sounded strained.

He looked straight into her eyes, gaze so intense it almost made her weep. "I refuse to ignore that fact." When she started to speak, he quickly put his finger to her lips. "I'm not afraid of what you are, Cass, but I'll need time to learn what it all means. And be warned—I have every intention of understanding you completely."

At his words, a huge burden left her. She smiled tentatively. "I don't think men are capable of completely understanding women. But feel free to try with me."

"Oh, I will." He grinned then pulled her into a loose, one-armed embrace.

"Here's something to think about." She kissed his chin. "That nose-twitching thing they did on *Bewitched*? Strictly Hollywood."

"I figured that." He laughed softly, then sobered. "Nothing I said last night came out the way it should have, Cass. And I didn't say the most important thing." He circled her waist with both arms and pulled her close. "I didn't say 'I love you.'"

"You said that a minute ago."

"And I'm going to keep on saying it until you believe it."

As she stared into his grave eyes, her doubts went up in smoke. She hugged him tight. "I love you, too, Mick."

"Will you still love me when I say I'm quitting my writing career?"

She could feel the sudden tension in his body, see the strain in his face. "What brought you to that decision?"

He relaxed marginally at her question. "With all that's happened . . . The serial killer copycatting my work . . . I just can't keep writing horror novels." The look in his eyes was one of pure longing when he asked, "Can you live with a *former New York Times* best-seller?"

"I doubt I'll be living with one long." His shocked expression made her take pity on him. She hugged his waist, then nipped his chin with her teeth. "You're a writer, Mick. That's the core of your being. You may leave the horror genre, but you'll never leave writing. And your brilliance will shine through in whatever type of writing you do."

His fierce embrace nearly drove the air from her lungs. "God, I love you so much, woman. I should have known you'd understand."

"Only writers truly understand other writers."

"Will you marry me?" His face fell when she stepped back, pulling from his arms. "Please don't walk away before we've talked."

Moving quickly, she plopped down on the sofa and looked up at him. "I don't plan to. It's just that I . . . Well, I . . . um . . . " Her cheeks suddenly felt hot. Taking a deep breath, she swallowed hard before baldly stating, "I can't think at all when you're holding me." Now her whole face burned. "All I can think of is sex."

He had the audacity to laugh as he grabbed his beer and moved to a chair opposite the sofa, body language radiating smug pleasure. "And that's a bad thing, how?"

"Don't get all cocky on me, lover boy," she admonished, smiling. "You said yourself we need to talk about this marriage thing. If I can't get my mind off anything but your body, no way I'll contribute thoughtful comments to a crucial discussion."

"I've got the same problem," Mick stated, mischief lighting his blue eyes. "You drive me wild and, unfortunately, there's not enough blood in the male body to power both the brain and the genitals simultaneously. So let's make love first, get it out of our systems, then talk."

Cassie practically leaped from her seat and threw herself at him. "Works for me."

They both laughed like naughty children as he caught her up and carried her to bed.

***

An hour later they were sufficiently relaxed that confronting their problems was possible. Propped against the headboard, Mick cradled Cassie to his chest.

"Have you ever compared notes with Sting," she asked, lazily running her hand across his pecs. "I can't imagine him being better at this than you are."

Mick caught her hand and brought it to his lips. "Lofty praise, indeed. Next time I see Gordon, I'll have to talk to him about his legendary sexual technique."

She glanced up at him. "You're on a first-name basis?"

"Actually, yeah. But, hey, met one superstar musician, met 'em all. Just like best-selling authors. I'd much rather convince you to marry me than discuss Sting's Tantric strategies." He grew still for a moment. "You told me our lovemaking is magic, and instead of acknowledging the truth, I said some really nasty things. I was wrong. What we have between us *is* magic, and I'm selfish enough to want to keep that for the rest of our lives."

She sighed. "I want to marry you, but—"

"Hush." Mick squeezed her tight. "Before you list all the reasons against us, let me tell you a story."

"Is it true, or a product of your amazing imagination?"

"Absolutely true." He shifted a bit to arrange the pillows behind him. "Back in Slovakia my great-uncle Teodore married a Rom. A Gypsy. Despite a complete lack of support from either family, they married in the mid-nineteen twenties."

Her hand stopped caressing his chest. "Did your grandmother

oppose the marriage, too?"

"*YaYa* had come to the States right after the first World War and wasn't even in Slovakia. Her three older brothers, Teodore included, stayed in Europe. The brothers and their families were enraged Teo had married Magda without their blessings."

"Why? Aren't Gypsies also Catholic?"

"That didn't matter. They were outcasts. But Aunt Magda's background didn't stop Teo. He married the woman he loved, family opinion be damned. For years they lived in Prague, where he taught linguistics at the university. He also occasionally was a visiting professor in Warsaw."

Cassie sat straight up. "By the Goddess, the Nazis were rounding up Polish intellectuals at that time."

"Exactly. And that's where Great-aunt Magda becomes a heroine. She had 'The Sight,' as the Rom call ESP. In November of Thirty-eight, she had a vision. In it, the Germans captured and killed Teo's entire family, including him and Magda. Since he was an intellectual and his brothers government officials, the danger was very real. She convinced him they couldn't remain in Europe, that they all had to make their way to the States or face certain annihilation."

Cassie found that she could barely breathe as Mick's story unfolded. "Did Teo's brothers believe her?"

"They weren't stupid. They'd heard the rumors, seen what was happening to the Jews, Gypsies, political dissidents. They converted their assets into gold and snuck out of Europe in Thirty-nine, just as the Nazis were occupying Bohemia and Moravia. And placing Slovakia under 'protection.' They had several close calls, but Magda's sight kept them ahead of their pursuers at every turn. In August, they arrived in New York. In September, Hitler invaded Poland."

"And World War Two started." Cassie let out a long sigh. "What an incredible story."

Mick took her face in both hands and kissed her tenderly. "You see? My family not only believes in but respects powers beyond the normal human's. Both my sisters and several of my cousins are psychic, and even though none practice professionally, not a single relative mocks their abilities. Or doesn't believe them."

"So, you're saying if I show up at a family gathering and telekinetically burn all the food to ashes, they'll just laugh it off?"

"I wouldn't go that far." Mick couldn't keep a twinkle from

his eyes when he stated, "It's extremely dangerous to come between a Slovak and his meal. We're a forgiving people, but not in regard to food."

Cassie's grin faded. "You're not lying to me, are you?"

She immediately found herself crushed to Mick's chest.

"God, no. How can you even ask that question?" He kissed her forehead. "I love you. My family will love you."

"I've barely come to terms with what I am," she whispered against his shoulder. "It's hard to believe strangers will accept me."

"Believe it." He shifted to see her eyes. "Come to think of it, you might not want to announce to all and sundry that you're a real witch. All my adolescent relatives will likely think it's so cool they'll constantly pester you to cast spells."

She lifted her head from his shoulder and looked up at him. "Maybe I should meet your family before deciding how to approach the situation."

She could feel Mick catch his breath.

"Does this mean you'll marry me?"

"This isn't going to be simple, Mick. I'm not easy to live with. Ask Endora."

He exhaled. "I was raised to believe that anything worth having is worth working for. Don't you think our love qualifies?"

"Absolutely." She flashed a huge smile. "Now, I just have to convince my family to accept your puny human ass."

"Shit! I forgot about them." Mick ran his fingers back through his hair. "Now what?"

Laughing, Cassie gave him a brief peck on the cheek. "Relax. Endora's in your corner. That's a major plus. And even more important, my mother's on our side."

"You're kidding."

Cassie shook her head. "She's really the only relative whose approval you need. So we're good to go."

"That calls for a celebration." Mick glanced at the clock. "It's six. We don't have to make an appearance until eight . . . ."

Cassie arched a brow. "Going for Sting's record now, are we?"

"I'm definitely up for trying."

Growling, Cassie launched herself at him.

Fourteen

Despite Cassie's assurances that he had Medusa's approval, Mick's nerves were stretched taut. A man would have to be completely insane not to dread meeting his future mother-in-law, especially when the term "she's a real witch" meant exactly that. He found himself swallowing around a softball-sized lump as he watched the formidable woman approach across the ballroom. Thank God Cassie had invited her to the booksellers' reception. Now, she couldn't really turn him into a slug or anything without someone noticing. Of course, he couldn't prevent awful things from happening later, but right then he felt somewhat safe.

Cassie touched his forearm, and the energy that passed from her hand felt like the old static electricity machine he had played with in junior high science classes. He vaguely wondered if he'd cause a spark by breaking contact, but for a couple of reasons didn't want to test the idea. First, everyone would notice a spark. Second, he needed all the confidence he could muster for this meeting, and Cassie's touch helped tremendously in that department.

Apparently, Medusa had shed her usual flamboyant apparel for the reception. She wore a gothic-styled black dress decorated with subtle astrological symbols stitched in thin, silver thread, and a heavy silver necklace with matching earrings fashioned in a Celtic love knot pattern. Simple in its elegance, the outfit suited her perfectly.

In contrast, Cassie wore an emerald business suit, white blouse and sensible emerald flats. The skirt, just a few inches above the knee, didn't show as much of her spectacular legs as Mick would have preferred, but this was, after all, a business function. Besides, if any of those horny old booksellers scoped out his fiancée's legs, he'd be forced into suitably Neanderthal mode and plant a fist in one of their smirking faces. He doubted that would impress Medusa.

Cassie obviously sensed his growing nervousness. She took a half step in front of him and reached to embrace her mother, kissing the older witch on both cheeks. Then she turned to Mick.

"Mother, I want to officially introduce you to Mirek Sandor, known to his fans as M. S. Kazimer. Mick, my mother, Medusa Bishop."

Mick grasped Medusa's hand, barely keeping from pulling it back when contact with her fingers felt like he'd grabbed a joy buzzer. "Pleased to meet you, Mrs. Bishop," he ground out between clenched teeth, happy he didn't yelp in pain or stumble through his acknowledgment. His palm vibrated like a live wire. Were all witches closet stand-up comedians and practical jokers?

"You're not at all pleased to see me," Medusa countered smoothly, releasing his hand. "You're as nervous as a cat on a hot tin roof." She glanced over at Endora, "No offense, Dora."

Mick hadn't realized Endora had flanked him opposite Cassie. "None taken."

"Mother—"

Black eyes that seemed to crackle with energy shifted focus. "Cassandra, dear, I'm merely sporting with your man. How will he fit into the family if he can't take a joke?"

That comment answered his question. Knowing Cassie would jump to his defense if he let her, Mick seized Medusa's hand, brought it to his lips and softly kissed her knuckles. "I think it only fair to warn you, Mrs. Bishop," he said softly, raising his gaze to meet Medusa's over their joined hands, "check your chair before sitting. I'm unmatched with a whoopie cushion."

Medusa's startled look gave way to a genuine smile. "Call me Medusa, Mick."

"Why don't we get a table and sit for a while?" Cassie suggested.

Mick sensed her relief that he'd easily countered her mother's outrageous behavior, and his nervousness eased. "Good idea. I'll get the drinks."

He memorized everyone's order and headed off to the bar. When he returned ten minutes later, Medusa, Cassie and Endora were seated at a round table near the buffet. The plush purple alligator with the green swamp hat sat on the table in front of Endora, Special Agent Robert Jamison next to her. Cassie and Medusa were opposite them. Curiously, no one else was within hearing distance. It didn't take Mick long to guess why they had such amazing privacy, but he wasn't going to dwell on his conclusion. Cassie had left a seat for him between her and her mother, and after delivering the drinks, Mick took it.

He'd barely settled when Medusa began speaking directly to him. All vestiges of outrageous behavior disappeared as she addressed both him and the table at large.

"Cassie has told me the real reason for this book tour," she stated without preamble. "And I want you to know, Mick—and Agent Jamison—that I will do whatever is in my power to help. I can also call on dozens of local friends—many in the Craft, many Voodoo practitioners, and many psychics—to help if need be."

Jamison shifted, looking uncomfortable. "I, uhm, appreciate your offer, Mrs. Bishop, but I'm not authorized to allow civilians to help in this operation."

Medusa raised a razor-sharp brow. "The authors on this tour are all trained Federal agents?" She shot a glance at Cassie. "Odd. My daughter failed to mention her new career."

"Point taken," Jamison conceded. "But, with the exception of Mick, the authors are window dressing."

"Be that as it may, they are involved. My daughter is involved. That prompts my motherly concerns. And my offer of help."

Jamison flushed and obviously tried to avoid running his finger under his collar to loosen it. "With respect, ma'am, if civilians hung around, interfering with my agents, this operation would be impossible to run."

"I understand your position, Agent Jamison," Medusa said on a rather predatory-looking smile. "But you won't even know we're there unless we choose to reveal ourselves."

"Take her word for it," Cassie interjected, "Mom's the real deal. What you saw in the Peabody lobby a couple nights ago is nothing to what she can do." She hoped the pride she felt in her mother's abilities shone in her eyes as she turned her look to Medusa. For once, Cassie's heritage wasn't something she felt uncomfortable acknowledging. That realization was incredibly liberating.

Mick gave Cassie's hand a quick squeeze, telling her he understood the significance of her statement. If possible, her heart swelled with even more love for him. When he firmly told Jamison he wanted Medusa informed of the FBI's plans, Cassie knew exactly how the Grinch felt following his Whoville reformation.

"I can't do that," Jamison protested, glaring at Mick, then at the three women at the table.

"My dear boy." Medusa interjected just enough lofty pretense into her tone to draw the agent's immediate attention. "Whether you choose to tell me or not is irrelevant. I'll simply read your thoughts and learn your plans that way."

The usually unflappable Jamison was on his feet. "That's outrageous!" He glared at them. "You're all crazy."

"No," Cassie interjected wryly, "that would be Uncle Mordecai. He was so obsessed with Eleanor Roosevelt that he transformed himself into a pair of her shoes in order to always be close to her. Unfortunately, FDR's dog Falla chewed him to pieces."

Robert Jamison looked like he'd been poleaxed, but Medusa and Endora beamed obvious approval at Cassie.

She took in their expressions and stated flatly, "Hey, I didn't completely ignore our family history. Give me a break."

Jamison looked toward heaven in an obvious appeal to a higher power then, on a sigh said, "All right, you win." He glanced around at the other guests.

"Don't worry," Medusa said serenely. "No one except those sitting at this table can hear what's discussed."

Robert blinked, then looked back at Mick and the others. "Well, I . . ."

Medusa raised her brow again.

"All right," With what sounded suspiciously like a *harrumph*, Jamison sat back down and leaned toward them. "This is our plan of attack . . . ."

***

Fifteen minutes later, after Jamison had finished his debriefing and walked away on the pretext of having work to do, Mick met his future mother-in-law's shrewd gaze and said, "Thank you, Medusa. You have no idea how much I appreciate your offer to help."

The older witch gave him her best enigmatic smile. "Oh, I think I do." She rose from the table and moved behind Mick to Cassie. "Darling, I really must be going. I'm supposed to meet Mandrake at midnight down in the Quarter. Some haunted history tour he wants to take." She laughed. "As if I don't know all the haunted places in this city."

Cassie rose to kiss her mother; Mick stood also.

"Mick, I'll do everything I can to help you catch this killer." Medusa placed the index and middle fingers of her left hand on either side of her nose and stated solemnly, "Witch's honor."

While Endora stifled a giggle, Cassie admonished, "Mother—"

"It's all right, Cass," Mick interrupted. He gently grasped her elbow, never taking his eyes off Medusa. "I know that's just television hokum. Your mother's testing me a bit."

Both of Medusa's eyebrows rose, and her voice was filled with genuine respect when she said, "I think I like you, Mick."

"Good, because I'm not going away. Not by choice, at any rate."

"Well said, human. Tah, darlings." With a wave of her hand, Medusa was gone.

Despite his resolve not to let anything he saw shock him, the witch's theatrical exit rattled Mick. "Jesus, Mary and Joseph," he muttered under his breath. "Did anyone else see that?"

"If they did, they won't remember it," Cassie assured him. She tucked her hand into the crook of his elbow and turned him toward the buffet. "Time to mix and mingle, oh New-York-Times-best-selling author." She had to tug him to get him to move.

"Can *you* do that?"

Cassie shrugged. "I doubt it. I'm way out of practice, and Mom's incredibly skilled. That's a trick not many witches will even attempt."

Mick was finding it hard to take his eyes off the spot where Medusa had been standing moments before. "She made it look like some movie special effect."

"Like I said, she's incredible. Don't expect every witch you meet to have that ability. Only a few can pull it off." She tugged harder. "Come on. I'm starving, and we have to do the PR thing here tonight, or they'll kick us off the tour."

"Fat chance of that happening, but where there's life there's hope."

Cassie gave him a wry smile. "In case you didn't notice, things just tilted heavily in the good guys' favor here tonight." She grabbed a plate and selected several warm appetizers. "Mom's got some very heavy artillery at her disposal. Her contacts in New Orleans alone reads like a Witchcraft and Voodoo Hall of Fame lineup."

"There's only one witch I'm really interested in," Mick murmured as he stepped up behind her. "And she's eying the fried chicken even as we speak."

"What can I say?" Cassie grabbed two drumsticks and set them on her plate. "You have amazingly good taste."

"It would be hypocritical to deny it."

Across the street, a cold-blooded killer sat plotting his final act, the *piece de resistance* of five years of destruction. At last having discovered the true purpose of this book tour, he had memorized the hotel's layout, including which rooms housed each of the tour's participants. It had taken amazingly little effort to find that information. As New Orleans was the last stop on this tour, he knew the trap would be set for him at the site of the last murder in *Mortal Sin*. The FBI had no idea just how final a stop this would prove to be. He laughed at the stupidity of the agents guarding his former idol from him. With their profilers and psychologists and mental illness dossiers, they thought they knew him. Thought they could predict his next move. Their efforts would be in vain, as his brilliance at misdirection would assure they looked in the wrong place. It would prove to be a fatal mistake for the greatest of them.

All was in readiness. All awaited the appropriate time, now only a scant few hours away. He would go over every detail one last time.

And then he would rest until the time came to kill again.

Leaving the latest tour function at a reasonably appropriate time, Cassie, Mick and Endora found a quiet corner of the bar to have a nightcap.

He picked at the label on his bottle of ale. "Endora, your being the bait for Jamison's scheme makes me really uncomfortable."

"Thanks for the concern, Mick," Endora said coolly, "but I think I can handle myself."

"You know that's not the issue. I don't want you in danger. Being right on the front line certainly isn't a safe spot."

Cassie placed a pacifying hand on Mick's shoulder, then turned to her familiar. "I've got to agree with Mick on this one, Dora."

Endora took a gulp of her kahlua and cream then licked the moustache off her upper lip. But her usually saucy smirk was nowhere to be seen. "There's nothing you can do to stop me this time, Boss. So don't even try."

Mick sensed Cassie's tension even before her grip on his arm conveyed it.

"Dora—"

"Not negotiable, Cass." Endora set her drink down with a dull thud, grabbed the purple 'gator from the small table they sat around and tucked it under her arm. "This is an opportunity I'd be a fool to pass up."

"But, Dora, what if—"

"Don't!" Endora was on her feet and backing away. "Just don't say anything. Not a word." Her raised hand stopped Cassie's argument before it left her lips. "If you say something, I'm going to second-guess myself, and I can't afford to do that. You know I have no choice."

She turned and fled.

"What in hell was that all about?"

Cassie's sigh was pure melancholy. "Atonement."

"Atonement for what?"

Cassie leaned her head on Mick's shoulder, still watching the door Endora had practically flown through. "You wouldn't understand."

"Are you kidding? I'm Catholic. We wrote the book on atonement." Cassie's slight chuckle encouraged him. "I don't want to pry, but this sounds like a really big deal for her."

"It is." Cassie straightened from her comfortable position on Mick's shoulder and motioned to their server. "Check, please." As the server headed to the bar, Cassie faced Mick. "It's Endora's story to tell, but I can give you a sketch. She must make reparation for a very serious past indiscretion. Apparently, she feels helping in Jamison's sting will count toward her debt." She shrugged. "I assumed being the bait appealed to her sense of irony. And that maybe in part she wanted a payback for the killer's hurting her so badly in St. Louis. I'd never heard her say she was thinking in another direction until just now."

Mick's gaze sharpened. "The killer attacked her in St. Louis?" When Cassie nodded, an expression of understanding lit his face. "That whole incident in the lobby, when I could have sworn I lost fifteen minutes."

Another nod. "I'll fill you in on all the details some other time. Suffice it to say that, when I told you Endora wasn't feeling well, it was the result of the killer hurling her against a wall while she was in feline form."

"My God. It's a good thing you were close by."

"Even then, I almost lost her." Cassie felt her throat tightening. Tears stung her eyes.

Immediately, Mick's arm was around her shoulders, and he was hugging her close. "She's all right, baby," he soothed. He held her for a moment. "Is she in a lot of trouble for this old indiscretion?"

Cassie smiled as she pulled from his embrace. "Telling you any more would betray her confidence. You'll have to ask her, as it's not my place to say."

"It's the old 'I can tell you, but then I'd have to kill you' deal, right?"

"Something like that."

Mick nodded. "I can respect your loyalty to her. She's a good friend. Tell her I hope things work out."

"You should tell her yourself. She values your opinion, just in case you didn't know that." Cassie signed the drink bill and handed it back to the server. Then turned to Mick and whispered seductively, "Let's get out of these stifling clothes and into nothing but silk sheets."

He smiled. "If this is how you distract me from the fact you just picked up the tab, it's working."

"Good."

***

Miles away, a small motel near the Fontainebleau State Park on the northern shore of Lake Pontchartrain experienced an unusual lack of vacancies and an even more unusual level of activity for a late March night. Ten vehicles, ranging from sedans to huge delivery-style trucks, filled the parking lot. Fifty people buzzed around the vehicles and the strip of fifteen guest rooms.

Endora fretted while an FBI technician showed her how to attach a surveillance wire to her chest. She and Jamison had agreed that her psychic abilities would not be revealed to the rest of the team, making the ritual of wearing a wire necessary to maintain the ruse.

"Glad I'm not built like Dolly Parton," she cracked. "The metal from her underwire would likely cause amazing static."

"Actually, just the opposite," the technician said placidly. "It's more like using twin broadcast towers."

Endora gaped at the woman who had just finished securing Endora's mic and was checking the pick up volume. "Dolly goes undercover? As *what*, a Dolly Parton impersonator?"

The technician laughed. "I was joking."

"Somehow, that knowledge disappoints me," Endora replied. "Knowing Dolly, she could pull something like that off, and I'd certainly pay good money to see her try."

"Believe me, so would every man on this team." The tech grinned wickedly. "And they'd all volunteer to put the wire on her, too."

Endora snorted. "I'll bet."

She was just pulling on her jacket when Jamison entered the

small guest room. More somber than she'd ever seen him, he unconsciously fidgeted with his tie. It amused her that he didn't seem to be able to meet her eyes.

Finally, his gaze zeroed in on hers, intense. "Ready?"

Endora gave him her patented bland, feline stare. "Yes."

"You sure you want to go through with this—" That tie fidget again.

She waved away his concerns, but her tone was deadly serious when she said, "Look, Jamison, this bastard is scum and deserves to go down. He nearly killed me, threatens my boss and the man she loves, and has murdered innocent people. I'd kill him myself if it wouldn't result in countless uncomfortable questions. The good guys need a win here." *I need a win here. Big time.* "So don't give me that 'In the event you are unable to perform your duties, the First Runner Up will take your place' crap. I'm not buying."

All fidgeting and nervousness stopped. "I don't want you to get hurt. This guy's hurt way too many civilians already."

"Not me," Endora stated. *Not again, anyway.* She buttoned her jacket at the waist and shot her wrists out the sleeves. "Last time he caught me by surprise. This time, he won't have that advantage."

Jamison hunched his shoulders in a sign of resignation. "I'm just trying to do my job."

"I know." Endora smiled with real warmth. "And I'm trying to do mine."

"Let's get to it, then."

With a saucy look, she tucked her hand through the crook of his elbow. "Lead on, oh Fearless Leader."

Jamison's glare at the technician dared the woman to make a comment. She refrained.

***

As planned, the tour's authors met the local book sellers at a grand reception. The hotel where they were lodged hosted the elegant event which boasted a Mardi Gras theme. It coincided with the sting operation miles away at Lake Pontchartrain.

"Well, that's the last time I'll ever do that," Mick commented as he squired Cassie back to his suite.

"You mean, you won't come to any of *my* book seller receptions? " she teased.

He laughed. "Of course. I meant the last one where I'm the bug under glass."

"Yuk." Cassie screwed up her face in mock horror.

Mick laughed again and planted a quick kiss on her nose. "I love you."

If she hadn't so completely shared Mick's sentiment, she might have been forewarned. But, intent on her love as they walked hand-in-hand, she failed to notice that no FBI agents guarded the penthouse elevator lobby. Or the ends of the corridor. Completely missed the aura of evil tainting the hallway air, so poisonous it had a dark color of its own.

As it was, she never even sensed the blow that caught her behind the right ear and smashed her head in. Suddenly boneless, she fell to the hallway carpet so quickly and silently, Mick took another step before he realized she'd let go of his hand.

"Cass—" He turned to look over his right shoulder and saw a man dressed like an FBI agent raising a ball bat to strike again. Mick had only a split second to register the blood in Cassie's dark hair before he leaped over her inert body and charged her attacker. "You sonuvabitch!"

Using his lean two-hundred fifteen pounds like a battering ram, he hit his enemy with a cross-body block that drove him into the wall. The force sent the bat flying. Both men dove for it. Grunting and swearing, they rolled on the carpet, grappling for possession of the weapon. Mick had a definite size advantage, but his opponent fought as if literally possessed, negating Mick's physical edge.

They thrashed down the hallway back toward the elevator, neither gaining the upper hand. Then Mick decided to use his bare hands rather than a club. Straddling Cassie's attacker, he grabbed him by the shirt collar and cocked back his fist, ready to break every bone in the bastard's face.

He never threw the punch.

Searing heat suddenly raced up his thigh from just above his knee, and he looked down to see a hypodermic needle the size of a B-horror movie prop sticking out of his leg. Just that quickly, he felt himself losing all muscle control. "You mother-fu . . . ."

The killer rolled away before Mick crashed down on top of him. Rising slowly, he straightened his very official-looking, government issue suit coat and adjusted his tie. Then he meticulously checked each piece of clothing to assure no blood had soiled them when he'd struck M. S. Kazimer's whore girlfriend. Skull fractures inflicted by baseball bats were rarely neat. He glanced over to see a widening pool of blood beneath the woman's head.

Pity he'd killed her. It might have been amusing to torture her in front of Kazimer, to prolong that faithless swine's horrified anticipation as he was given a graphic preview of his own fate. But two unconscious people would have proved far too problematical. He'd have to sacrifice the amount of enjoyment to be derived from making her last hours on earth agonizing in the extreme. Of course, M. S. Kazimer would suffer unspeakably before being allowed to die. Thus was the fate of those who betrayed their faithful worshipers.

He bent to lift his victim in a fireman's carry. Then he disappeared into the nearest service elevator to begin their descent into hell.

***

"Medusa, she's coming to."

A voice Cassie didn't recognize penetrated the wall of pain substituting for her skull, reverberating—though likely a mere whisper—like a launch pad at liftoff. She couldn't help it. She groaned. Loudly.

Instantly, a hand caressed her forehead. She knew without looking it was her mother's. As Medusa chanted in a low voice, Cassie's pain subsided dramatically. She opened her eyes a crack. The small room was typical of an older house in The Quarter—high-ceilinged, with elegant French doors that led to a balcony—and the pleasant hum of positive paranormal energy. She heard the low background sound of New Age music along with a bubbling water fountain. But ambiance was the least of her concerns as her head began to clear.

"Where's Mick?"

The four strangers standing around what appeared to be some type of examination table all looked at Medusa.

Her mother's expression told Cassie the news was bad. "Abducted. About an hour ago." When Cassie made to sit up, Medusa gently restrained her. "You're in no condition to go anywhere right now." Cassie's dark look had her mother quickly relating how they'd found her very near death in the corridor outside Mick's suite. The obvious traces of a struggle had indicated he had been drugged and carried off. "You were too badly injured for me to leave you, so Mandrake volunteered to search for Mick's aura. But he's never met him . . . ."

Heart hammering with dread, Cassie couldn't manage any volume in her voice. "You must have arrived just in time to save my life," she whispered. "How'd you know we needed help?"

If anyone in the room noted that she'd used "we" instead of "I" no one commented.

Medusa sat beside her daughter on the examination table and gently smoothed her hair back from her face. "I had two very trusted friends watching of you. The moment they heard your telepathic cry, they moved in." With a sad shake of her head, Medusa added, "If they hadn't been respecting your privacy and were closer when that beast attacked, they'd likely have prevented Mick's kidnaping."

Cassie was startled to see tears well in Medusa's eyes. "Mother, stop!" She grasped her mother's hand then looked around at the circle standing attendance. "None of you are to blame here. I thank the Goddess you rescued me as quickly as you did. Otherwise . . ." She had to swallow hard to continue. "Otherwise, I doubt I'd have survived that blow."

"You have Trish to thank for that." Medusa nodded to a dark-haired, pale-skinned woman of average height standing at the foot of the examination table. "As soon as we got to you we stopped the bleeding. But your survival wasn't assured until we brought you here. Trish is the South's best energy healer and graciously treated you on short notice and at this late hour."

"I was glad I could help," Trish quietly stated.

Cassie nodded her thanks as Medusa silently gathered her in her arms and hugged her. Before her mother shut the telepathic connection between them, Cassie caught a gruesome image. A skull crumpled like a crushed aluminum can, and a pool of blood three feet across. The flood of parental horror and grief at the death of a child. Cassie knew she'd seen herself as Medusa had—lying in the hotel corridor, mere seconds from death. She also knew Medusa would never describe that scene to her, or tell her how very close she'd come to crossing over.

"Thank the Goddess for all of you." Drawing strength from her mother's embrace, she very soon pulled back. "What time is it?"

"Close to midnight," Trish stated in a calming tone.

Cassie's heart did a flip. "Mick's been gone nearly ninety minutes." She sat up gingerly, waving off Medusa's supporting hands. "All right, I survived that maniac. He's not going to kill Mick." She swung her legs off the bed, woozy but determined. "I'm going after him."

"Not alone," Medusa stated, her hand steadying on Cassie's

shoulder. "You've been badly injured. I'm coming with you."

"So are we," the other witches chorused as if they'd been auditioning for the parts of the three weird sisters in *Macbeth*.

Trish smiled wryly. "Midnight. The witching hour. A bit out of my area of expertise." She handed Cassie her jacket. "I'll stay here and see if I can locate your friend and perform a long-distance healing. He'll need the drugs he was given cleared from his field."

"It might be better if you rested up, Trish. In case we need your healing skills after we locate Mick," Medusa pointed out. "The amount of energy you expended on Cassie's behalf has likely left you very drained."

After seeing herself in Medusa's memory, Cassie had an inkling of the tremendous effort Trish had made.

"I could certainly use a nap," Trish said with a nod.

"And a strong cup of green tea."

This brief exchange bemused Cassie slightly. Trish, obviously, was outside the Craft, yet Medusa spoke to her with the tone of long acquaintance and great mutual respect. Another human her mother regarded highly. But Cassie had no time to ponder this latest revelation. Mick was in danger. Saving him took priority over all else.

She glanced around, smiling grimly. "Thank you for the help, but understand one thing. None of you are to interfere with my right to take the first crack at this bastard." She met each gaze with steel-eyed determination. "He kidnaped my fiancé and almost killed both my familiar and me. This is personal."

Medusa could hardly contain a proud smile. "Tell us what to do, Cassandra."

***

Mick awoke with the severe case of cotton mouth typical of the anaesthetized. He fought the drug, but it kept hauling his eyelids down. And when they closed, all he could see was Cassie lying in a steadily-widening pool of her own blood. That image snapped his eyes open, and he silently prayed that help would arrive before her life drained away into the motel's carpet. He'd just found her. Losing her now would kill him.

If the lunatic who'd abducted him didn't manage that first.

He couldn't fight the reflex to swallow, but doing so was agony. When had his throat been lined with sandpaper? Clamping his lips shut proved the only way to stifle the groan that desperately sought escape.

Things went downhill from there.

"Shit!"

He'd tried to raise his hand only to find himself immobilized on a type of operating table. His heart skipped a beat, and he had to force his breathing to deepen. To calm. As long as he didn't panic, he had a chance. He refused to calculate the odds, but someone always won the lottery, right?

Although he could move his head, it was difficult to see much of the room he lay in. He used his other senses. The unnatural silence seemed to indicate he was alone for the time being. Dampness and the smell of mildew indicated water, perhaps somewhere below sea level. Lake Pontchartrain? No. It was unlikely his attacker had taken him there. The killer had broken pattern—if he hadn't, Endora and Jamison would have caught him in the sting they'd set up based on the climactic murder in Mick's last book.

Instead of going after a lone woman in a back water bar near a Louisiana state park, he'd ignored the lure and gone after Mick and Cassie at the hotel.

Cassie. His throat tightened. Tears burned the backs of his eyes. God, what if he'd gotten her killed? And even if she'd survived a baseball bat to the skull, she'd likely be in some emergency room right now, fighting for life. He said a prayer that that was the case. Even if he didn't get out of this alive, at least she would.

As for the others—Endora, Jamison and most of his Feds were at the sting site. Most likely, Medusa and her colleagues were also near Lake Pontchartrain. Help was miles away, meaning Mick was completely on his own. No comfort there, considering he didn't think well on his feet. Then his rather macabre sense of the absurd kicked in, and he wryly thought that, since he wasn't exactly standing, he shouldn't have a problem.

Either he had gone completely insane from terror, or had found some kind of courage he'd always hoped he had but never had the opportunity to discover. Either way, he began smiling stupidly over his mental joke.

Then suddenly he wasn't smiling anymore. A slight noise had his pulse kicking into overdrive and a cold sweat breaking over his body in a clammy wash.

Off to his right, a door had opened.

***

Dora, get back to the hotel immediately.

Endora jerked as Cassie's voice filled her head, the urgency in her tone nearly overwhelming. Even though she knew her friend wasn't physically there, she glanced around the bar anyway. Just as she suspected, the smoke-filled room revealed no members of The Craft, known to her or otherwise. No, Cassie hadn't come in person to drag her back. But she'd summoned her just the same. Endora hissed in anger. Cassie had no idea how important doing this was to her. Of if she did understand, for some reason she didn't care.

I'm working here, Cass, she retorted. *Call me back later.*

I need you back here now, Endora.

Although Cassie couldn't see her gesture, Endora slammed her shot glass down on the bar, sending a double-shot geyser of whiskey into the air. *By the Goddess, Cass, this is the lowest you've ever sunk. I can't believe you're so set against my working this sting that you'd—*

The killer attacked Mick and me. He nearly took my head off with a ball bat, then abducted Mick.

Endora suddenly found it very difficult to breathe. *Great Mother Goddess! Are you all right?*

Yes.

The strain in Cassie's voice said it had been a near thing.

Dora, the sting won't work. The killer somehow figured out Jamison's plans, and he didn't bite.

Instead, he tried to kill you.

And now he's going to kill Mick if we can't find them and stop him.

I'm on my way.

Pulling the front of her blouse away from her chest, Endora leaned down and spoke directly into the microphone. "Jamison, the killer hit the hotel." She was off the bar stool and halfway to the back door as she added, "Take your team back to the city as fast as you can. I'm afraid you've likely got agents down."

She tore the wire from her chest, tossed it away, and had transformed to her feline state in two strides.

Inside the FBI command post, Jamison was snapping orders to his stupefied officers. "Drake, Wilkins, O'Brien—pack the com equipment and meet us at the hotel ASAP. Garcia, get out of the bar and haul ass for base." He checked his watch. "I want everyone but the com guys there in fifteen." When they sat gaping at him, he snapped, "What the hell about 'back at base in fifteen' didn't you geniuses understand? *Move!*"

The scramble behind him as he grabbed his coat and bolted

from the command truck indicated his rant had roused them from their collective stupor. He didn't look back, concentrating instead on covering the dark pavement between him and his car as quickly as possible.

* * *

Back in the Quarter, Medusa and her three friends had joined Cassie in a circle to conjure Mick's location.

Cassie swallowed hard, fighting sudden panic.

"Don't waste energy in doubt," Medusa murmured, giving Cassie's hand a squeeze. "We'll help if you need us. But the operative word is 'if.' You can do this without us, Cassandra."

"Please don't test that theory by leaving right this minute." Cassie tried to make light of her fears, but was certain everyone in the room could sense her near-desperation.

"Cleansing breath, then clear your mind," Medusa ordered. "Concentrate on Mick. Allow no distraction."

Ignoring the dull throbbing behind her right ear, Cassie closed her eyes and followed her mother's instructions. She pictured Mick in her mind's eye as they'd walked toward his suite just before the attack. He was laughing at something she'd said. Holding her hand. Then, the blow to her head had rendered her unconscious. She fought through the darkness to keep Mick in her vision. He struggled with a man dressed like an FBI agent. He was winning the fight. Then a hypodermic needle flashed. Penetrated his thigh . . . Cassie's vision faded, but just as quickly Mick reappeared in her mind. He was strapped to a table in a dank room.

Her eyes blinked open, and she looked around the circle. "I saw the ruins of an amusement park."

"Lakeshore Drive," the tallest witch answered immediately. "The old Pontchartrain Beach Amusement Park. Near UNO."

"That's at least thirty miles from where the FBI set up their operation," Medusa observed.

Dora, go to the old amusement park. Near the university on Lakeshore, Cassie relayed to her familiar. *We'll meet you there.*

The wizened little witch who looked to be older than Medusa by fifty years shook her head. "This is a total departure. He's completely broken the pattern of killings."

"And now it's up to us to make sure he never establishes another pattern," Cassie said grimly. She looked at her mother. "Any suggestions?"

"A protection spell. Now that you know where Mick is, you

can keep him safe until we arrive." When Cassie's brow shot up in disbelief, Medusa added, "You have the greatest power of all at your disposal, Cassandra. Love. Let your love for Mick strengthen your ability to protect him."

It was all Cassie could do to keep from gaping. "You haven't been reading Leo Buscaglia lately, have you Mother?"

Medusa actually laughed. "Goddess, no."

"Because you're sounding frighteningly hokey, and I don't need that right now."

Medusa broke the circle to grasp both of Cassie's shoulders. "True love is pure white light, the most powerful form of energy at our disposal. Only light can drive out darkness. Use yours to protect your loved one."

"We'll help you," the old witch added, and the other two nodded.

Cassie bobbed her head, her throat too tight to allow a verbal response. Taking a deep breath, she closed her eyes and concentrated all her love on Mick.

***

Mick's biggest crazed fan had changed from his dark business suit to surgical scrubs. That fact raised the hair on Mick's nape, but he didn't allow his fear to manifest itself in physical tension. Supremely confident, the man stood in the doorway, a slight smile on his face. Since he was of average height and slight build, Mick had to assume that the bastard's amazing strength came from the fact that he was pure evil incarnate. He'd fought like a man possessed, and Mick was just starting to feel the bruises from their encounter at the hotel. If he lived through this, he imagined he'd be incredibly sore in a couple days.

Having decided to approach what was coming the same way he'd prepared for a hockey game, Mick lifted the corners of his mouth in a slight smile that perfectly matched his enemy's expression. A deep breath steadied his nerves, and he pictured himself playing his very best. In this case, he pictured himself at the top of his writing game, his most erudite and glib phrases ready to spring from his mouth instead of from his fingers onto a manuscript page. Losing a hockey game never had fatal consequences. Here, failure was not an option.

"Awake at last, I see, Mr. Kazimer. I assure you, very soon you'll wish you were still sleeping."

Fifteen

The killer's rather high-pitched voice surprised Mick. Was he gay, or was that just a far too cliched stereotype that wouldn't provide insight into the man who had killed to impress him?

Focus, Sandor. No fear. You're on top of your game. Despite his mental pep talk, he cleared his throat before saying, "You have me at a disadvantage, I'm afraid. You know my name, but I don't know yours."

The man stopped an arm's length from the table. Close enough for Mick to see the fanatical light of insanity burning in his dark eyes.

"My name is unimportant."

Get him talking, Mick commanded himself. *Get him talking, then keep him talking.* "It's certainly important to me. I'd really like to know the identity of my biggest fan."

The man's entire body went rigid. "Why do you say that?"

Keep him talking. "Only the person who knows more about my writing than anyone else in the world could do what you've done."

"I don't know what you're talking about."

He raised his right hand, and Mick saw he clutched a lethal-looking scalpel.

Shit. After sending up a quick mental prayer to St. Jude, Mick forced himself to say nonchalantly, "I have to have something to call you. 'Biggest Fan' somehow sounds sarcastic, don't you think? Just plain 'Fan' doesn't accurately describe your status. 'Big' sounds like a rapper, and 'BF' is out of the question for lots of reasons."

"You don't need to know my name."

"Of course I do. I love knowing who my fans are. And, let's face it, you're a genius, and geniuses are great to know. No need to be modest. Lots of people are familiar with your work."

The hand holding the scalpel jerked convulsively.

"I think you're the only person who could have pulled off what you have," Mick hastened to say, eyes riveted on the shiny blade. "All the planning, laying the groundwork. Only a true genius—only you—could be capable of that."

A smile curled the killer's lips as he pulled up a high stool and sat down next to the table. Then he began to roll the scalpel handle slowly between his palms, and Mick felt himself sweating a river.

It took all his self-control to maintain a conversational tone. "However did you manage it?"

"I simply followed your blueprint."

The chillingly calm tone in which those words were spoken was somehow more frightening than if they had been screamed from a frothing mouth. Mick dug deep within himself to find the courage to say, "You made fact out of fiction. That was none of my doing. It was all yours." *And you're going to burn in hell for it, too, you bastard.* Anger abruptly began to drive out fear, and Mick's mind sharpened. "So what do you say, 'Biggest Fan'? What's your real name."

"Fred White."

"Really? Got any relatives in the Detroit area, Fred? I went to school with quite a few Whites—"

White leapt to his feet, sending the stool crashing to the floor. "Shut up! Shut up!" He raised his left hand to his head and grasped a handful of sandy-colored hair, then stalked away from the edge of the table.

The explosion of insanity Mick feared he'd triggered manifested itself in a far more sinister way than merely a sustained rant. By the time he'd crossed the room twice, White's frantic pacing had slowed to a controlled walk. Holding the scalpel with the blade down, he approached Mick's side again, and when he raised his eyes, Mick almost gasped. The nearly black orbs looked like obsidian. The evil, obsidian eyes of a mindless killing machine.

The clock had almost run out.

***

"Dora, did you find him?" Cassie emerged on the dark street near the ruins of the amusement park just as Endora transformed herself back to human form.

"Just got here." She tilted her head. "My guess is they're in an underground room, though."

"This way." Medusa indicated a set of steps off to the right. "I sense a great evil very close by." She turned to the eldest witch. "Millicent, would you put a containment spell on this area?"

The old witch's smile was just a bit smug. "I did before we left the Quarter. Right after Cassie cast her protection spell."

"Excellent." Medusa turned to Cassie. "Do you want us to come with you?"

She nodded. "Backup only, though."

"It's your show, Daughter."

***

"You stopped writing," White said, his calm tone terrifying in its detached simplicity. He tested the edge of the scalpel with his thumb. A drop of blood beaded where he'd touched the blade to his skin. "I worshiped you. Patterned all my killings after those in your books. Made my life's work a testimony to your writing brilliance. And then you stopped writing." He raised the scalpel and brought it down into Mick's right thigh. "Now you must die for betraying me."

Adrenaline prevented the searing pain from racing immediately to Mick's brain, giving him time to stifle the scream that clawed upward from his chest. As it was, his breath hissed through his teeth as he fought to keep his stomach from emptying. To keep from crying out in pain.

White pulled the blade from Mick's leg, went to the stand beside the operating table, and calmly wiped it clean on a white towel. Then he turned back, sneering. "So, the great M. S. Kazimer can control his reaction to pain," he said softly. "Well done." He tilted the blade to study it in the glare of artificial lights. "I assure you, however, before you die, you'll scream like all the rest. Beg to die like every last one of them."

Although he couldn't control the trembling of his leg, Mick kept a cool head. He wasn't about to let White torture him. His chances of escape dimming, he decided to go out with a bang. To see if he could inflict some pain of his own. "You know why I quit writing, you pathetic bastard?" he taunted. "Because of you."

White whirled around, scalpel again at the ready.

"That's right, Freddie Boy." Mick put every ounce of contempt he could muster into his words. "I got tired of carrying your stupid, sorry ass. Tired of giving you step-by-step killing instructions. So I quit writing. It's high time you stop copycatting and do something original."

White's eyes blazed, and he moved back to the table. "I *am* original. I'm a genius. You said so yourself."

"Genius?" Mick snorted. "You're an unimaginative thrall who can't think of a novel way to off someone. Instead, you stole my ideas."

"I did it to honor you!"

"You did it because you're a nobody who wanted to be

somebody."

"No!"

The blade slashed across this time, opening a six-inch long wound in Mick's thigh and wrenching a moan from his lips. He noted dispassionately that, although his leg bled profusely, the lack of a pulsing spray indicated White hadn't hit an artery. Somehow, that didn't make him feel any better about his chances. In fact, he figured that was his captor's goal all along.

Mick fought to control his panting breaths as he gasped out, "Describe one murder you committed that wasn't patterned after my books." A sneer curled his lips. "You can't, can you, Freddie Boy?"

"I worshiped you!"

White raised the blade and slashed again.

Mick saw the path of the scalpel was headed toward his chest, and he braced for what would most likely be a killing blow. *I love you, Cassie.*

The blade had traveled only a few inches in its downward arc when, suddenly, a shimmering light surrounded Mick. The scalpel point struck the light and slid harmlessly away.

"What the——" Only momentarily distracted, White struck again. Again the blade was deflected. With a guttural cry, he raised his hand again and again, slashing repeatedly in a frenzy of hacking blows. None of them came anywhere near hitting his target. The blade snapped in half, and he threw it aside, replacing it with beating fists that were likewise deflected.

"How is this possible?" he screamed, cool demeanor melting into total panic. "Not again. It can't be!"

Eyes rolling in his head, spittle at the corners of his mouth, White raced to the exit door. Throwing it open, he managed to ascend only two steps past the doorframe before being hurled back into the room. He landed flat on his back beside the table where Mick lay.

"I guess it *can* be," Mick said through clenched teeth.

No words could describe his feelings when he realized White could neither escape nor kill him. That someone was protecting him. Dared he hope that someone was Cassie? *Jesus, Mary and Joseph, please make it so.*

Knowing the impossibility of success, Mick nonetheless strained to loosen the bonds on his wrists and ankles. The effort only made the bleeding worse.

"Dammit." He'd have to sit there and leak blood until help

arrived. Which, if the growing pool of red under his leg was any indication, needed to be soon.

White made to scramble to his feet.

"I think I'd stay right where I was if I were you, Fred."

"Betrayer!" White launched himself at Mick only to again meet the invisible barrier.

"Slow learner," Mick retorted.

The rebound from this encounter with the force field threw White to the floor. Scrambling across the concrete on hands and knees, he grabbed the broken scalpel blade and rose in a half-crouch to stare wild-eyed at Mick. Then he slashed his own throat.

"I loved you," he gasped as blood gurgled from his lips. He fell face-first to the floor.

"Mick!" Cassie burst through the door, Endora and Medusa close on her heels, and flew across the room to his side.

"Cassie! Ohmigod, Baby, are you all right?"

Cassie's enthusiastic kiss answered that question for him. "We came as soon as we could," she explained, pulling back.

"Just in time, believe me." Mick planted a quick smack on her lips.

Ignoring the two love birds, Endora knelt beside White's prone form. "He's almost crossed over. Should I bring him back?"

Cassie's gaze met Mick's. "Your call."

He swallowed hard. Was he being judge, jury and executioner? He glanced at the man who had performed so much evil in the name of love. So many deaths. So much devastation.

"Let the bastard go," he answered quietly. "He should pay for his crimes, but maybe it's best he killed himself. His evil is expunged from the world, not locked away where it could even remotely infect others."

Suddenly, Cassie looked down. "You're bleeding."

"He managed to get in a couple licks before your barrier kicked in." At Cassie's guilty look, he quickly added, "Hey, the cuts don't even hurt."

"Liar." She gripped Mick's wounded leg with both hands, closed her eyes, and gently squeezed.

"Ouch!"

She didn't even open her eyes to look at him. "Quit being a baby, and sit still."

"Oh, so I go from a brave liar to a baby," Mick groused.

"So much for tender loving care."

It was a sham complaint. Soothing heat had permeated his wound the moment Cassie touched him, and the bleeding soon stopped, along with the pain.

As Cassie worked, Endora freed Mick's arms and legs.

Medusa moved to the center of the room. The master witch closed her eyes and tilted her chin upward, raised her hands palms up and began a low chant. The light in the dim room brightened until its intensity resembled sunshine in a midday desert. White light permeated every corner and crevice—driving out all vestiges of the dark evil that had been there—then faded to the original glow of the artificial lights.

"I sent his soul to the light," Medusa said simply.

Endora bristled, snapping, "After all he did, he deserved eternal damnation."

"It's not our place to decide, Dora. We—"

The sound of pounding feet on the stairs interrupted. A split-second later, Jamison and his agents burst through the doorway, guns drawn.

"You're too late, Robert." Mick, now sitting with his feet dangling over the side of the table, found he couldn't take his arm from around Cassie's waist. With his free hand, he indicated White. "Meet Fred White, serial killer. Fred took the coward's way out."

Jamison looked down at the scalpel still in White's hand, then glanced around at the group. "Sure he didn't have help?"

"You can check the blade for fingerprints, but you'll find only his," Medusa stated regally.

"No doubt."

The older witch crossed her arms over her chest and gave Robert her haughtiest stare. "I assure you, Special Agent Jamison, we would not have let him die so easily had we been involved–."

"—Point taken." Jamison turned to his agents. "Call in the name Fred White. Have O'Brien process the body, then all of you get back to base. I'm going to escort Mr. Kazimer and his party there myself." The look he gave Cassie, Endora and Medusa dared them to suggest they'd return to the hotel in any manner other than via a government vehicle. Then he looked at the torn leg of Mick's slacks and the blood on the operating table. "Need to go to Emergency, Sandor?"

"No, I'm fine," Mick said, grinning. "Why do you ask?"

The agent only gritted his teeth in response.

***

"I'll call you when I get home, Mother." Cassie stepped back from hugging Medusa and turned to embrace the others who had helped rescue Mick.

The group stood in the living area of Mick's hotel suite as dawn was breaking over New Orleans.

Medusa gave an uncomfortable-looking Endora a quick hug, then turned to Mick. "Still want to join the family?"

"Absolutely." With a grin, he wrapped his future mother-in-law in a gentle bear hug and squeezed. "I can't wait to break out the whoopie cushion at the first reunion."

Medusa swatted him on the shoulder and then kissed his chin. "I must warn you, dear boy, that you're about to enter the Big Leagues. Witch practical jokes are very sophisticated and complex. A mere whoopie cushion won't compete."

"I sense a challenge here." Mick bussed her on the cheek, and then, cinching Cassie around the waist with his arm, turned to Medusa's friends. "I can't thank you all enough for your help. You literally saved our lives. Please come and visit Cassie and me any time."

Millicent stepped forward, a twinkle in her ancient black eyes. "I have a favor to ask you, young man."

"Mick, please."

With a smile, she produced a copy of *Mortal Sin*. "I'm a huge fan. Have read every single word you ever published. Would you autograph this for me?"

"It would be my pleasure." Mick took the book and the pen Millicent offered with it. "Do you want this signed to anyone in particular?"

"Madigan." She spelled it for Mick. "My husband. He's read all of your titles, too."

Cassie wrapped her arm around Mick's shoulders as he handed the book back. "Be sure to tell Madigan this is a special edition. The last autograph M. S. Kazimer will ever give."

The tall witch cocked her eyebrow. "You're really retiring from writing?"

"Probably not for good," Mick stated quietly. "But there will definitely never be another title penned by M. S. Kazimer."

"Too bad," Millicent said. "You're great at spinning a tale of mayhem."

Mick and Cassie shared a look. "Unfortunately, some people

couldn't just see them as that—tales. One made fiction a reality. It's time for me to move on to other challenges."

"Like honing your practical joking skills." Medusa linked arms with Cassie and then gave her a quick kiss. "There's a big voodoo function in the Quarter tonight. Want to come?"

"Tonight?" Cassie glanced out the window of the hotel suite. "Mother, it's practically dawn, and I haven't slept in a day and a half."

"Well, you've got until midnight to catch up." Medusa glanced over at Endora. "Dora, you up for partying?"

The familiar shook her head. "My boss is a slave driver. I have to work."

"Dora, you do not!"

"That's my story, and I'm sticking to it." Endora nodded to the room's other occupants as she moved to the suite door. "See you around."

"Dora—" Cassie started after her, but Medusa held her back.

"Let her go, Cassandra. She needs to work through some things."

"I know, but—"

"Let it go. When she's ready, she'll talk to you about it." Medusa gestured to her friends. "Let's be off, then, since we can't convince those much younger than we that they need to have some excitement in their lives."

"I've had enough excitement for a while, thanks," Mick said.

Cassie nodded her agreement.

"Be well, both of you." With those words, Medusa and the others disappeared.

Mick shook his head. "I don't think I'm going to get used to that one any time soon." When Cassie had no ready remark, he took a good look at her. "You're really worried about Endora, aren't you."

Cassie's eyes filled with tears. "Yes. Oh, Mick, she's in such need right now. But Mom's right. I can't help her. At least not at this point."

"Is there anything I can—" Seeing her expression, he broke off. "I know. It's Endora's story to tell, not yours."

He suddenly found himself engulfed in a hug of epic proportions.

Cassie kissed his cheek, then said, "That's one of the reasons I love you, Mick."

He raised his brow in question.

"Understanding a person's privacy. Being a writer, I know you're insatiably curious. You want to know things, want to understand how things work. But you draw the line at invading someone's privacy. I find that quality very sexy."

"How sexy?" His grin was purely wicked.

She gave a heartfelt sigh, smile wistful. "You don't need any excuse to drag me off to bed, if you're angling for a reason." He growled, but she held her hands to his chest to ward him off. "But I really truly do have a headache."

He stilled completely. "God, I forgot about your injury!" Grabbing her by the elbow, he gently propelled her into the bedroom and made her lie down. "I'm so sorry, Cass. It's just that you came charging into that room like Elliott Ness, and I was all cut up and not thinking about your being hurt, and then White killed himself—"

"Mick, enough!" She stopped him from pushing another pillow beneath her head. "I'll be all right. Really. But I probably overextended myself after the energy healing last night, and now I'm paying for it."

"What was I *thinking*?" He pulled the covers up to her chin. "You're spending the day in bed resting. We can order in if you want. Or you can just sleep."

She accepted his tucking the blanket around her, reaching to caress his cheek with her fingertips before he stood back up. "Thanks."

"I love you," he whispered as he bent to gently kiss her forehead.

"Right back at you."

After drawing the curtains on the brilliant New Orleans day, he turned back to her. "Get some rest. I'll go find Jamison and get instructions for what happens next. I'm sure there are still plenty of hoops he's going to have me jump through before this investigation is truly over."

She muttered a sleepy, "See you later," as he quietly left the suite.

***

Six weeks later, Mick and Cassie sat in her sunny kitchen in Salem, enjoying the warm spring day.

"If this guest list gets any bigger, we'll have to get married in the Crystal Cathedral."

"It's probably not open on Halloween." With a flick of her

wrist, she sent the coffee pot levitating across the room to refill his cup.

He added cream and sugar and took a long drink. "Wonder if the New Orleans Saints rent out their football stadium."

Cassie sighed and set down the prop pen she'd been pretending to write their guest list with. She knew it annoyed Mick when she used psychic dictation, although he never said anything, so she made it look like she was actually doing the physical work. "Maybe we could just elope."

At her suggestion, his expression brightened. "That's an idea . . ." His enthusiasm just as quickly waned. ". . . that would get us both killed by our families. If we eloped, we'd have to make Jamison get us into the Witness Protection Program."

"I think he owes you one."

On those words, Endora sauntered in, long tail swishing. "That will never work, and you know it." She leapt into the pile of papers and lists of addresses on the table.

Mick grabbed his coffee mug before it spilled over everything, shooting her an exasperated look. "Thanks for that adrenaline rush, pal."

"The pleasure's all mine."

Cassie and Mick exchanged glances over the top of Endora's head.

"Dora, you're out of line, and you know it," Cassie said quietly.

"Hey, a week of being grilled by the FBI in D.C. can put anyone off her game," Endora rejoined, but her tone didn't have its usual cocky humor.

"This has nothing to do with wrapping up the White case." Cassie's annoyance was evident. "This started on the book tour."

Rising from his chair, Mick grabbed the coffee carafe and his mug. "I'm going for a walk. No sense wasting this weather by staying inside." He missed seeing Endora's look of gratitude as he turned and left the room.

"All right, familiar mine, spill it."

***

Out of respect for Endora, Mick decided a constitutional around Cassie's five-acre Salem farm was in order. He needed to stretch his legs after several hours of work on wedding plans, and the women needed to talk privately. He set off across the field behind the barn, headed for the woods.

He could relate to Endora's remark about being off her

game. The week of meetings with Jamison's superiors had been surprisingly grueling, despite the Bureau's insistence that Mick was not responsible for White's activities. Going over the details of his working with the Feds had forced him to articulate his memories of every minute of the book tour—the public ones, anyway—and doing so had dredged up every emotion he had. Primarily guilt.

"Your writing did not trigger this guy's actions," Jamison had reminded him yet again. Repeatedly.

But it was one thing to hear that from a professional lawman and another to believe it in his heart of hearts. His conviction that he had somehow unleashed this monster had led to his retirement as M. S. Kazimer. The tour hadn't changed his mind about that. It had merely convinced him his decision was right. Further, he'd pledged twenty percent of his earnings from every Kazimer book sold in perpetuity to programs that trained law enforcement agents in forensics and profiling. Had Jennifer still been his manager, she'd have had apoplexy over that.

Mick had to laugh at the pledge. He knew it wasn't Catholic guilt at work—though likely some would think that. It was more giving back to the people who'd solved the White case. He'd always supported law enforcement institutions. Now he was just doing it on a larger scale. It felt good to think that the very books which had inspired a sick individual would now provide funding to keep those individuals from hurting others.

And there was something else. At the edge of the pond, he sat down on a huge boulder, set aside the coffee cup and carafe. From his shirt pocket, he withdrew a folded envelope containing a single sheet of his publisher's letterhead.

Even though he'd already committed the contents to heart, he scanned the letter.

Dear Mick,

Your proposal for a series of children's fantasy books written as Mirek Sandor is very exciting. I'm sure by now Miles has contacted you about our offer of a three book contract, but I've been given permission to add the option for three more.

You'll be working with Lillian Davis, our top children's editor, and I can't tell you how thrilled she is to have the chance to collaborate with you.

Have Miles call me next week to set up a date to get you to New York for some face-to-face time with Lillian.

> *Sincerely yours,*
> *Louis Van Sykle*

He laughed and returned the envelope to his shirt pocket. His agent, Miles Bednarek, had certainly informed him of the offer. However, since Mick hadn't bothered to warn his long-time agent that his writing career had taken a one-eighty, words like "excited" and "thrilled" hadn't entered their conversation about the offer. "What the hell are you doing?" had been Miles' question to Mick.

He'd calmed down somewhat when Mick had explained the whole reason behind his change of genres, nonetheless reminding his client that children's authors almost never made anywhere near the amount of money *New York Times* best-sellers did. But Mick was perfectly happy with his decision. He was a writer, and thus he had to write. But he'd found a different channel for his creative energy, and the money wasn't the issue.

***

Cassie found him an hour later still sitting on the big rock, throwing pebbles into the pond.

"Penny for your thoughts," she said as she hugged him from behind.

He turned and kissed her cheek. "Hey, pretty lady. Did you and Dora work some things out?"

"We discussed the situation, and I think cleared the air somewhat."

"But—"

"But the bottom line is Endora's got until the Winter Solstice to resolve this situation, and no one can help her." Cassie moved to sit beside Mick on the sun-warmed boulder and put her head on his shoulder. "It's so hard to watch her struggle and not be able to do anything about it."

"Guess we'll just have to give her all our love and emotional support while she's dealing."

Cassie looked up at him. "Have I told you recently just how much I love you?"

"Yes, but don't let that stop you from saying it again."

She laughed, then sobered. "How are you doing?"

"Better." He tossed another pebble. "Ending my horror

writing career is going to be a very good thing. If I can keep Miles from having a stroke over my change of focus."

"He'll survive the genre switch. Now, if it was a *gender* switch, that might do him in."

Mick laughed. "Becoming a woman is just not an option for me. I couldn't find high heels big enough for my feet." He shot her a heated glance. "Besides, I enjoy making love to you too much to change."

"Good answer, human. If you'd said you wanted to stay a man because you liked standing up to pee, I was going to have to brain you." She grew momentarily quiet. "We really haven't talked about New Orleans, Mick. Should we?"

"You first."

Cassie made a face. "Typical male. Not in touch with his feminine side."

"Actually, I really want to hear your take on this. It might help clarify mine."

"Wow." Settling back against Mick's shoulder, she said, "Let's work back from the most recent events. I'm glad they kept the case's major details out of the media."

Mick shifted her until she was sitting with her back against his chest. He held her in a loose hug. "Why's that?"

"Publishing such bizarre details would just encourage copycats, and feed some very sick people's need for grisly events. Closing the case quietly was the best thing for all, especially the victims' families."

"How'd you feel about signing that nondisclosure statement?"

Cassie shrugged. "No problem. There is no earthly reason to bring much of that to the light of day. And all the others did the same thing."

"They're great people. Any one of them could have written a blockbuster book about the situation, but they all agreed to protect the secrecy of the case." Mick paused. "Something that bothers me most about this whole thing is, even if the Bureau had publicized the details, they wouldn't have gotten as much media time as my retirement announcement."

Cassie sat up and looked at him over her shoulder. "You're right. Media sharks in a feeding frenzy. All those fans trying to call. All the requests for interviews. The only thing that would have made the White case more interesting to the public was if they discovered you helped bring him down."

"And that I helped create him."

"We're not going there, Mick."

"Sorry." He hugged her. "But it's going to take a long time for me to reconcile the fact that my writing influenced someone to kill so many."

"Influenced is not the same as made," Cassie stated firmly. "And that's all I'll say on the subject. Now, it's your turn. What's your feeling on the whole thing?"

"It was the best of times. It was the worst of times."

"Thank you, Charles, but I was speaking to Mirek Sandor, my fiancé."

"Actually, Charlie got it right," Mick said with a shrug. "It was the worst time of my life for the most obvious reason, but it was the best time, too, because you and I met and fell in love."

Cassie could feel her eyes filling with tears and her throat closing. Still, she managed to ask, "Even having to deal with what I am? Even knowing I'm going to outlive you by so many years?"

The hug tightened. "My family is very long-lived, Cass. *Yaya's* nearly a hundred and four, and she doesn't show any signs of slowing down any time soon. Practically every relative I have, unless they had an accident or were killed in a war, has lived well into their nineties. Several have gone over the century mark. That means I'll likely go for another sixty years, or even more."

"I'll still have about fifty more years without you."

He kissed the side of her neck before he said, "Is sixty years with me going to outweigh fifty without me? Won't our children and grandchildren be there to comfort you?"

In a flash, Cassie turned sideways in his lap and threw her arms around his neck. She kissed him hard. "I love you so much, Mick. I want you, need to be with you, for all the time we have together. For how ever many years that may be." She paused. Gathered her courage. "But if you can't handle what I am, then I don't want you to feel obligated to me for any reason."

His arms crushed her to his chest. "Don't turn ditzy on me now. I love you, Cassandra Hathorne. For who you are. My life will be a complete waste of time if you're not with me. *What you are is part of the package, and I'm buying the whole bundle.*" Mick paused. "Besides, I've wondered more than once why you picked me when you could have married someone who has your same types of abilities."

Relief flooded Cassie, and she smiled. Finally at ease. "At the risk of sounding unoriginal—I love you for who you are. So what if you're pathetic at practical jokes."

With a twist of his body, Mick pinned Cassie beneath him. "That's below the belt."

"It certainly is," Cassie purred. Wrapping her arms loosely around his neck, she rubbed her breasts against his chest. "And I think you need to show me just how far below the belt that hit."

Mick chuckled. "You little witch."

"Absolutely. And proud of it."

Printed in the United States
21348LVS00001B/299